Illusions of Immortality

also translated and introduced by Brian Stableford:
Anonymous: Sâr Dubnotal vs. Jack the Ripper; *Anthologies*: News from the Moon; The Germans on Venus; The Supreme Progress; The World Above the World; Nemoville; *Allorge*: The Great Cataclysm; *Bérard*: The Vampire Lord Ruthwen; *Bessière*: The Gardens of the Apocalypse; *Bleunard*: Ever Smaller; *Bodin*: The Novel of the Future; *Brown*: City of Glass; *Caroff*: The Terror of Madame Atomos; *Champsaur*: The Human Arrow; *Derennes*: The People of the Pole; *Driou*: The Adventures of a Parisian Aeronaut; *Dunan*: Baal; *Duvernois*: The Man Who Found Himself; *Eyraud*: Voyage to Venus; *Falk*: The Age of Lead; *Féval*: Anne of the Isles; The Black Coats ('Salem Street; The Invisible Weapon; The Parisian Jungle; The Companions of the Treasure; Heart of Steel; The Cadet Gang; The Sword-Swallower); John Devil; Knightshade; Revenants; Vampire City; The Vampire Countess; The Wandering Jew's Daughter; *Féval, fils*: Felifax, the Tiger-Man; *Haraucourt*: Illusions of Immortality; *Joncquel & Varlet*: The Martian Epic; *Kahn*: The Tale of Gold and Silence; *La Hire*: The Nyctalope vs. Lucifer; The Nyctalope on Mars; Enter the Nyctalope; *Lamothe-Langon*: The Virgin Vampire; *de Lautrec*: The Vengeance of the Oval Portrait; *Le Faure & de Graffigny*: The Extraordinary Adventures of a Russian Scientist Across the Solar System (2 vols.); *Le Rouge*: The Vampires of Mars; *Lermina*: Panic in Paris; Mysteryville; The Secret of Zippelius; *Moselli*: Illa's End; *Nizet*: Captain Vampire; *de Parville*: An Inhabitant of the Planet Mars; *de Pawlowski*: Journey to the Land of the 4th Dimension; *Pellerin*: The World in 2000 Years; *Ponson du Terrail*: The Vampire and the Devil's Son; *Renard*: The Blue Peril; Doctor Lerne; The Doctored Man; A Man Among the Microbes; The Master of Light; *Richepin*: The Wing; *Robida*: The Clock of the Centuries; The Adventures of Saturnin Farandoul; Chalet in the Sky; *Rosny Aîné*: The Givreuse Enigma; The Mysterious Force; The Navigators of Space; Vamireh; The World of the Variants; The Young Vampire; *Rouff*: Journey to the Inverted World; *Ryner*: The Superhumans; *Spitz:* The Eye of Purgatory; *Steiner*: Ortog; *Tiphaigne de la Roche*: Amilec; *Varlet*: The Xenobiotic Invasion; *Vibert*: The Mysterious Fluid; *Villiers de l'Isle-Adam*: The Scaffold; The Vampire Soul; *Ward & Miller*: The Song of Montségur.

Illusions of Immortality

by
Edmond Haraucourt

translated, annotated and introduced by
Brian Stableford

A Black Coat Press Book

ISBN 978-1-61227-075-3. First Printing. February 2012. Published by Black Coat Press, an imprint of Hollywood Comics.com, LLC, P.O. Box 17270, Encino, CA 91416. All rights reserved. Except for review purposes, no part of this book may be reproduced or transmitted in any form or by any means, electronic or mechanical, including photocopying, recording, or by any information storage and retrieval system, without permission in writing from the publisher. The stories and characters depicted in this novel are entirely fictional. Printed in the United States of America.

TABLE OF CONTENTS

Introduction

There is no entry on Edmond Haraucourt (1856-1941) in Pierre Versins' *Encyclopédie de l'utopie et de la science-fiction* (1974), but there is a passing mention in one of the theme entries of a work entitled *La Traversée de Paris* (1904), as one of a group of stories modeled on Alfred Bonnardot's "Archéopolis" (1859; tr. as "Archeopolis" in the Black Coat Press anthology *Nemoville*)[1], in which future tourists visit the ruins of Paris.

Because Versins does not distinguish between books and short stories in such subsidiary references, the brief mention in question started numerous collectors searching for a book with that title. The fact that no such title appeared in the catalogue of the Bibliothèque Nationale only resulted in the BN joining in the wild goose chase; the fact that a second-hand book dealer listed the book in question in a catalogue in 1983, as a joke, only added to the confusion.

The text to which Versins had referred was finally "rediscovered" in the 1990s in the pages of the Parisian daily newspaper *Le Journal*, which—as befit the most ostentatiously "literary" of the Paris dailies—ran a weekly feuilleton section whose contents were noticeably more pretentious than the general run of popular serial fiction. That rediscovery was enabled by a reference in the introduction to a new edition of one of the other stories in which futuristic tourists visit the ruins of Paris, Alfred Franklin's *Les Ruines de Paris* (1908; originally 1875), and gave rise in its turn to the discovery that the only futuristic fantasy by Haraucourt to have appeared in a separate edition, *Le Gorilloïde* (booklet version, 1906), had also been serialized in *Le Journal*. The search was then ex-

---

[1] ISBN 978-1-61227-070-8.

tended, turning up three more unreprinted futuristic fantasies from the same periodical.

This story is told in an essay by Jean-Luc Buard, which was employed as one of the appendices to a collection that was then made of four of the stories in question, published by Éditions Apex in 2001 as *Le Gorilloïde et autres contes de l'avenir*. In addition to "Le Gorilloïde" and "Cinq mille ans, ou la traversée de Paris," the collection reprinted "La découverte du docteur Auguérand" (1910) and "Le conflit supreme" (1919). All four stories are translated in the present collection, as "The Gorilloid," "A Trip to Paris," "Doctor Auguérand's Discovery" and "The Supreme Conflict."

Unfortunately, given that it was supposed to be making an item legendary for its obscurity available to a wider audience, the Apex collection is extremely elusive; I would have no idea it existed had I not happened to run into the publisher one day in the book room at a French convention. It remains unpublicized outside of a small community of French collectors, and is by no means easy to obtain by conventional means; the publisher, also being a book-dealer, likes to keep a monopoly on sales. This is a great pity, because three of the four stories in the collection—the first three—are very striking indeed, qualifying, in my opinion, as masterpieces of a sort. They entitle Haraucourt to be considered in the first rank of French "Wellsians"—which is to say, those pioneers of French scientific romance who published their best work in the wake of the introduction of H. G. Wells' work in the genre to France, in the pages of the *Mercure de France*, between 1898 and 1901. The three Haraucourt items rank alongside the key works of Maurice Renard and J.-H. Rosny aîné as type specimens of what French scientific romance might have achieved had the Parisian marketplace not become swiftly hostile to such works when they failed to win sufficiently wide popularity.

The serials in *Le Journal* were not Haraucourt's first ventures into futuristic fiction; one of his earliest published stories had been a remarkable, if somewhat disorganized, portmanteau piece entitled "La Fin du Monde," which appeared in the *Revue Hebdomadaire* in 1893, and which Haraucourt reprinted in a collection of *contes philosophiques* entitled *L'Effort* [Effort] (1894). Two of the other stories therein, "Immortalité, conte philosophique," which was Haraucourt's first-published short story, in the *Revue Bleue* in 1888, and *L'Antéchrist*, first issued as an illustrated booklet in 1893, are also fantasies with a futuristic element, and the fourth, "La Madone" (*Revue Bleue*, 1890) is closely linked to them thematically. Those four stories, which fill in some of the ideological background to the later futuristic fantasies, are also reprinted herein, as "Immortality: a *conte philosophique*," "The Madonna," "The Antichrist," and "The End of the World."

"Immortalité" suggests, among other intriguing ideas, that every great author only has one fundamental idea, and that all his individual works are variations of it (what is nowadays knows as "*auteur* theory"). Whether that is true or not, the fact that Haraucourt asserts it so positively invites us to consider his work in that light, and if we do so, we can easily see that the four stories in *L'Effort* all share the same underlying theme, which is carried forward with varying degrees of brutality in the four stories in *Le Gorilloïde*, and also lurks in the background, albeit fugitively, in many of the *contes cruels* that he produced in some quantity for *Le Journal*—including one another fantasy that I have included in the present collection, "Les Sabots de Noël" (1906; reprinted in *La Peur*, 1907), here translated as "A Christmas Gift."

I have elected to title this collection *Illusions of Immortality* because Haraucourt's own fundamental idea seems to have been a preoccupation—almost an obsession—with the impossibility of immortality and the illusory nature of all the dreams orientated in that direction: not merely the trivial dream of a literal afterlife, which he can only consider as a joke, but—much more importantly, in his world-view—the artist's dream of acquiring a kind of immortality through his works and the popular notion that one might acquire another kind of immortality by virtue of one's posterity: the children of humankind in general, if not one's own children. Haraucourt's imaginative work is all orientated to the task of putting the boot into that set of ideas, and further corollaries associated with it, in a fashion that seemed to many of his contemporaries to be intemperate and embittered. It was not a task that was ever likely to make him popular, even among his fellow artists, let alone the general public, but he thought it noble as well as necessary, and whether one approves of it or not (I do, as it happens) there is no doubt that it took him to some magnificently strange literary extremes, and gave his best work a unique and highly distinctive flavor—always something to be welcomed in the literature of the imagination.

In order to understand the world-view that Haraucourt tried so hard to encapsulate and embody in these philosophical fantasies it is useful to know something about the forces that shaped him, as a human being as well as a writer. Fortunately, he began (at the age of 79) to write his memoirs, feeling the need to explain himself, if not to apologize, thus providing us with some invaluable information about his peculiar childhood. Unfortunately, he died before completing the task, but the posthumously-published fragment, *Mémoires des jours et des gens* [Memories of Days and People] (1946), extends, albeit vaguely and somewhat confusedly, into the early 1890s, so it overlaps the period in which the stories in the collection began to appear—which, in a sense, pick up the intellectual narrative where the memoir leaves off.

In my book on *Scientific Romance in Britain 1890-1950* (1986), I pointed out the seemingly-interesting point that many of the pioneering British writers of scientific romance were sons of clergymen who had converted to freethought, who seemed to be using speculative fiction as a means of building a cosmic *weltanschauung* capable of substituting for the one they had deserted, by way of self-justification. That pattern could not be reproduced in France, of course, because French clergymen, being Catholic, did not have sons—but they did have nephews,[2] and there was no shortage in France of devout men outside the clergy, whose offspring simulated the generation gap in question. Edmond Haraucourt was not the son of a clergyman, but he was the nephew of no less than four, with a further two nuns thrown in as aunts for good measure.

Haraucourt begins his memoirs with the ironic proclamation that he owed his very existence to the Church. His mother was one of seven children, and was the only one not to be sent into Holy Orders, not because she was not sufficiently pious, but because her parents needed someone to do the housework and look after her younger siblings. (Haraucourt diplomatically refrains from mentioning the family's name, although it had worked so determinedly to eliminate its posterity that there was no one left to offend, but it was Biet.) When the rest of the Biet children had been packed off to the Far East as missionaries, Edmond's mother remained behind, but when her own mother died, her father had difficulty adjusting to celibate life, and naturally turned to the Church for help.

The Church, ever obliging, not only volunteered to find Monsieur Biet a new wife, but also offered to provide his daughter—who would thus be made redundant as his housekeeper—with a husband. His confessor apologized to M. Biet for the fact that M. Haraucourt senior was penniless and came with blots on his escutcheon—not only was he an orphan but his grandfather had joined the Revolution and fought for Napoléon—but offered assurances of his utter respectability. Thus, Edmond's mother was introduced to a total stranger on the day of her betrothal, the banns having already been posted, and was married within three weeks.

---

[2] International variants of the word "nephew" were used euphemistically during several centuries of Catholic history to refer to the illegitimate sons and catamites of clergymen, especially in the College of Cardinals, but I mean the word literally here; those sorts of shenanigans were not as common in provincial France as in decadent Rome.

Haraucourt was thus brought up in a household which was, at least to begin with, very poor and exceedingly devout—except that his mother had never forgiven the Church for taking away her six siblings, and she refused to send Edmond to the seminary where he was inevitably offered a decent education. She also refused to end him to the local community school, as his father wanted, and insisted—although it involved considerable financial sacrifice to begin with—that he go to a *lycée* (a private boarding school) in order that he could learn Latin and Greek, thus being prepared for entry into the professions without being simultaneously indoctrinated and groomed for Holy Orders.

A precocious child, Haraucourt began writing poetry at the age of five, and became a dedicated book-lover—extremely dedicated, in fact, in the only way that a child in a devout and poor household can be. Having access to very few books other than the Bible he treasured the few to which he did gain access enormously, and from the age of six to eleven lived in the near-exclusive company of just one book: *Don Quixote*, which he describes in his memoir as "the secular Bible of the Occidental world," arguing that Quixote and Sancho Panza are, in combination, the perfect symbols of the divided self, containing between them an entire account of human being.

In imagining human being as fundamentally divided, Haraucourt was, of course, thinking firmly in the tradition of all the great philosophers, from Plato onwards—but the vast majority of those philosophers had considered the "higher" self to be that of sane reason, and the "lower" one to be that of dangerously wild passion. In selecting his own idiosyncratic model, Haraucourt overturned that hierarchy: his Quixotic higher self is a noble dreamer of dubious sanity—the archetype of a particular image of the artist—while the lower component of the duo stands for not only for commonsensical rationality but a keen appreciation of life's pleasures.

For the remainder of his life, Haraucourt seems to have compartmentalized himself in exactly that fashion, creating such a sharp distinction between his Quixotic art and his hedonistic everyday life that no one who knew him could ever understand how such a cheerful *bon vivant* and relentless womanizer could possible write books that seemed so deeply pessimistic and embittered. In his memoir, Haraucourt explains that, while he had always been grateful for his personal good fortune and fully appreciative of the joys available to him—whose indulgence he did not stint, when he could afford them—far from preventing him from observing the miseries and mistakes of others, that had only made him more acutely aware of them, prompting him to lament them in no uncertain terms

He *was* lucky—at cards as well as in love, if his own account can be believed—but not always. The *lycée* might have taught him Latin and Greek (which did ultimately come in useful) but he learned sterner lessons there. The sharpest of all the memories recorded in his *Mémoires* explains that, because he was an apt pupil, he tended to finish his assigned work—done in class under the supervision of a master—more rapidly than his fellows, but still had to sit there for the requisite time. At the age of twelve, he began to use the time thus made available to write his first novel, in a blue notebook. For weeks on end he painstakingly constructed a conventional melodramatic romance. From time to time, the master would come to see what he was doing, read a few lines, and then pass on without making any comment. When he completed the novel, however, and wrote the ultimate *fin*, with a feeling of great accomplishment, the master summoned him to the front of the class and methodically ripped every single page of the notebook to shreds, one by one. Haraucourt reported that the incident impressed him with a lifelong hatred for the abuse of authority, which echoed through all his subsequent work—and indeed, much of his savage cynicism can be seen, in part, as a reaction to that moment of cruelty and his helplessness in the face of it.

Haraucourt presumably saw no more of that particular master, because he attended a different *lycée* almost every

13

year as his father, a civil servant in the Ministry of Finance, was transferred at regular intervals to various far-flung provinces; although he was a boarder, he was always transferred in order to be within reach of his family. He reports, a trifle resentfully, that although his father's transfers always involved promotions, and eventually lifted the family out of poverty, his own situation never changed; he was never given any money, but only supplied with exactly the number of postage stamps required by his obligatory letters home. Even so, he contrived to get occasional access to books other than the Bible and his schoolbooks, and took deep impressions from those he loved, most especially the poetry of Victor Hugo and Charles Leconte de Lisle, who became the key models of his own poetry.

His final year of school was spent at the prestigious Lycée Henri IV in Paris (where Maurice Renard would later be a pupil), and soon after completing his set of diplomas he had assembled his first collection of poetry, modeled on Hugo's *Légende des siècles* and Leconte de Lisle's *Poèmes barbares*, but focusing more narrowly on the subject that most occupied his thoughts and endeavors at the time; it was entitled *La Légende des sexes*. Haraucourt noted in his *Mémoires* that the collection went everywhere with him for the next few years, and continued to follow him for the rest of his life, but between 1876, when he completed it at the age of 20, and the day when it finally crept into print, he had considerable difficulty even placing individual poems in periodicals. He claimed that it never occurred to him for a moment during that time that he might actually make a career, or even a vocation, out of writing; it was something he did for pleasure in his leisure time, like chasing women—and, indeed, was intricately interlinked with that other pastime, imaginatively—whereas work was merely a means of making a living, in order to support his higher and hedonistic pursuits.

Initially, Haraucourt had a vague notion of preparing for a career in law, and worked in a notary's office for a while, but could not settle there and tried out the civil service—an attempt not helped by the time he spent working directly for his father. After various other brief positions, and a few intervals when he occasionally had to sleep rough, he was recruited as secretary to the Prefect of Corsica. He spent a year on the island in 1879, but then had to serve his compulsory turn of duty in the army, and wound up back in Paris on his release, where he fell in with members of a political group carrying forward the ideas of Léon Gambetta, one of the great men of the Third Republic, and became the editor of their campaign newsletter.

The chronology of the memoir becomes slightly confused at this point, but it appears to have been at the farewell dinner of this group, whose candidate had not fared well in the elections of 1881, but would no longer have needed a campaign newspaper anyway, that the idea was broached of using the group's printing press to run off a few copies of *La Légende des sexes* for private distribution. The copy of the text in the Bibliothèque Nationale catalogue, bearing the signature "Le Sire de Chambley" is dated 1883 and the place of publication is given as Brussels, but if Haraucourt's memory is accurate that might be one of the several unlicensed editions that appeared because he neglected to deposit the copy necessary to register copyright in the work. It does, in fact, seem likely that he had at least a few printed copies available in 1881, although the text was not published then in the sense that it was ever offered for sale through the normal channels.

After the end of the Gambettist campaign, Haraucourt got a job as an electrician in a theater, managing the lights. It was, according to the *Mémoires*, this job that led to a conclusive split with the Biet family, who heard that he had been seen hanging out with actors, decided that the black sheep had finally strayed too far, and demanded that his mother cut off communication with him. His parents disappear from the memoir thereafter, but it is hard to believe that they really never communicated with him again, and he certainly continued communication with his Uncle Félix, with whom he seems to have maintained a friendly correspondence while the latter was the Bishop of Tibet, and with whom he remained on good terms when he returned to Paris. (Although he doubtless did sterling work for the church, Félix Biet is now remembered primarily as a naturalist, who sent numerous specimens of plants and animals back to Paris from the Far East, and has a species of bird named after him.)

According to Haraucourt's memoir, the extraordinary stroke of luck that transformed his fortunes in 1882 occurred when—unknown to him at the time—the editor of *La Jeune France*, Albert Allinet, was moved by the submission of some of his poems to burst into laughter at their absurdity while Leconte de Lisle happened to be in the office. The great man asked to see the poems, did not laugh—perhaps recognizing his own influence—sternly instructed the editor to publish them, and then sent Haraucourt an invitation to his *salon*, where he introduced him to some of the other grand old men of French letters, including Théodore de Banville and Ernest Renan. Those three appear to have decided—apparently on a whim—to take Haraucourt under their wing, and promote him as a promising young poet. Banville published a glowing essay on his work in *Gil Blas*, and within a matter of weeks he had been invited to numerous other salons, including dinner at Alphonse Daudet's house—on which occasion he met Georges Charpentier, who took him to dinner at Sarah Bernhardt's house the following evening.

Almost instantaneously, Haraucourt became so famous within the limited circle of the Parisian literary community—without yet having published anything substantial—that when Rodolphe Salis decided to save his ailing *cabaret*, Le Chat Noir, by promoting it as the capital's leading literary café, Haraucourt was one of the two young writers—the other being Maurice Rollinat—that he invited to the planning meeting, along with Emile Goulot, whom Salis instructed to re-form the Hydropathes, in order to help him do it. Haraucourt was drafted to the editorial staff of the periodical *Le Chat Noir*, to which he also became a contributor, and he joined the café's cast of regular performers, although Rollinat—with whom he became fast friends—was much a better singer and musician, and he was also outshone in that regard by Jean Richepin. Even so, some of Haraucourt's songs, and musical versions of his poems, still survive, and can nowadays be found on CD. Not only did he become a fixture in *Le Chat Noir* from 1882 onwards, but he was also introduced to Victor Hugo, a few months before the great man's death, and was recruited to help carry his coffin—the surest sign of all that he had *arrived* in the Parisian literary community.

One suspects that the real story was somewhat more complicated than the truncated version offered in the *Mémoires*, and the passage in "Immortalité" that describes the narrator eagerly handing his work around to the great writers in paradise, one by one, suggests that any copies of *La Légende des sexes* that were made in 1881 might have passed through numerous prestigious hands before the 1883 edition made its rather fugitive appearance. At any rate, Haraucourt's reputation was already made before the 1883 version appeared, and he was confronted from the outset with the challenge of living up to it. He did not shirk the challenge, of course, but he must have had doubts about his ability to answer it adequately, and cannot possibly have forgotten that poor Don Quixote had been unhorsed by one of the windmills he had mistaken for giants.

It seems probable that the only reason that *La Légende des sexes* was not prosecuted for obscenity is that no one likely to initiate such a prosecution ever found out that it existed, although Haraucourt notes proudly that when he was hauled into court, as part of a group action leveled against *Le Chat Noir*, the case came before a liberally-minded substitute magistrate, who not only ruled that the prosecution was absurd and the senator who had occasioned it was an utter fool, but took the defendants out to dinner thereafter. In spite of the largely private critical acclaim it won, however, the book remained virtually invisible, and Haraucourt still had no thought, nor any realistic possibility, of actually making any money from his writing. He settled into a clerical job at the Ministry of Commerce, where, as at the *lycée*, he was able to do his assigned work rapidly enough to allow him abundant time to write, and he blithely composed poems, plays and prose fiction in his office before going off to spend his evenings in Le Chat Noir or at various salons. Uncle Félix tried to save him from his life of debauchery by arranging for him to go into retreat in a monastery for a while, but Haraucourt loftily informed the superior that, although he considered himself to be a good Christian, he had never felt the slightest need or inclination to believe in the divinity of Christ, and he simply used his cell as another quiet place to write.

It was not until 1885 that Haraucourt contrived to publish a book with a commercial publisher in Paris: his second poetry collection, *L'Âme nue* [The Naked Soul], and not until 1887 that he followed it with his first novel, *Amis* [Lovers]. His first play, inevitably, was written for Sarah Bernhardt, whose coterie of male admirers he had joined with typical enthusiasm—a *Passion* in which she was to play the Virgin Mary—but it became embroiled in controversy and the first scheduled performance had to be moved and drastically reduced in scope; some years passed before it saw production in a theater and publication (in 1890). He fared better with his second play, a musical comedy based on Shakespeare, *Shylock* (published 1889) with music by Gabriel Fauré, but *Don Juan de Mañara* similarly languished unproduced and unpublished for some while, ultimately surfacing in 1890.

It was in this context that Haraucourt published "Immortalité," a piece whose theme and development reflects his continuing dubiousness regarding his ability to live up to the reputation he had acquired in advance of any real achievement. He must have been well aware of the fact that, although he had written *La Légende des sexes* by the time he turned twenty, he had been twenty-six by the time the 1883 edition appeared, and was now in his thirties, not really "young" by the standards of young Parisian writers—although his closest friend, Maurice Rollinant, was even older, and had made a similarly-belated début as a Decadent Hydropathe in 1883, having earlier published an isolated volume influenced by George Sand.

18

Indeed, all the writers whose attention Haraucourt courted and who befriended him were older than he was, often much older. That had its advantages—Leconte de Lisle, Banville and Renan recommended him for the Légion d'honneur as part of their publicity campaign on his behalf, and he was appointed a Chevalier, much to the astonishment of his superiors in the Ministry of Commerce, and probably to his sponsors too—but it also separated him somewhat from the writers of the up-and-coming generation. He was probably seen by them as a kind of weak imitation of his fellow *Chat Noir* performers Maurice Rollinat and Jean Richepin, and was deemed to have moved almost without transition from being scandalous to being *passé*. Even his cycling companions, who included Anatole France, belonged to an older generation—although the author of "L'Antéchrist" and the author of "La Tragédie humaine" doubtless found one another congenial company.

At any rate, it is not entirely surprising that Haraucourt had begun to feel intimations of literary mortality when his career had hardly begun in earnest—he was not to know, in 1888, that it would extend over another forty years, bringing him a certain measure of further critical acclaim, and even making him a little money. That helps to explain the rather jaundiced view presented in "Immortalité" of the conduct of the great writers in their private heaven—but any number of writers might have done that, while no other writer would have gone on from there to end the story as Haraucourt did, and it was that extension of perspective that not only laid the groundwork for his other futuristic fantasies but made them truly exceptional, unique in the annals of French scientific romance.

A downbeat spirit similar to that of the stories collected in *L'Effort* is reflected in his "novel in verse," *Seul* [Alone] (1890), but the critical reception of that book was more muted than that of *L'Âme nue*, and he must have felt that the backlash against his initial welcome was beginning to take form. By that time he was increasingly diverting more effort into drama and prose than the poetry that had been his first love. He must have had high hopes for *L'Effort*, which appeared as an elaborately decorated book with colored or monochrome illustrations on every page, framing the text, but it was not a commercial success, and there was a marked hiatus in his publications thereafter. It was not until he began working on a regular basis for *Le Journal* that he resumed publishing prose in a relatively steady fashion.

Haraucourt had another stroke of luck in 1894, however, when someone he met in a café—whose name he never discovered, but who obviously knew who he was—suggested out of the blue that he would be the ideal candidate for a vacancy as a curator of the sculpture collection in the Musée du Trocadero. He applied for it, and got it, and at last discovered a day job in which he could take a real interest, and in whose exercise he could be content. He spent the rest of his working life as a museum curator, transferring to the Musée de Cluny in 1903. Although he had had no interest in archeology prior to 1894, except insofar as it bore upon his love of Classical art, he took to it like a duck to water—and the stories in this collection will serve to illustrate exactly how well he was prepared in advance to take a long view of human affairs. Perhaps there was a mysterious heredity at work; although he only mentions the aristocratic d'Haraucourt family once in his *Mémoires*, when he comments that his Revolutionary great-grandfather had ended up fighting in battle against his own uncle, an *émigré* d'Haraucourt, it might be worth noting that the annals of the French Archeological Association are replete with d'Haraucourts, who seem to have formed a significant clique within its membership throughout the 19th century.

Not long after starting work at the Trocadero, in 1896, Haraucourt married. All that the *Mémoires* contains relating to the marriage is a handful of fragmentary notes that he never organized into a chapter, but he does take the trouble to observe that his friends were amazed by the fact of the marriage but not at all surprised when the immediate comment of one of them—"I'll wager she hasn't a *sou*"—turned out to be spot on.

He does not even mention his wife's name (it was Mathilde), let alone say anything about her background or the circumstances of their meeting, but she must have been considerably younger than him, as she outlived him by twenty years in spite of his surviving to the ripe old age of eight-five. The amenable job and the marriage—which was presumably amenable too, although it remained childless—seem to have mellowed him somewhat, although they did not change him. His work at the Trocadero undoubtedly fed in to the work he was doing, subtly, as in the thematic collection that he considered to be his poetic masterpiece, *Les Ages. L'Espoir du Monde* (1899)—a much closer analogue of *La Légende des siècles* than *La Légende des sexes*—and unsubtly, as in "Cinq mille ans," but the overall impression given by the work he published after the turn of the century is that it was more relaxed, and not quite as personal.

That was certainly true of the bulk of the work he did for *Le Journal* , to which he was a regular contributor for some two decades, The newspaper had been founded in 1892, but it was not until it was taken over by Henri Letellier in 1899 that Haraucourt was recruited as a routine supplier of copy. In spite of the paper's literary pretensions, he had to modify his output to fit the requirements of *feuilleton* fiction, and much of the work he did for the paper consisted of short domestic melo-dramas and *contes cruels* that could be fitted into the weekly *feuilleton* section (which had space for between 1500 and 2500 words) in their entirety. He reprinted numerous pieces from that slot along with a previously-unpublished novella in *Les Naufragés* [Castaways] (1902), and a further batch in *La Peur* [Fear] (1907), both of which volumes reflect the miseries of the human condition in a series of depictions of tragedies and disasters, often involving an element of physical horror, but in a detached and rather casual manner. Five stories from the former collection and three from the latter were combined with three further items from *Le Journal* in a new collection, also (confusingly) titled *La Peur* (1914), but the Great War

21

followed hot on the heels of that collection and he published nothing similar thereafter.

Haraucourt appears to have tested the waters of *Le Journal* with regard to publishing futuristic fiction there with a short piece about the abolition of dueling, "Point d'honneur. Contes de l'avenir" [Point of Honor: Tales of the Future] in 1900 (although he had served as a second in several literary duels Haraucourt refused to fight himself and disapproved strongly of the institution), but the seeming promise contained in the subtitle remained unfulfilled—although "Conte de l'avenir: Le Dernier Pape" [A Tale of the Future: The Last Pope] appeared in another periodical, *La Grande Revue* in 1903, presumably having been rejected by *Le Journal*. The editor appears to have relented, however, and "Le Gorilloïde" appeared in three parts in January 1904, to be followed by the six parts of "Cinq mille ans" in September/October of the same year. Nothing more of a similar kind appeared thereafter, however, and although the former story was reprinted as a booklet, Haraucourt never managed to reprint the latter item in any form at all, either because it was considered too unconventional in its form or because it was considered insulting to the inhabitants of Paris, France, and Europe.

Alongside his work for *Le Journal*, Haraucourt published several longer prose pieces, including the novel *Les Benoît* (1904) and a book containing two short novels, *Trumaille et Pélisson* (1908), all of which were ironic tales of luckless humans implacably crushed by cruel fate and the hostility of their fellows. The book he undoubtedly intended to be his prose masterpiece, however, was *Dieudonat* [the tile is a name, but it means "godsend"] (1912), an extended *conte philosophique* somewhat reminiscent of Voltaire's *Candide*, although he presumably thought of it as his own *Don Quixote*.

It is probably significant that Haraucourt did not publish any more futuristic fiction for six years after his account of the ruins of Paris and the stern lessons to be leaned therefrom, and that when he did, it was a story of a markedly different kind, being set in the imminent future. "La Découverte du docteur

Anguérande" appeared in seven parts in *Le Journal*, but not quite as a serial. The first part appeared three weeks before the second and there was a fortnight's gap before the third appeared; that must have made for slightly difficult reading, and no one ever got a chance to read the story *en bloc* during the author's lifetime. Small wonder, therefore, that it remained unknown and unhailed, even among dedicated fans of antiquarian proto-science fiction. It is, however, a very remarkable story, as brilliant in its own way as "Le Gorilloïde" and "Cinq mille ans," whose scope and sarcasm are slightly undermined by the inevitably awkwardness of their presentation.

At a much later date, Isaac Asimov was to complain bitterly about the dire effect on speculative fiction of what he dubbed the "Frankenstein complex"—the tendency of writers about technology to use the same story-arc as Mary Shelley's novel, introducing a new technology only to cause it to run amok, thus requiring destruction. Whatever its convenience as a plot-formula, and the reassurance provided by the apparent restoration of the *status quo* in the conclusion, the endless repetition of this ritual, in Asimov's view, was bound to breed an extremely unhealthy technophobia in its readers. The problem facing writers wanting to do things differently, of course, is that if new technologies are *not* introduced into stories merely in order to be canceled out again, the project of literary extrapolation becomes much more difficult and the results much less likely to provide readers with a comforting sense of closure.

"La Découverte du docteur Anguérande" is one of very few scientific romances not only to recognize this problem but to react against it, decisively and fiercely. It deliberately inverts the formula, so that when the new technology makes its definitive appearance, it is not the invention that runs amok but the society into which it is introduced. Whereas Victor Frankenstein was represented as "the new Prometheus"—J. B. S. Haldane was later to complain that biological inventors following in the footsteps of Daedalus actually got an even worse literary deal than Promethean chemists or physicists—

Haraucourt's biological inventor is explicitly likened to Christ, recapitulating God's role by bringing humans the gift of new life. Whereas Frankenstein became the archetype of a whole species of "mad scientists" threatening to upset worlds whose sanity is taken for granted, Anguérande is represented as a quintessentially sane individual caught up in a whirlwind of violence that exposes the inherent madness lurking just beneath the surface of civilization. The story thus became the first, if not the ultimate, parody of the Frankenstein complex, and warrants classic status of a sort on that account.

Classic or not, though, it is easy to see that "La Découverte du docteur Anguérande" was not calculated to win its author any widespread popularity. If what he had done to Paris in "Cinq mille ans," in a relatively good-humored fashion, had seemed to some readers to be a mortal insult, then what he did to it in "La Découverte du docteur Anguérande," in a spirit of fervent wrath, was ten times worse; not only did Paris become an insane city stupidly rejecting the gift of life, but it did so partly because the good doctor had won entirely sane and reasonable support from Germany: the arch-enemy of all French scientific romance. If that support automatically made Anguérande a traitor in the eyes of the Parisians of the story, it presumably did exactly the same for Haraucourt in the eyes of his Parisian readers—as he had obviously known that it would.

Given that observation, there is a certain irony in the fact that when Haraucourt returned to the future on last time the pages of *Le Journal*, it was not long after the conclusion of the Great War, when "Le conflit suprême" appeared there in four parts in March 1919, reflecting with extremely sarcastic bitterness on the manner in which the war had proved everything the author had always believed and stridently proclaimed about the long term future—or lack of it—of humankind. Reflecting the disillusionment and disgust of the war's aftermath, the story lacks the majestically-distanced calm of "Le Gorilloïde" and "Cinq mille ans," and even the combative flamboyance of "La Fin du monde" and "La Découverte du docteur Anguérande" but its sheer relentlessness preserves a certain impact in spite of its slapdash disorder.

In between those last two futuristic stories, however, Haraucourt had found the editor and readers of *Le Journal* much more sympathetic to tales of the distant past. Between December 1912 and June 1914 he published a long series of vignettes featuring the inventive exploits of the "first human," which were rearranged in book form as *Daâh, the premier homme* (1914). That seems to have been the most popular of all his books, except for his oft-reprinted guidebook to the Cluny museum. Immediately after *Daâh*'s publication, however, the Great War interrupted Haraucourt's career decisively, and, like many other French writers, he was not the same man by the time it had concluded. "Le conflit suprême" was, in a sense, a sad gesture of farewell to what had been before— "*Adieu, et bon ennui*," as St, Peter's stand-in says, tellingly, to the protagonist of "Immortalité."

Although Haraucourt did go on to publish two more novels, *L'Oncle Maize* [Uncle Maize] (1922) and *Vertige d'Afrique* [African Vertigo] (1922) he dedicated most of his subsequent writing career to the production of a supposedly-definitive historical study of *L'Amour et l'Esprit gaulois à travers l'histoire du XVe au XXe siècle* [Love and the Gallic Spirit Through History from the 15th to the 20th Century], published in four volumes, after his retirement from Cluny, in 1927-29. He lived thereafter in a cottage on the Île de Bréhat off the cost of Brittany, apparently doing very little until he decided to write his memoirs, and not doing enough thereafter to bring that work to a conclusion.

The literary legacy that Haraucourt left behind is undoubtedly a peculiar one, but that surely ought to be reckoned a good thing, there being no virtue in unoriginality. Whether or not it certifies the greatness to which he once aspired is, of course, a matter of opinion, but he probably did enough to have got into the kind of impossible writers' paradise described in "Immortalité," even if he never got into the actual Académie. He offered himself as a candidate once, in 1909, in competition with Henri de Régnier (whom he had first met at that very first *soirée chez* Leconte de Lisle) and Jean Richepin (whom he knew well from the early days of *Le Chat Noir*, and had greatly admired for his flamboyancy), but he lost the election. The many people who were surprised that Richepin won would probably have been astonished had Haraucourt won instead, and he never tried again; Régnier simply waited for another seat to fall vacant, offered himself for a second time, and was accepted. As readers of this collection will clearly see, however, Haraucourt knew perfectly well that, in the long run, it really didn't matter whether the Académie acclaimed him or not, because all illusions of immortality are utterly vain. The trick is to make the most of mortality while it lasts, and he certainly seems to have done that.

Brian Stableford

IMMORTALITY

A conte philosophique

I was a little frightened to discover that my last hour was about to sound and that it was necessary to die.

I had got the most out of life, knowing the joys and the suffering that it permits a frail organism with our body and our soul. I had possessed everything that one can possess down here, since my imagination, making up for the insufficiencies of fortune, had given me internally, by turns, all the intimate enjoyments that the real world had refused me. On my whim, I had been powerful, rich and beloved. What emperor ever imposed a more sovereign autocracy than the one it pleased me to invoke in miraculous realms? What king or sultan handled more gold or precious stones in vaster coffers, or built a more sumptuous palace in which to dwell? What Don Juan embraced lovers more superb in the midst of more terrible or sweeter dramas? I had only had to close my eyes to see everything—which is to say, to merit everything and hold everything. The universe had been submissive to my desire and, unlike those who possess material things, I had not wearied of anything, because I created them at the caprice of my changing needs, and in each one I had cherished my work—which is to say, myself; an affection that is never deceived.

I said to myself: "There are only two things in life that make it worth living: the love of art and the art of love." I had divided my human duration between the two. I had been wise enough to be a fool; I could die content.

What a treasure I was about to forsake, though, in the consciousness of my thinking being! At a stroke, I was about to lose, not only everything that exists, but everything that can be conceived; not just the essence of a human being, but that of the gods!

At least, like Horace. I thought that I was not dying *entirely*.

Frankly, I had reaped little glory thus far. I had just passed through half a century without raising much veritable enthusiasm, and I could not help finding that quite legitimate—certainly not by virtue of any doubt as to my vast merit, but by reason of the fact that curious minds are the last to solicit the curiosity of the crowd: the crowd that all prodigies attract except those of thought, which runs after a fossil tree, a guillotine, an acrobat or a beast, which understands them, but which finds intellect boring.

But I anticipated future justice; across the future, I saw my soul perpetuated in the memory of fraternal souls; I heard, with a hint of jealousy and rancor, some amorous beauty reading one of my amorous sonnets, and lending my words to the lips of someone absent.

"So what? What can it mean to you that, in twenty years, a woman who might once have given herself to you can only contemplate your bust in the foyer of a theater? She would be the first to be frightened and disgusted if you came back from your immortality to ask you for a caress...

"Imminent cadaver, what good is glory, if love is not its end? An end avowed or unavowed, conscious or unconscious, love is the terminus of everything, the only valid hope, and what love does not recompense is not recompensed. You have mocked Woman, but for her alone you have amassed labor in dreams, for her smile, for her kiss, and what you pretend to pursue in the beyond is merely a lie of your vanity. All glory is a decoy, if it is not proven, when night sleeps over the city, by a mouth with beautiful white teeth..."

These reflections had too much truth in them to soothe my death-throes, and I turned my head toward those who were weeping around my bed. Their faces gave evidence of a profound affection and a sincere grief; I was both satisfied and chagrined. The desolation of those good people pained me on their behalf and pleased me on my own. I experienced a mixture of pity and pride at seeing so much regret on my behalf, and the pity was soothing, since I rendered it in proportion to the regret devoted to my person.

My beloved was sobbing, her forehead supported on the bed, and occasionally raised her tearful eyes toward me. She had a rare beauty thus, so beautiful and so young that I was anxious for her; I understood that she would either die of despair within a matter of months, or, too deprived of love, would replace me at the end of a year; egoism and affection struggled within me, and I did not dare to wish for either one of those misfortunes.

"Darling," I said to her, "when I am no longer here, will you love someone else?"

She straightened up, her arms extended, sublime in fear, prayer and faith, and I was severely punished for my foolish and cruel words, for she fainted; someone carried her out and I died without seeing her again.

Softly, without effort and without pain, I expired, so gently that it was impossible for me to discern the precise moment when life was, and then was not; I even believe that the moment in question does not exist, for I persevered in waiting for an end when the end, it seems, had already come. Someone murmured: "The heart's no longer beating." I sensed that it was true, but I still sensed it; I retained a confused perception of the fuss that was going on around me, and almost of the causes of the sounds—and when someone approached me to close my eyelids, I had an infinitely subtle notion of the touch of a finger, which trembled over my eyes.

Increasingly, however, I was detached from any interest in things and of life, and the ephemeral, incomplete sensations did not awaken within me any need for analysis or comprehension. After my death, I lived a special life, diminishing by degrees, which would have appeared incomplete to an animal, but was a life nevertheless: the life of plants that have been cut and are etiolating in vases. That vegetal persistence was succeeded by another, even more meager, doubtless created by the chemical work of various elements united in my remains, which were gradually being transformed and disaggregating.

Thus, I was declining toward a more imperfect state from one minute to the next—which, by a series of ungraspable transitions, a slow progress through organic metamorphoses, was going to take me lower still—and during that play of bases and salts, acids and metals, during that alembic warmth, parts of me fled toward other bodies, disseminated to infinity. I forgot them, while new beings appropriated them, in order to enjoy, with the debris of myself, something they called their self. Thus came, in the gradual cooling, the slumber of inert minerality.

These logical evolutions, and the minimal apperception that remained within them, permeated my defunct being, bearing nothing within them that could offend our conventions regarding the laws of eternal matter. But alongside that, outside of it, a phenomenon was produced so strange that I cannot succeed in convincing myself of it, even though it has lasted for several thousand years, and I would not dare to relate it here were it not for the hope I have of bringing to human lips the scornful smile with which they welcome every mystery or simple dream: the smile that brings joy to the greater number, and does honor to its victims.

Scarcely was I dead than I perceived that my soul was immortal, no longer in the diffuse fashion of my body, which was beginning to crumble, but immortal in all its force, with a clear and total possession of its essence.

I had difficulty comprehending it at first, so much did the revelation astound my reason, which had always affirmed the impossibility of a result without labor and a effect without cause. I was humiliated by my long error, and all the more vexed that my dialectic continued to rebel against the admission of such a hypothesis, refusing the possibility even in confrontation with the manifest fact.

In that state of mind I found myself on the threshold of a vast domain enclosed by railings and planted with magnificent trees. The gate opened before me and an old man dressed in an antique fashion came toward me with a hospitable gravity, asking to know my name. I had no difficulty replying, for we are always proud to hear our own name pronounced, as if an entire synthesis of genius and glory were magically contained in those few syllables.

"A poet, no doubt? Only poets name themselves with that simple pomposity. Please wait here."

He drew away, and came back almost immediately with a rectangular package that he was generous enough to offer to me."

"Here's your paradise," he said, "and your inferno. If you'd care to follow me now..."

My immortal soul took the bundle that was held out to it, and started walking alongside its host. I framed a thousand questions internally, of course, regarding the nature of that enigmatic gift, but I dared it ask a single one, for fear of seeming too ill-informed. The old man, doubtless accustomed to that noble attitude, smiled beneath his white beard, either out of compassion for my humanity or simply because he wanted to exchange a few words, and asked whether I didn't want to know what my burden contained.

"It's the shade of your books," he added.

I scarcely understood any better, but I tried not to let anything show.

"They'll be useful to you in the region that awaits you, in the Garden of Letters, where those who mirror their soul in words reside. There you'll find your predecessors, those you love, and others, just as great, permanently unknown in your homeland, whom you'll revere for their misunderstood majesty. There you'll live together, in the communal exile that you have been able to merit, far from ordinary people..."

At these words, I felt a profound joy, and I appreciated all the serenity of a happiness forbidden in the world of nations. Is not exile the true fatherland? O Paradise, more-than-promised land, since nothing promised it in slavery! I was about to penetrate into a world that passers-by do not enter, where one converses with one's peers, where impotence is no longer there to judge as a sovereign mistress, where one is

31

delivered from the antagonist who makes us respect our failures, and the complimenter who makes us blush over our merits!

"I beg your pardon, amiable old man—one more word: are there, at least, women there?"

"A rich windfall, in a wood where they only retain their intelligence!"

"Then, truly, we shall be alone..."

"As in the course of life! For you're not unaware that the perpetual labor of thought is the calmest of egotisms, and that the furtive memory of emotions is engulfed therein. What use are they, profound as they are, if not to re-enter into the dream, to descend within yourself? Alone—and that will be, I tell you, your reward and your punishment—alone, the rare monsters who, falling in love with infinite problems, and seeking, and digging, knead errors mingled with truths; those who deign to think..."

"Do human beings exist who have never thought?"

"They're small in number; but less numerous still are those who link a few judgments and erect an entity. The members of the near-universal crowd, having only attained embryos of purely contingent whims, only survive death in a fashion as incomplete and as sterile as their life. Puny in ideas, they wear an appearance of soul that now procures them an appearance of prolongation—floating in limbo, as the Christians put it, among the souls of infants and beasts."

"Which is infinitely flattering for dreamers, and which avenges them."

"Oh, they don't all get in here."

"I thought as much," I replied.

"I know. Artists are scornful of those who do not have the gift, and prefer those who have."

I noticed once again that the old man professed, with regard to the human species and our failings, a disdain that was slightly shocking to a son of woman; so, by virtue of a need to rebel, which is sometimes dearer to us than our ideas, I felt honor-bound to come to the defense of suspect artists of whom I had been ashamed on earth.

"They don't all get in here, you say? And how do you separate the bad from the good? Have you an esthetic tribunal, and has that tribunal the right to judge? Nature might be eternal, but not Beauty; it's the appropriation of nature to the temperament of an individual, or a race, or an epoch. Can you quote an absolute formula, then, for eternal Beauty? Great artists have devoted their lives to its embrace, but you can't name two who agreed on its definition; sages have pursued the True, and all by different paths, but we have venerated them all as sages; religions have discovered the Good, heroes have professed it to the point of martyrdom, and we have built temples, sanctified prophets, while contrary religions have, in turn, charged one another with anathemas and one cult's apostles have damned another's saints!"

"You deny the absolute! Know it, therefore, now that it is too late to repeat it to your brethren! There exists between the laws of the body and those of the soul a correlation of which humans have no suspicion, but which science will perhaps one day reveal to you. The domain of thought and that of matter arise from one unique principle, and all things are directed according to one unique method. The same harmony presides over everything, regulates everything, orders wills as well as stars and plants, and one primal law dwells in the abstract of which all the others, physical and moral, are only corollaries."

"God?"

"As you please. One of the corollaries is the law of Beauty. But what does it matter? Your merit, humans, lies not in knowing the divine thing, but in seeking it, wanting it, cherishing it and giving its love the blood of your flesh and the effort of your soul. Your grandeur is in the worship and the will.

"That alone, my friend, is judged at the esthetic tribunal which you were pleased to imagine just now—which we do not have, but which resides in the sincerity of your own consciences."

"Our consciences?"

"Yes—as with animals, there are warm-blooded artists and cold-blooded artists. As with animals, the former have their personal temperature, the later participate in the ambient temperature. The former are souls, the latter reflections; the former create, the latter assimilate. Some, at the price of a sacrificed fortune or happiness, pursue the adorable ideal and—repudiated more often than not by the skeptical or hateful indifference of their contemporaries—dream with their eyes upraised to the heavens, without seeing anything around them, and seeing nothing even in the heavens at which they gaze but their own soul. The others are unconcerned with their Beauty or their Truth, but with the affirmation that it is necessary to present to people in order to please them or shock them—which comes to the same thing, since the end they are pursuing is public attention. They sacrifice their self—doubtless worthless since it cannot triumph—to the crowd, and in that bastard compromise their renown and wealth is erected. They do not produce, they produce themselves; they are full, not of talent but of their own talent; their sufficiency is made of their own insufficiency, as furtive and temporary as the moment and fashion; they are born to die, and, before art, live as if they had not been born; but they are the great men on earth, while the valorous are the great men in heaven.

"So it's those praised by the vulgar to whom you close your door?"

"They have no wish to open it; having been their own judges; if they were conscious, they have opted for success rather than pure art; if unconscious, their name is impotence, and what right would they have?"

Fearing that the eloquent old man was no longer building abstruse theories, I permitted myself to interrupt, and was about to take a look at the beauty of the location when he told me that our journey was at an end.

I consoled myself effortlessly, thinking about future friends, beautiful conversations with the demigods, giants of poetry and great thinkers before whom I would be proud to humble myself, and to whom I would express my admiration in emotional terms, and who might perhaps render me some sympathy in exchange...

"*Adieu*," the old man say to me "and *bon ennui!*"[3]

When he indicated the remainder of the route to me with an extended arm, I continued on my way.

There were, in turn, paths through woods, amid thick vegetation and unfamiliar flowers; walkways of opaline sand that sparkled in the light, like crushed pearls; abrupt clearings inviting dreamy repose; and shady nooks on the banks of streams, above which hung long hammocks that one might have imagined to be woven out of blonde tresses. Sometimes, a melodious aroma passed on the breeze, like the tune of a song, and sometimes unexpected music emerged from magical tree-trunks or rained down from high branches.

Above the foliage, a changing sky was radiant, and toward the distant horizons, a line of mysterious mountains slept, roseate and violet.

But no one was living there; I walked for a long time.

Suddenly, I perceived, crouched at the foot of a tree, a man dressed in animal-hides, who was protecting with his hand, like a miser guarding his treasure, a large heap of gray objects resembling bones. He ran toward me brandishing a kind of club; he shouted incomprehensible syllables at me, and the same sounds were repeated perpetually in his mouth. When he reached me he put the object I had taken for a weapon in front of my face: a ewe's shoulder-blade on which symbols were engraved. Alternately, he tapped the bone and his chest with his finger, looking at me anxiously, and the syllables that he was hurling at me like a madman, with a plead-

---

[3] This pun on the conventional *bonne nuit* [goodnight] is untranslatable, but easily comprehensible.

ing voice, were still the same. Occasionally, he darted a suspicious glance toward the tree he had just quit, as if he feared that someone might steal his wealth.

The man was suffering profoundly from my silence, and I was sorry not to be able to reply to him; I shrugged my shoulders and shook my head in a gesture of helplessness—but that gesture was doubtless terrible to him, for he extended his arms despairingly and fled toward his tree.

Then others came, who also repeated unique syllables, in the same anxious and pleasing tone; they surrounded me and crowded me, jostling one another in order to speak to me; some showed me hieroglyphic cylinders or pieces of wood covered in colored streaks, others held out coarse figurines of fallen deities; one held fire in his hand. Then, I was shown wax tablets or long scrolls of papyrus; and the crowd was still growing, with monotonous cries, and the further I advanced in order to escape them, the greater their number became, and everyone who perceived me immediately ran to meet me.

Finally, amid that dolorous clamor, I discerned the language of a Greek; taking him to one side, I understood that he was telling me his name, and asking me whether that name was glorious on earth...

Misery! Human misery, to that extent!

They were all calling out their names and asking me whether humankind had lost their work and their memory!

Before my ignorant gaze they stood aside, some angrily, others full of resignation. Immediately, others came to take their places, and my pity wept for them.

I saw some who did not even deign to disturb themselves as I passed by, for after a hundred centuries, they had ended up despairing.

Finally, I found myself among those who shared our language.

The most ancient—having gradually, by the accumulation of days, detached themselves from our hypocrisies—solicited a terrestrial memory without any pretense. The more recent greeted me with an exaggerated benevolence and questioned me as to the present state of letters, without interrogating me about themselves. I replied to them in friendly terms. More human than they had remained, I was a better liar and concealed my thoughts; could anyone blame me for having thought that I was fulfilling a duty in concealing the unjust scorn heaped on one of them, or the diminished grandeur of another, or having hesitated to torture those shades with the ignorance or stupidity of my contemporaries?

By dint of multiplying kind words, however, I ran out of formulae, and warm as my eulogies seemed to me, I soon observed that they remained insufficient for those in favor of whom I was inventing so much glory. Those dead men were insatiable; they hungered for nothing else. Those who, when alive, had been best able to preserve the courage of the sincerity of their dream from the vain noise of renown, no longer thought of anything now but collecting posthumous fruits, as if they had formerly worked for nothing else, as if the renunciation of present favor had only been possible for them once by virtue of their faith in the favors to come.

I had been introduced to great men, whose conversation taught me nothing beyond their books and almost diminished their greatness for me. Through their acquaintance, I was able to convince myself more exactly of an aphorism that I had once tried to establish: the vastest minds only possess, in reality, one sole idea, which haunts and dominates them, constitutes their entire personality and is perpetually reproduced in various manifestations, which they mistake for different ideas. An event in which they are involved, a sensation that touches them, a sentiment that moves them, will excite in the depths of their soul that unique wellspring of thoughts and cause it to gush; every impulse of their heart, every pronouncement of their brain is a formulation of it, the analysis of which denounces its parentage; everything emanates from that idea and everything is brought back to it; it is a trunk with a thousand branches, which generates flowers of fruit thanks to the strong trunk that assembles and fuels them.

On observing this unity of origins in an intellectual organism, I recalled the doctrines of the old man concerning the unity of the primordial law regulating the universe; every moral being appeared to me as a little world constructed in the resemblance of the great. "And," I said to myself, "if the cosmic forces are called God, is it not this judgment that the holy books signify in declaring that human beings are made in God's image?"

This posthumous psychology occupied the early days of my sojourn, but egotism soon claimed its rights.

A few immortals, in order to talk to me about their books, deigned to direct the conversation initially toward mine, and I discreetly expressed the desire to know their opinion of me. I therefore undertook to play for them the role that they were playing for me, but I excused myself without constraint. They, I thought, were only preoccupied with the banal impressions of the public, while I was enquiring of a chosen elect, and my case seemed honorable by comparison with theirs. Thus, I allowed several of them to extract from me the promise to confide the only copy of my works to them, and the list of my promises immediately became so long that it was necessary for me to keep an exact account of them.

The attention of that society became more welcome thereafter, and I welcomed with genuine joy the visitors whose words brought me a judgment of myself alongside a question about them. As soon as it was returned, the book passed into other hands; it deteriorated somewhat, but I heard with a broad smile the friendly apologies mingled with just eulogies. Was a slight rip paying too much for the compliment of so august an ancestor? And I gave no further thought to the fact that the exemplar was the only one to which my immortality had the right.

People talked about me; the officious quoted the favorable remarks made about me, and I adapted myself so well to that pomp that I could no longer envisage without a certain anxiety the prospect of a new arrival who might steal my importance.

With that dread, however, was mingled the unacknow-ledged desire to know what eloquence had declared over my coffin. "Adieu, dear and noble friend..." Oh, the beautiful speeches I could have improvised on the edge of my grave!

One day, I learned that he had arrived...that the latest dead man had just been born.

Run toward him, listen to him, interrogate him? What need would I have, anyway, to ask him questions? He must be full of me...

But all those old ghosts barred the way and gave evidence of a truly indecent avidity. I would at least inform them of the way that a shade worthy of the name behaves! I would teach them by my example not to hurl themselves voraciously at the heads of poor deceased individuals! I waited, without moving, with an apparent impassivity—with which they were all familiar, by virtue of once having simulated it themselves.

He appeared. He was nothing but a black bard, a misera-ble Griot[4] whom his people and his king, according to the prevailing custom with regard to poets, had immured in the hollow trunk of a baobab, and the nation had had held a great feast as a sign of rejoicing.

The sorcerer could not be of interest to any civilized soul and was soon left in peace. Uncaring, he went to sit down by himself under an odorant linden tree and began to sing again, accompanying his chants with the rhythm of a drum. People went by but he was oblivious to them—and some of them envied him.

But what about a man? Is a man so rare a thing, then?

Finally, someone died on the old continent, and he came from the cities of France.

---

[4] Griots were a kind of ethnographic fantasy, allegedly a caste of magically-talented wise men recognized by Central African tribes in the French colonial regions of Sudan and Senegam-bia, analogous—as the text acknowledges—to the (equally fantasized) bards of the ancient Celts.

"Oh," he said to me, "what a triumph, my dear friend. You're the god of fools. After the pitiful funeral rites and the obligatory necrology, a brave bureaucrat protested in a long analysis and conferred genius upon you—you know that we gladly attribute genius to dead men who, like you, only had talent. Young men became excited and gave lectures in which humanity entire was honored by your spirit; your play was produced! When sane people wanted to raise a few reservations, the old critic who had derided your poems so forcefully, and made so many bourgeois laugh with your verses, cried shame upon those who were insulting a hero in his sepulcher and the fatherland in one of its glories. He was the one who as able to march at the head of the Young, organizing their enthusiasm and enlisting them.

"The most foolish of your detractors became, with him, your most respectful disciples; and, as they had mocked you by virtue of not being able to understand you, logically, they extolled you for the same reason. A eulogy devoted to you is nowadays a qualification of intellectual delicacy and esthetic sensitivity; fundamentally, they praise you in order to be esteemed, and not for what you are; no one reads you, any more than they did before, but people buy your books. Your glory is an investment, and your statue a bid at auction. People criticize your widow for having married her lover! Apotheosis, my dear, or fashionability, which comes to the same thing. Would you like to know a secret? It will pass."

An augury of misfortune! His prophecy was accurate. Another few months, and I was dethroned—by the author of some seductive crime, or a mob, the inventor of a machine or a microbe, or a star... My fatherland, France, had this for its motto: always possess a great man, and change him every spring. It thus established a rotation of glory in conformity with its democratic aspirations, which permitted every citizen to hope for his moment of history.

I consoled myself for such a rapid fall by counting on a future rediscovery. I thought: "Truth informed by art does not act directly upon the masses; it impresses a few distinguished minds, and is plundered in turn, for their own use and by trade, by the ostentatious acrobats, vague keepers of dancing bears who assemble the crowd and are the only ones able to please it, because of their mediocrity; they only understand half of it and only explain a quarter of it, but no one else has the voice to be heard, and the respects of vain people only return later to the ultimate origin."

We formed in the other world a group of malcontents whom the world has maltreated. When one of us became famous again he rendered his esteem to the living and left us. By way of compensation, however, the group was incessantly swelled by all the illustrious individuals fallen into desuetude, geniuses in retirement from employment who came to wax indignant in our midst and return scorn for disdain. Oh, how they legislated in vengeful adages!

"What good is effort," they cried, "and for whom? Superior beings, in the course of their lives, are submissive to rules followed by fools; they submit, being too few in number to resist, but they plant the seed on their wisdom and die; then, slowly, their solitary thought becomes wisdom for the crowd; but the crowd, in touching it, makes foolishness of it in order to assimilate it more easily; other sages suffer from it in their turn, dream, die, reform, are reformed, and so it goes on, forever..."

When the band of the triumphant passed by, and waved to us, we banished added:

"Patience... Do you know what endures better than the most superb creations? It's conventional banality. In the whole of your soul, the representatives of posterity, guided by their instinct, will be able to discover in some poor corner one miserable phrase that formulates in a synthesis the noble stupidity of peoples: that is what they will choose of you, because it resembles them; that is what they will put in your name in anthologies, which worldly people will cite appropriately, by way of erudition, and which will follow you in the esteem of

41

electors, until you disappear in your turn beneath a deluge of more modern ineptitudes."[5]

I do not know whether these insolences are creditworthy, but the fact is, so far as I was concerned, that the third generation displayed of me a few verses plagiarized from Boileau and a few parliamentary aphorisms; the latter got me into schools, and the baccalaureate examination became my only hope.

To show that I deserved better, I quietly put my library at everyone's disposition, but the poor books were already becoming tattered; when they were returned to me, I returned them and caressed them with loving care.

Everyone, in any case, was doing the same, and we talked in between times about art, its nature and its goal; each of us presented an authoritative definition in conformity with his own temperament, almost always contained in a chapter of his work: the supreme homage!

One said: "Art is an interpreted malady."

Another: "Talent is accumulated will."

A third: "Genius is an obsession."

And everyone: "Prettiness in art is the agreeable form of ugliness."

As befit people placed outside the struggle, who watch the foundations of their work being undermined, we easily fell into agreement in issuing recriminations against the tendency of letters.

"What remains in the sphere of publishing?" an epic poet declaimed. "Two classes: the executioners of books and the gilders of syllables. Rival classes, and both are right to cover one another with insults. The former cannot write and the lat-

---

[5] Edmond Haraucourt could not know, of course, that more than a century later, a search of the world wide web would repeatedly turn up one single line of his poetry, preserved in popular song, which he would probably not have regarded as his most profound thought. ("Partir, c'est mourir un peu" [To depart is to die a little].)

ter do not deign to think! If it were forbidden to quote the former, what would become of the latter? Exclusive concern with form leads an author fatally and progressively to refinements so complex that they are confined to aberration; it is little more than a monomania, and bears its own death within it twice over: absence of idea, folly of form..."

Etc.

In that he went astray, paying no heed to the fact that such a literature is that which suits an era in which art is no more than a recreation.

Alas, it would soon be even less...

From time to time, abrupt reactions brought one of us back into the light, and I observed that every epoch collected, from the racial past, the poet who had had a soul analogous to that of the new days; every civilization sympathized with its brothers of another age, and when it was extinguished in a transformation of the species, the elected poets returned to a second era of forgetfulness, and others emerged for an ephemeral period, until changing humanity gave them in their turn successors more appropriate to the tendencies of its thought. Of all of them, successively, it was said: "How modern he is!"

I understood then that immortality is merely an intermittence.

Watching over the centuries, I looked forward to my resurrection. One day, people of small importance adopted me in good faith, and I was moved, without vanity.

"Yes," I said, "to do one's work is a duty, not for the masses, about whom it is permissible to care as little as they care about us, but for the few, who will find joy in it, and the consolations of a stainless friendship, for the unknown brothers we would have cherished, and who will cherish us, whose soul will bathe in that momentary communion, the quiet confidence of the book that listens, in order to persuade itself of the duty of amity."

But then, again, buried in the distant dust of accumulated books, I was only touched by those who plagiarize, devourers

43

of the dead, vampires of letters, who know how to rob tombs and nourish themselves on the cadaver of glory.[6]

Meanwhile, the chronicles of the earth were becoming increasingly rare. Poetry could no longer flourish. Practical and positive life unified the minds of races. Art gave way to business; publicity called itself glory, comfort happiness and desire passion; joys having become enjoyments, money was the sole origin of everything, and the skillful heaped it up. Renown was no longer a favor stolen by intrigue but, like love, merchandise that only the rich could buy. Some undertook, hopefully, to write books, paint canvases, sculpt marbles; then the press set the tariffs for them at which talent, genius and publicity were sold. Ambition wore away determination and need oppressed ideas; no one spent his life anymore; everyone earned a living; profit was law, worship being poverty, and nothing else existed.

Sometimes, nevertheless, the world, in a spirit of dandyism, offered itself the luxury of a bad poet to pamper; sometimes, also, some demigod who had died of starvation would come to tell us about the sumptuous distress of our descendants.

Humanity advanced thus.

---

[6] Ouch. In this depiction of waxing and waning fame, however, Haraucourt is not deliberately setting out to insult those who might one day take an interest in him, but meditating on such exemplars as Charles Baudelaire, who was adopted as a role model by the members of the Decadent Movement of the 1880s a generation after his death. Haraucourt was routinely assumed to belong to that Movement, although he would have denied it. He would also have had in mind the manner in which Leconte de Lisle was adopted by the Parnassians as a hero when his initial fame had dwindled, and then dropped again by the younger members of the association, who found his company a trifle boring.

At that time, the most fortunate among us saw themselves denied in their very existence, and commentaries were published to demonstrate that they never existed.

Then, increasingly, humans detached themselves from things and, while the slowness of the ages extended in ennui, we learned nothing but the number of the years from the stories of the most recent arrivals.

Our old planet was impoverished by its artificial luxury, and the soil, exhausted by over-hasty production, dried up like the human heart.

A silence fell then, and lasted so long that the heavens thought the Earth extinct; it lasted so many centuries that we watched, with amazement, other beings arrive. They were hirsute and stocky, with dark eyes, bare torsos and menacing arms. To savage rhythms, in curt and bitter words, they sang violent battle-hymns.

The Earth had, therefore, oscillating in its orbital course, inverted its poles, in order that new continents might surge from the hollows of the seas, in order that the oceans might invade the empires with their waves and foam, with forests of poisonous algae.

Everything was about to begin again.

Nothing any longer remained of our ancient passage; definitive death had erased everything and confounded the pride of the great and the petty alike; our time fled so far away from us that we lost the memory of it ourselves, and Dante became the contemporary of Orpheus.

Beneath the immensity of our ennui, some crouched down in the contemplation of their books, in order to find some vestige therein evocative of their abolished existence. In the restricted circle of their unique idea, those spirits turned and returned about themselves, indefinitely, and the pettiness of their human aims then became clear to their judgment, enlightened by a gleam of infinity. On the threshold of one oblivion, they became able at that moment to imagine another, which was called the oblivion of thought. And the disgust of having been was the only thing that survived of so much pride.

But life was renewed upon the globe, and that other humankind, whose newborn we had seen a little while before, undertook its own voyage through the recommencing series of centuries.

Then, weary of seeing, avid to die a second time, leaving the heap of our illusory dreams to molder under the trees, we all set off along a route that took us far away from the races that had succeeded us, toward the mysterious world of the horizon.

Thus our exile progressed, voluntarily seeking the darkness.

But when, beyond the frontiers of snow, we came to a gray land that lay beyond a colorless sky, we found a vast host sleeping on the sands: ashen faces, with lightless eyes, the shades of shades, who had once, like us known the miseries and the vain splendor of life and thought, in the very distant past, before the first Deluge...

The people whose anterior existence we had not suspected roused themselves from their torpor to watch us file past, and, without asking who had troubled their sleep, lay down again in total indifference.

Beyond!

In order to sleep like the elders, our renunciation demanded bleaker darkness!

Finally, in the obscure silence of an inviolable desert, we recognized our true abode. Everyone lay down on the ground, desirous, since everyone had forgotten him, of forgetting himself, in order to bury the inanity of his dreams and his pride in the depths of a sleep that would be endless.

THE MADONNA

There was once—a long time ago—a painter who possessed a great artistic soul and cherished his art above everything. He adored it and cultivated it for himself; he saw it as
an end and not a means, the objective of life and not a road
leading to fortune or renown. Never, moreover, had he pon-
dered or rationalized that way of feeling; he experienced it
naively and lived according to his nature. When he had imagined something beautiful he tried to realize it, and worked
on it fervently, without caring whether the people around him
thought that it was good or bad. He searched, he loved—
which is to say that he searched himself and loved his dream.

That had quickly brought him to solitude; to live within
oneself is to live at a distance. He was, therefore, adequately
disdained, and his merit was so great that no one had any inclination to believe in it.

But what did that matter to him? If, by chance, he provoked a sincere emotion, he was more excited than flattered
by it, simply deeming that he had encountered a mind in conformity with his own, something akin to a friend. He went
through life without being very familiar with it, having never
looked at it save through the lens of his thought, with the result that it seemed to him to be sweet, tender and serene, like
his soul.

For that dreamer, everything was transformed into the
nourishment of dreams; the pleasure of others give him pleasure in passing, their misery implanted within him a compassion fecund in sadness; noble actions seemed to him sugges-
tive of courage; as for villainies, he never had occasion to suffer from them because he was never able to perceive them,
and if anyone had demonstrated them to him they would have
been wasting their time, because he would not have been able
to understand them.

In his hours of leisure, he went out of the city and refreshed himself in the calm of the fields; he only liked tranquil spectacles; he contemplated sunsets, children at play, the gazes of virgins, and the pairs of oxen that paused as night fell to plunge their shiny muzzles into water-troughs, in which the pale sky was mirrored and cradled.

One evening, as the livestock were returning to the barns, he arrived at a well at the gates of a town. A young girl had set her full pitchers down, and was resting on the stone rim before going home.

Above a slender torso, her sad and serious face, lit by the reflections of the setting sun, stood out against the background of a golden sky, and the low sun, hidden behind her, dispersed tremulous gleams amid the clouds. That radiance, filtered by the child's blonde hair, made her a mobile nimbus, and in that glorious light, she resembled the saints of paradise.

He drew nearer in order to examine her more easily. She did not move, and did not see him, doubtless absorbed in some meditation. She had a smooth forehead, a slender nose, frank eyes and a mouth devoid of a smile. As austere as the evening, she was in harmony with it, became part of it, completed it and, poeticized by it, poeticized it in her turn. She was redolent with religion. The serenity of her attitude expressed a vague mysticism, a pious and resigned astonishment, an adoration; one might have thought that she was striving to hear some enigmatic phrase, simultaneously impenetrable, divine, happy and heart-breaking.

"What are you thinking about?" he asked.

"Nothing."

"Why do you seem to be lost in a dream, then?"

"It's a beautiful day."

She picked up her pitchers, and departed.

"Do you often come to the well?"

"Every day."

He went back too.

"Sit down, as you did yesterday," he said, "and look at the sky."

As soon as he got back to his house, on the first evening and all the following evenings, he took up his pencils and tried to reproduce on paper the face that was haunting him. Every night, he dreamed about her in his sleep, always reminiscent of the saints in the chapels, aureoled by the dusk, opening her eyes upon a mystery; she showed herself thus, even more beautiful than in reality, for thought idealizes and fecundates nature.

Twenty or a hundred times a day, behind the lowered eyelids of the man who evoked it, that virginal face sketched itself, first in a mist, then becoming more precise by degrees, taking on warmer colors, penetrated with life—so much life that, in the end, it poured out around her; and always, the virgin with the golden hair was manifest in the same fixity, with that same gaze directed straight ahead, and that anxiety which was scrutinizing infinity. For hours on end, she was immobilized like a statue, as unshakable as marble, and always interrogating her enigma.

With the result that, for the solitary man, she had become something other than a passer-by, and more than a tangible being.

At that moment, she incarnated her own astonishment; she was a hieratical stupor; she was an idea; she was a symbol. Assuredly, God was speaking to her; she was listening to a voice from outside the world; an angel had just revealed to her a terrible glory, and her dazzled eyes were hesitating to see clearly into a future of triumphs and tortures.

Was it not thus that the Mother of Christ must have stopped in mid-gesture, when she had felt awaken within her the germ of the divine infant? The angel had said: "The Messiah will be born of you." The angel had disappeared; the Virgin Mary was still trying to hear him, not daring to doubt or to believe, overwhelmed by the prodigy, she was imploring the Lord and trembling for her son.

Oh, to fix on canvas that soul and that moment! To grasp the ungraspable, to imprison that fugitive emotion in a work of art, to erect as a pious homage the durable evocation of someone bearing her God; and to put all his artistry, all his faith, his two religions, into a page that would be a prayer!

He saw that so clearly, felt it so profoundly, that he would certainly be able to reproduce the holy vision with which he was filled. His idea had conquered him to the point that soon, nothing any longer existed alongside it—nothing. The child of the well was no more than an element of the internal poem; she scarcely rekindled it any more, she merely represented it; and as art is a kind of love, the day came when she, like any lover, was not cherished for her merits, but by reason of what our thought adds to her fragile charm.

Is not loving a woman to love all the beauty and all the virtue in the world, in order to adorn the chosen one therewith? Is not loving an idea, embracing it madly and plunging oneself thereinto, to imagine God and create him in his turn?

That is why he felt himself penetrated with reverence when he went to the well now, and his knees were trembling, as if in a confession of love, when he dared one evening to say to the blonde girl:

"Would you like to come to my house, and I'll draw your image? I'll give you a mantle of roseate silk, with a blue dress. You'll live as you wish, without doing anything; I'll look at you, and when I've painted your portrait on a golden background, we'll offer it to Our Lady; then it will be blessed in the church, and the faithful, believing that they're looking at the Holy Mother, will kneel down around it.

"Visit my father and talk to him."

Three days later, she came to the painter's home; he sat her down near the window and placed himself in front of her.

For a long time he contemplated her, and they both remained immobile. At times, the man's lips parted as if to say something; his staring eyes were shining and his hands trembling. She thought that he was suffering from some grief when she saw two tears swell in the corners of his eyes and run down his cheeks.

Suddenly, he launched himself toward the easel on which the canvas was standing. But he stopped in front of that pale surface, on which his mind's eye saw lines and colors in advance, the work finished, perfect, total. That virginal whiteness was like the mirror of his soul, a screen reflecting the ideal. He was already admiring therein the realization of the long-cradled dream, and the fruit of future labors.

What can I say? He admired it again, and for the last time, sensing that as soon as he tried to embrace the chimera it would fly away, and that nothing would any longer remain of its charm or its splendor as soon as he had violated the magical vision with his heavy hand.

The girl was looking straight ahead.

When evening came, the master put down his brushes.

"Come with me," he said, "and sit down at the well."

The next day, when he examined his sketch, he blushed at its poverty.

He went back to work, but the next day, he pitied himself.

He took up the task again and, every morning, was invaded by shame before he results of his effort.

Soon, shame turned to anguish.

He began again, however, sadly, tenderly and slowly. Then fever flared up, and there were hours of joy, minutes of delirium, paid for the next day with the same suffering and the same discouragement, endlessly followed by the same renewals of valor and despair

Fixedly, the girl always looked straight ahead.

O mothers! You know it, the life of those who create: to conceive in folly, to gestate in pain—and how long that expectation is!

He worked until nightfall, and, returning to his oaken easel as soon as dawn broke, let his hands hang down in renunciation. He searched for the fault, thought that he had found it, and the discovery restored his courage.

He rubbed it out and began again; this was better; it was good—almost good, the dishonor of art!

"Another day lost!"

He was astonished to have been able, the evening before, to experience some satisfaction before that erroneous thing.

"Perhaps tomorrow—perhaps!"

The next day resembled the day before.

"How long have we been working?"

"It was three months yesterday."

He groaned internally; then he became enthusiastic again.

"Oh! I will!"

But the work will not. It fights, it defends itself and runs amok; it escapes and allows itself to be caught.

"I have it!"

It is further away than ever. It is the monster that slithers and scorns, the Proteus with a thousand forms, which does not want to be vanquished.

Henceforth, he has neither rights not strength. He is the slave of an idea; he believes it to be his own, and belongs to it. He is the possessed, whom no baptism can exorcize. The more his demon resists him, the more he persists; the more it is vanquished, the more it desires victory. Does he really want it? He pursues it. He runs after it dizzily. He does not want anything; he just goes.

Can one say that a stone dropped into a gulf wants to fall to the bottom? It falls without being able to avoid falling, and will fall because it must, with ever-increasing rapidity, and fury, incapable of stopping; to go is to obey; obedient to something more than a desire, more even than an instinct: a law!

"How long have we been working now?"

"It will be a year tomorrow."

Was that not life, after all? But the painter was searching for a soul. So he was unable to grasp it, that impalpable gaze, and set it there forever! Folly! To make of thought a line that one marks, to put infinity into a blue patch! That the rose should be a stupor and the white should be a prayer!

"I can't, I can't!"

The soul! But is she not changing from week to week, that child devoid of gesture and voice? Unless, at this moment, exhausted by effort and killed by impotence, he can no longer study nature, since he finds in those great open eyes even more sadness than before...

"Why do you seem so grief-stricken?"

"Because I'm mourning for you."

"Why are your mourning for me?"

"Because I love you."

When she spoke, he knew that he loved her too.

After the wedding, he went back to work, and for as long as the daylight filtering through the window permitted, the two spouses remained seated facing one another, she petrified in her Madonna's pose, he with head bowed over his palette or his neck craning toward his canvas.

"Have courage," she said, softly.

One day, she uttered a small cry and put her hand to her side; the hope of being a mother was radiant in her paned eyes.

Whether he is born to be a god, a king of a vagabond, a child is never anything but a child, no more desired or beloved by the woman who bears him, and the Queen of the Angels had no other suffering or ecstasy in her gaze when the Redeemer was stirring in her entrails.

Wonderstruck, the painter straightened up.

"Don't move, please! Stay like that!"

He threw two years' work into a corner, and took up another canvas.

He could see now; he understood; he knew; he would be able!

The difficulties were forgotten, the time wasted no longer regretted. To work! He too had his empty cradle; he too, in his eyes and is heart, bore a maternal voluptuousness; in him too the sacred child was stirring anew.

Yes, he would be victorious!

What does it require to be victorious? One hour in life! And to win that hour, scorn and faith are sufficient: scorn for the past, faith in the future; disdainful pity for the work accomplished, always miserable; valiant love for the future work, still adorable; do not judge that one has done well, but affirm that one will do well; observe one's impotence but retain pride in one's potency; doubt one's work but believe in oneself.

Like worthy writers consoling themselves for the pages they have written with the pages they will write, worthy painters forgive the canvases completed when they salute the majesty of new ones.

He worked, feverishly, hastily, and the months went by.

As our ideas are modified with our souls, and our souls with our lives, he said one morning: "Put your child on your knee."

The hours seemed less slow to the woman thenceforth. In the evening, she smiled affectionately when she contemplated in the painting the image of the little blond figure, so frail and so dear, of baby Jesus, pink and soft, holding out his lovely bare arms.

And when the child died, she wept tenderly at still finding him there.

But she resumed her seat next to the window, her seat and her pose, and looked straight ahead, imagining that the precious burden was still warm in her hollow hands.

"We won't work tomorrow; we'll pray, because he's been asleep for a year."

Then the time went by, as time does, and the woman remained seated; her face no longer had the freshness of yore, but it was sad, mortally sad, and its sadness was more beautiful than beauty.

To see her so desolate in her nimbus, holding Jesus in her arms, one might have thought that the Holy Mother was thinking of destinies to come, and that she had already glimpsed the cross on the mountain.

But that was not the Ideal—it never had been—and the master worked relentlessly.

"Your hair is going white, my poor man."

Many others were whitening as well.

"There are wrinkles in your cheeks, my poor wife."

Many other wrinkles were to come.

"On Sunday, we'll be finished."

That Sunday never dawned.

"I'm very tired; would you like to go and rest by the well?"

On an evening like that one, he had met her, but now they were almost old; the wife, as they went back to town, leaned painfully on the husband's arm; she murmured:

"I can hear our child calling me."

Face to face, each on their seat, they were two phantoms: the specter of folly examining the specter of suffering...

Soon, the man came back alone to sit on the stone rim of the well—and the work was not finished!

He had turned it to the wall; twice widowed, by his companion and his dream, having no longer any will nor any objective, he was waiting to die in his turn.

That was a long time coming, too—as slow as the ideal work.

One day, however, he dared to set the dolorous canvas on the easel.

He knelt down in front of it, and prayed.

How pitiful she was, the Madonna, with her poor mortal god, and how well she spoke, with her mute gaze, of the somber fatality of life, the inanity of hope, and the anguish that looms over joys! How human she was, the divine being! How well she knew the eternal secret of the abyss, and how frightened she was of the oblivion promised to al dreams! One might have thought visible in her the emblem of the vain religions in which our race ecstasizes, and which death awaits, one after another, and which slowly go on their way to martyrdom, from the cradle to Golgotha.

Only one dot, there on the canvas, to extinguish that overly bright and confident light, as the last ray of daylight dies away: one point near the lip, further to attenuate that shadow of a smile, that sweetness of hope...and it would be the idea!

He did not dare.

But he saw the dead woman sitting in her accustomed place, who wanted to say, as before: "Work."

He took up his desiccated brushes, and with a supreme gaze, contemplated the model. Then, getting down on his knees, he dared.

One dot, one shadow.

He stepped back into the room.

Night fell.

Then, standing in the silence, he recognized before him his entire soul, his entire life. The unique thought of which his life and thought were made stood up immutably, and gazed at him.

The dream had triumphed! The soul had tamed matter!

After the brushes, the palette slid from the painter's hands. Weeping his first tears of joy, he went to his beloved's seat and kissed her pious lips.

He had no more to do thereafter but depart and join them, the dear absentees—and the hour soon sounded.

In memory of them, until his last day, he kept their almost holy image close to him; when the angelus rang, he knelt down before his Madonna, uniting in the same prayer the adoration of the heavens and the affections of the earth, and the monument of gory was to him but a monument of love...

After the master's death, the canvas was famous for a long time in the land, for one of the honest drapers of the city, having acquired it, had written on the background: "The House of Our Lady—Probity—Confidence."

Admired by children coming home from school, the sign remained suspended over the shop's threshold for thirty years, but the merchant's son had it painted over one day, in more cheerful colors.

THE ANTICHRIST

At that time, as Matthew, Mark, Paul, Anselm and Jerome had predicted, the imitator of Christ, the filthy profaner, was born in Babylon, in the city of civilization where evil triumphed, clad in pride under the double name of vice and virtue. And he was the man of sin, the son of perdition announced to the peoples for the day in which the Earth would be in great affliction—so great that there would have been nothing similar since the world's beginning.

Armed by his Father with the forces of nature, he came among the peoples in order to be the last god.

He belonged to the race of Dan, born into a poor Jewish family, his name was Emmanuel David.

As no one knew that he had been created by the Evil Spirit, those who watched over his cradle never thought of connecting his birth with the marvelous signs that were to accompany it: the sky became dark; the sun was veiled by an eclipse; and the next day, when the full moon rose over the horizon, it was red, and cast sheets of ruddy gleams over the blue landscape.

The scientists and journalists, however, explained the causes of the eclipse, and only landscape painters took note of the astonishing light of the great lunar disk; no one remembered Saint Methodius and prophetic threats.[7] In vain, the stars shifted in the sky and the bolides traced their luminous streaks over the nocturnal backcloth without any shepherd following them to the house of the newborn.

---

[7] The 7th century document nowadays known as the *Apocalypse of Pseudo-Methodius*, describing the rise and rule of the Antichrist, was falsely attributed to Saint Methodius of Olympus.

He grew up in tranquil poverty, playing on the sidewalks of streets until the day when the Prefect of Police gave the order to exterminate the innocents; then the poor little creatures were taken in sad groups to the prisons where their youth withered in the effort of learning to read, count and write; and when Emanuel went back to his mother, he had a paler face and his limbs had become thin. When he reached ten years of age, his eyes were darkly circled, for shame was already resident in his heart.

Doubtless he might still have been happy if he had remained simple, but he had a need to understand, a desire to know, and those things, in distancing humans from the naiveties of nature, take them away from possible happiness.

He therefore went into the places where adolescents are informed of the changing affirmations of science, and when the doctors interrogated him in the temple of Sorbon, he confounded their presumptuous ignorance.

In the Levite quarter, a great celebrity surrounded his name from then on.

The man who was to parody the acts of the Savior justified the prediction of Saint Hippolytus,[8] however, and during his early years he was gentle and merciful. His generosity, like that of Christ, led him to know our weaknesses, and also enabled him to forgive everything, because he understood everything. But while Jesus' forgiveness was inspired by love, his forgiveness was inspired by scorn, with the result that to the indulgence of God, he opposed the indulgence of the Devil.

He said: "For a long time, having seen human beings in books, I admired their genius; now, having seen them in life, I admire their foolishness."

---

[8] Saint Hippolytus of Rome really does seem to have been responsible for the text on Christ and the Antichrist attributed to him, written *circa* 202 A.D.

He withdrew to the middle of the desert: to that place where one only encounters men and women, which is called life. He fasted, and knew the horror of being alone. But he devoted himself to the labor of thought, and when he was hungry, he was tempted.

The angel that wanted to turn him away from his path came to him and said: "Exchange your books for bread!"

He replied to the envoy: "Man does not live by bread alone, but by every word that emerges from the Mind."

The angel took him to the high tower of bolted iron that rises above the Champ de la Guerre[9] and said to him: "If you want to teach men the language of nature, and if you think they will understand you, you might as well throw yourself off the top of the tower and break yourself on the pavement!"

The angel took him to the Montagne des Martyrs and showed him the city with the hundred thousand roofs: "Prostrate the pride of Thought before the omnipotent Stupidity of our peoples, and our peoples will give you the kingdom of the world, with its glory."

He replied: "Go away; you adore the sincerity of your soul, and serve that alone."

The angel abandoned him, and the One who possesses the Science of Good and Evil immediately recognized him as his son, and invested his power in him, in order that his terrestrial mission might begin.

Now, Emmanuel had learned all things: the art of thinking, the art of healing, and the Kabbalah. Philosopher, physician and mage, he possessed wisdom, understood matter and commanded spirits.

---

[9] The Eiffel Tower overlooks the Champ-de-Mars. Although I have translated the names of Emmanuel's disciples into English, I have left the wry references to Parisian locations in the original, in order to preserve their mostly-obvious wordplay.

His parents complained to him: "What do you do, monster of sloth and iniquity?"

He replied: "I think."

"Work instead, then, useless eater! We have made great sacrifices for you, and you study all professions, but you're good for nothing, and you can't even earn any money."

When the neighbors came to visit his mother, they said: "It's a great pity that you have such a son; we always said that your Emanuel would give you trouble, and we feel sorry for you." But the neighbors were pleased, because the mother had previously humiliated them with her child, who recited fables so well, but who now brought shame upon the despair of her old age.

He met Simon Peter and Andrew, who were guiding their boat through life, then James and John, and they became his first disciples. He said to them "Follow me." But they admired him enviously, and did not follow him.

"Are you denying me already, Peter? It's morning. I shall go on alone, then, and you will come back to me when they call me Master. Friends do not aid us at the foundation of our personality; it is necessary to conquer them among those unknown or among enemies, and bring them back, vivacious and luminous; then they accept one joyfully and defend one as their own work, or rather, as their own glory."

Thus he drew away from them, but without weeping or long over lost friendships, for he was absorbed by the abstract thought that gradually detaches us from things of the heart—with the result that he was soon able to experience all the emotions and all the affections, but was no longer capable of suffering for long, for the pure idea is a fount of forgetfulness for the heart.

Being in the liberty that we name Exile, Emmanuel went into houses in which healthy men detain the sick; he enabled a great many paralytics to walk, rendered sight to people almost blind, hearing to the deaf and speech to the mute, but always refused to render reason to the insane.

"Lunatics are happy," he said. "Thought is the torment of humankind. Reason only guides us through error; the monomania of an insane person procures more joy than the ever-disappointed aspirations of reasonable people. Happy are those who think they are holding something when they are holding nothing, for they possess more than reality, if they have faith in their possession. The man who imagines himself to be Caesar is more enviable than Caesar, for no one will dethrone him if no one cures him—and I shall not be the wicked person who commits such a crime."

Thus, his reputation as a clever man was combined with the prestige of what the Gentiles call an Eccentric, and his renown spread rapidly. And from all the points of the compass the suffering begged him to come to their homes, and although he was poor, being generous because of his youth, he asked for little money, and that created the belief that he had little merit.

Now, one evening, being a student of mysterious things, he read these words:

"The Messenger deceived the Jews by advertising himself as the Messiah, and deceived the Gentiles by means of magical incantations."

That sentence dazzled him, for there are abruptly-understood axioms that grip of immediately and fully; they strike our sympathy as if we had already known and loved them, but then forgotten them, and which we were predestined to apply to all aspects of our life; it is like a revelation of ourselves, and in them, so to speak, we discover a part of our soul, enlightened by the divine light of formulae.

He opened the book of Raban Maure[10] and read: "He will be born by the operation of the Demon."

---

[10] The 8th century writer in question signed himself Rabanus Maurus Magnentius because he was writing in Latin. The quotation probably comes from *De universo libri xxii sive etymologium opus*, a kind of encyclopedic dictionary.

And having gone to sleep, he had a dream in which his Father appeared to him and said: "I am Satan and you are my son. I have created you among humans because the reign of the One who died on the cross will soon vanish; the time of my glory has come; I have invested my knowledge and power in you, and you will accomplish prodigies. Go, and be. Above all, declare it, for humans only believe that which is affirmed to them, but believe everything that is affirmed to them with authority. They will publish the fact that you are great if someone begins to tell them so, and no one can certify it better than you. For he who is humble will be humbled, while he who stands tall will be raised up, and the hindmost will remain the hindmost."

Then Emanuel stood up and went down to the street. A Parisian he knew came up to him and said: "Where are you going?"

He replied: "I'm going to act."

The other was astonished by these words. "You, a dreamer?"

But Emanuel replied: "It is among men who dream that the only true men of action are found, for the idea is the origin of all force."

Now, night filled the city, and as it was the time of year when Easter was approaching, in the week of mourning when Christian peoples sanctity themselves by means of fasting and austerity, he saw at the crossroads and in the shops of those selling salted pork a great multicolored host of people. These masses of men and women, in theatrical dress, like phantoms escaped from legends, were rushing after one another with screeches; in order to celebrate ugliness, some were almost nude, and others had put masks resembling animals or diseases on their faces; and they were all waking obliquely, like monsters who had scared away the wind with their own songs, which were obscene.[11]

Except, at the corners of dark streets, the daughters of joy had desolate expressions, and the virgins whose lamps had run out of oil were forcing themselves in passing to smile at their friends the centurions, guardians of morality and order, who were walking two by two.

Emmanuel thought: "How said it is to be gay!"

That is why, drawing away from the Temple of Harmony, toward which all these discords of colors, sounds and epochs were hurrying, he sought the discreet house to which his disciples had retreated, and found them drinking hydromel from glass cups, with communal spouses.

Stopping on the threshold, he instructed them thus: "Happy are the poor in spirit."

And it was amid great joy, in which laughter burst forth in the idle of songs while cups struck the marble tables. One who was named Maria was spreading peppermint over the feet. And as Simon proclaimed: "Shut up so that he can speak," he raised his right arm over the seated people, who listened to him say, slowly:

"*Idem est beate vivere et secundum naturam.* Quintillian wrote that.[12] To live happily and to live according to nature are the same thing! But you have depraved the world and nature is dead in you, except for fornication. So many rules have been formulated, so many laws imposed on the feeble understanding of human beings through the centuries, and the races have changed so much, giving in turn the name of vice or virtue to the same things, that you are living in a Babel and no longer know what your duties are, and what you rights are. But now

---

[11] In 19th century France the forty-day Lenten fast was interrupted by the Mid-Lent festival, on which the excesses of Mardi Gras were renewed.

[12] Actually, it was Seneca, but he was probably quoting a familiar dictum of Stoic philosophy.

are come the ages of punishment, now is come the unity of humankind—which was once alas, perfectible, and now, alas, is perfected. The same law will reign over the entire globe, and that law is called the annihilation of all hope and all dreams, the annihilation of interior worship, the annihilation of mother nature. Hybrid and artificial beings, look upon the slackness of your arms and the emptiness of your hearts! Look into yourselves, and then around you; let nothing exist anywhere, and if anything still remains, hasten to demolish it!"

Immediately they knocked on the doors, which opened, and a cold wind penetrated into the hall; they shook the marble tables, which were fixed to the floor with iron crampons, and the drinks were spilled.

And David continued: "Everything is flowing away! Who, then, first left the door ajar? Do you not see that everything is flowing under the door, and that the loss of everything is called the modern Soul? In order to pillage distant lands, you have invented metal monsters that cross oceans and mountains in a day, and when you speak in your room, a wire carries your voiced to the antipodes and brings back replies. You triumph thus and peoples speak to one another. But in truth, humans no longer hear humans, and it is assuredly Babel, for in transporting the products of your fields afar, you have transported at the same stroke the produce of your moribund souls and the excessive appetite for profit, with the result that the world becomes unanimously frustrated as soon as it cannot make money."

The men said: "That's the way it is," and the women said: "For sure!"

Then he added: "People of the West, you have buried the bad seed; you have sown salt and you shall harvest dust. The Earth is a pregnant spouse that will give birth to death. People of the West, it is too late to look again toward the East. The East that fertilized you is sterile, because of you. No longer say: "Out there, on the two flanks of the Caucasus, new peoples are awakening to whom the mastery of the world will belong and who will regenerate it. Do not hope thus, for if they invade your fatherlands your soul will invade their soul, and if they devastate your provinces, you will devastate their consciousness—and you will be the definitive conquerors because you are the weak, and the weak attach the strong to their triumphant chariot."

The women uttered cries of approval again, but the doctors and magistrates who were present criticized him for deceiving confident minds with formulae to which they gave the name of paradoxes.

But he said: "Does not history teach that Asia killed Greece, that effeminate Athens tamed virile Rome, and that Africa died in Capua?[13] Does not Wisdom teach that the contagion of disease is to be feared by the healthy, without the contagion of health offering any hope to the dying? Old men with pasty faces, the Barbarians will not devour you, but you will suck the virgin blood from their veins! Those peoples, so young that they are child-like, have a child's spirit of assimilation, with the thirst for enjoyment and knowledge, will assume your decrepitude without having lived their youth. They will pass into the night scarcely having bathed in the vague and future light of the broad daylight of midday; thus their abrupt sun invades the entire sky at a stroke, and disappears at a stroke, casting them from shadow into bright light, and from brightness into shadow, without dawn or dusk. Do you still dream of a world rejuvenated? Then overturn the poles and wash the entire face of the world in a cataclysm! It will be the Deluge, or the Business Suit!"

When he had pronounced these words, he fell silent, but an instant afterwards, he added: "In truth, in truth, I tell you, the supreme conquest of Progress is Ruination."

---

[13] The Carthaginian general Hannibal wintered amid "the delights of Capua" in the course of his invasion, and his campaign against Rome never recovered its impetus.

Then there was a great noise in the crowd that surrounded him. Some cried: "Bravo! Bravo!" and struck their cups forcefully against the amphorae; others imitated animal cries; and everywhere, there was loud laughter.

James said to Simon: "He has spoken the word of truth."

And Martha said to Madeleine: "He's funny, for sure; one doesn't get bored when he talks."

And again, servants poured wine, and gaiety illuminated all the faces. But as the guests had spent their last drachmas, the servants came to declare, trembling: "The cellar is empty, and there's nothing left but reservoir water."

Then Emmanuel stood up again and said: "Let the water be changed into wine." He extended his hands, and as they were full of gold, the pitchers were full of hydromel and spiced wine.

Because everyone knew that he was poor, they were astonished, and thought that he had come into an inheritance or committed a crime; they approached him incontinently with a respect full of affection, and Martha came to sit on his knees, confessing: "You are my Lord and Master."

Immediately, Judas, who was good at arithmetic, counted those were at the table, in order to share out the drinks, and found that there were thirteen. But the young master reassured him, saying: "I shall lose one of my patients this year."

Madeleine was anxious, though, and asked: "Have I sinned, I who have no husband?"

He replied: "Yes, you have sinned in giving yourself to those you do not love, but you have acted well is yielding to veritable affection—for acts of love do not depreciate us, but raise us up; that is truly nature, and love, in spite of our pride in thought, is the strongest part of us. What human work of art is equal to a beautiful body, which is divine work? What poem is as exalted and superb as the folly of a true kiss? And do you know any inspiration equal to the delirium of an embrace? I have washed my soul clean of prejudices; I have washed my soul clean of modesty!"

Now, an aged scrivener, who belonged to the sect of the Bourgeoisie and had three daughters, took offense and censured Emanuel: "He is proffering blasphemies, for he approves courtesans against virgins and against holy marriage."

Calming the tumult however, he replied: "I do not criticize virgins, but I mourn for them, and what I reprove is you. Have you the right to constrain, by conventional morality, young women to chastity? Cheating the desire of nature under the borrowed name of virtue, are you sure that your virtue is anything but a crime, which God will judge sadly, in seeing in modify the order and harmony of the world? Fixing ages and maturities, he has organized a preconceived lot for us, but you have replaced those maturities and ages with the necessity of marriage, which comes too soon or too late, or does not come...

"Now, a virgin is a zero in nature, a dead number. And society by constraining to virginity a woman who is not married, commits a double crime: tyranny with regard to the woman, theft with regard to nature!"

But the old man said again: "He does not respect old age, who speaks to me thus."

Emmanuel confounded him in these terms: "Ought I to respect you solely because you have been stupid long than another?" And he added: "In truth, young men and old men ought not to live together. It is only necessary to demand of them a polite relationship of mutual and legitimate scorn."

Immediately, a few doctors from the École des Normes, becoming indignant, tried to laugh, and one of them asked mockingly if he esteemed the minds of children more that those of mature men.

David said to him: "The child is far superior to the mature man, because he enjoys, as yet without pretension and without vanity, his contemplative and assimilative faculties, and his instincts of intelligence, which he will later deprave by wanting to submit them to the direction of a reason, an intelligence and a logic that are always incomplete—which is to say, much more unreasonable, unintelligent and illogical than the total absence of reason, intelligence and logic. The child is still in the superior state of an intelligent dog; humans only arrive at the inferior state of unintelligent mind. The former only knows submission, but he knows it and can do it; the latter no longer wishes to submit, and can analyze, but he does not yet know and cannot yet do; for the mature man is a perpetual embryo of unrealizable wisdom; his entire life is ingrate age, a perpetual transition into something higher that he will never attain, toward which he appears desirous, but which, in the depths of his heart, he detests: the superiority of intelligence."

He noticed then, however, that no one was listening any longer, for he had talked too much, and said: "You have ears in order not to hear." And immediately, he resolved to be heard regardless. That is why he fell silent, and withdrew soon afterwards.

Then, the following day, having made the prescribed ablutions, he went to the home of a Parisian who possessed numerous houses and agreed with him to establish himself in one of them, choosing the most magnificent—for a son of man will not be esteemed unless he lives in sumptuous dwellings.

There, he cured yet more lepers, and the rumor soon spread that he effaced the slightest trace of secret maladies. Then the rich and the Gentiles came to him from every direction, and the women of Asia had themselves transported to his palace in hired chariots ornamented with painted coats-of-arms. All made him presents of works of art in bronze, antique vases kneaded by artisans of Sèvres or Saxe, and notes printed in blue that he exchanged for large sums of gold. Severely dressed servants watched over his door, where a tin-plated bell sounded, and the room where visitors waited under the chandelier with seven branches was upholstered in crimson velvet.

Nevertheless, he killed a few patients, and when Peter asked him why he acted thus, Emmanuel replied: "To set an example." Then he explained that answer by saying: "When I cured everyone, they had little confidence, but now that some of them die, I am named as the man to whom one comes in desperate circumstances."

And when Peter asked him whether that was not unjust, he replied: "Yes, it is unjust, but I am just in spite of it, for it is written: the just man is one who commits injustices and observes them subsequently for himself, without anyone demonstrating them to him."

Meanwhile, his reputation had grown to the point that there was not a single man in Babylon who was unaware of him. Then Peter, Andrew, James and John said: "He is my friend."

And the neighbors and relatives, when visiting his mother, repeated: "We always said that your Emanuel had a great future. He must give you plenty of money."

His former friends asked him: "How is it that, although you are so rich, people bring you yet more riches, but that no one offers anything to us, who are so poor?"

He replied: "Thus I tell you that people give to those who already have, but, as for those who have but one obol, that too will be taken away."

The Pharisees and the Gentiles wanted to have him at their table of honor, and held great celebrations because of his presence; mothers also thought of choosing him to marry their daughters. Whenever there was a feast, friends said to their friends, in order to persuade them to come: "Emmanuel David will be among us." And that is why several of them named him the Attraction.

When he was in his hosts' homes, he accomplished prodigies, to please and honor them. And as his speeches were not ordinary, people listened to them, without pleasure but in silence, with the smile that Gentiles put on to give the appearance of understanding. Afterwards, in order to be admired for their intelligence, they approved by nodding their hands or clapping their hands.

And when he went out he said to his disciples: "You see, I have explained to these men and women verities that shock them, but as they are in a magnificently-decorated room, civility constrains them to applaud me, and I have enjoyed having forced them, by means of their own social conventions, to approve of that which attacks those same conventions."

Peter asked him: "Why do you insult them, those who are your brothers?"

He replied: "They are not my brothers, for they are children of stupidity, and I am not their brother, for no man will recognize as his brother a man who is superior to him; but he will flatter him, out of cowardice or self-interest, unless he can destroy him out of envy."

Now, he invited to his palace the most distinguished of those he knew, in order to offer them enjoyment too, by accomplishing new prodigies before their eyes, and to give evidence of the power that was in him. Even though he was a bachelor, women came too, under the pretext of science. When they were all assembled, he ordered the tables to rise into the air, and the tables rose up; people who doubted were also levitated toward the ceiling and suspended in mid-air. Spirits appeared at his command to answer questions, and great men who were dead submitted humbly to the caprices of the idiots who were interrogating them. Then, fixing his gaze on the eyes of a few audience members, he revealed what they were thinking, and accurately; he also wanted to reveal publicly what they had been doing during the day, but even the most honorable were opposed to that. A pale hand that manifested itself over the table and had no arm wrote a poem.

Then the women came toward him, touched his sleeve and called dim "Dear Master." The Scribes said: "That's a clever man." And the Doctors, being envious, murmured in a low voice: "Charlatan."

Then, one of them who wanted to test him asked; "Can you prevent a stone from falling in empty space?"

"Yes."

"Can you prevent a man from sinking in the water?"

"Yes."

Then the man proposed a bargain, in the form of a wager, and challenged him to walk on the waves in order to cross the river with dry feet. Everyone having laughed, Emmanuel declared: "That I shall do tomorrow."

The women interrogated him, with soft smiles: "Are you not the Devil?"

But because their faces were pale, he replied: "I am the man who is awaited."

Meanwhile, a foreign woman came in, about whom bad things were said, and some said: "Why is the shame being inflicted upon us, we who are honest, of encountering a woman who is not? She left the conjugal house to follow her lover."

Then he said to her: "Hear what people are murmuring: you are accused of having abandoned your husband to go to your lover's house."

She replied: "Would it have been better to take him with me?"

The slanderers were thus confused.

Emmanuel asked again: "Did your husband love you, and did you love him?"

"No."

"Did you love your lover?"

"Yes."

"Go on peace, then, for the true marriage is that of love, and you have not belied your love—but a woman is adulterous who, having taken a lover, continues to sleep with her husband, and thus deceives two men at once."

Then he worked further miracles, which the spectators designated by the term Experiments. As the Gentiles lived

71

without any faith, they found these things very curious, but explained their causes and methods to their neighbors, and none was troubled in his consciousness to the point of thinking: "That is supernatural." On the contrary; they amused themselves competing with one another and examining David from afar, affirming out loud that he was very intelligent; but when they were in the street they said that his insolence was great, that he was badly brought-up, and several of them also called him: "Upstart."

Now, the following day, the Scribes write a long account of his marvels in the Dailies, and announced to the people the challenge that David had accepted—with the result that, by ten o'clock, a large host had gathered on the river bank, and the Prefect of Police was obliged to send numerous centurions to contain the crowd. As soon as Emmanuel appeared, he was warmly greeted by the people.

In the midst of the ovations, however, he thought sadly: "These people do not understand and will not understand. Alas, that which makes us superior to you and make us the Elect is not what we produce but that to which we aspire. Great in our conceptions, we are petty in our realizations, and that brings us closer to you. You perceive them because of their pettiness and their impotence, with the consequence that you know nothing about us but the worst, and honor us by reason of that which renders us despicable to ourselves."

Then he took off his gloves, and, having imposed his hands above the waves, he marched over them to the opposite bank; then he did likewise a second time and retraced his steps, while toll-collectors and vagabonds acclaimed him with cheers.

Now, the multitude pressed forward in order to get a glimpse of him, and several climbed trees. The centurions formed a double line to protect his passage, and James asked him: "Are you satisfied?"

He replied: "I am what you see, for people envoy manifesting their power more than exercising it; a man wants to have it in order to prove it, and would consent to lose it provided that people still believed that he had it."

A skeptic said, laughing: "Christ did not do otherwise." But he spoke thus to mock the Savior and those who believed in him, and no one thought that the person repeating the Messiah's works could only be God, or the Enemy of God.

Now, the man of little faith who had mocked thus was a doctor graduated from the École des Normes, and David said to his disciples: "In truth, I tell you, every time that our country has need of a pompous idiot or a blasphemer, he will always be found by locating a man emerged from that house."

All day long the Scribes came to his dwelling in order to interview him, and when he was weary of receiving them, he ordered that the doors should be closed; then, those who had been unable to enter recounted in detail how his house was organized and what were his mores.

Meanwhile, Emmanuel having been let alone, he thought about his Father and the kingdom that it was necessary to conquer, in order that the Mission would be completed and that he would be God in his turn.

"I am the envoy of the Natural Power, and the primary desire of nature of perpetuation. If beings and things down here have an ultimate reason for their brief existence it is, in animal life, not to agitate for an hour, but to reproduce; and in the life of the species, the task is not to move in the vain noise that renders celebrity, but to build in the shadows in order to transmit its soul."

But his Father's voice proclaimed around him: "The man who speaks in the shadows is no longer heeded by anyone. Speak in the light!"

At that moment, he found that a man had urgently implored his servants and had finally persuaded them to take him to the Master; and when he was introduced to him, that man,

73

who was a rich Sacrificer, offered him five hundred gold marks, and asked him to come to his temple, in order that he could talk and perform prodigies before a great many people—for that temple, which was called the Folies-Pharisiennes, contained ten thousand seats in a single hall.

Having meditated, Emmanuel replied: "You shall be rewarded because you have been audacious and indiscreet. Gather the publicans and the bankers, and when they are seated I shall appear before them."

Immediately, his name was written on walls in enormous letters, and, on the appointed evening, he presented himself to the people in order to instruct them; but the common people were absent, and the only ones who had come were those the people detest without knowing them, and who lead the people without knowing them.

First, he informed them on matters of wisdom, and they were disappointed, for pure verbiage does not interest anyone; however, they were all amazed to see that doctor who, dressed like them in a black double-breasted suit, accomplish marvels, and in the middle of the night they returned home and said to their wives: "In truth, we've seen astonishing things that no one expected."

Emmanuel said: "They aren't sufficiently astonished yet."

And Simon asked: "Why?"

He replied: "Because they're fools."

A Samaritan who was present asked in his turn: "What, then, is a fool?"

And the Master explained to them: "A fool is distinguished from a beast in that in ignorance, the beast is humble, while the fool explains. As he is ignorant of everything, he can explain anything."

Judas asked: "Do they are least love you?"

David replied, joyfully: "They detest me. Stupidity is sometimes full of indulgence for genius; foolishness will not admit it at all."

The crowd gathered every evening before the porticos, and the sellers of drinks whose tables were in the vicinity made large sums because they yielded to the rich the little cards thanks to which it is easy to get into the temple.[14] And everywhere, prodigal sons, who supported bad girls and lived in impurity, offered painted images representing the face of Emmanuel; and the latter were in the homes of merchants, alongside celebrated courtesans and foreign princes. Women widowed of their virtue sent him epistles full of affection and songs were composed in which his glory was celebrated in petty verses.

Even though he made a great deal of money, though, he was sad, because no one thought of saying: "He is the One who is awaited." And he feared the severity of the Father who had sent him. That is why he paid a scribe whose foolishness had rendered him famous among men to publicize the fact that Emmanuel's power surpassed Nature; that was done, and the scribe invited the priests to ascertain whether the newcomer's name did not correspond to the number 666, as John the Theologian had predicted in the twentieth chapter of the *Apocalypse*. And that was read in a daily newspaper just as the sun was setting. Immediately, great laughter spread through Babylon and Emmanuel's name was heaped with derision, and the scribe—who had for the first time, said something reasonable—was scorned, for no one was unaware that he had been paid.

Then David withdrew to the Jardin des Marroniers and prayed: "O my Father, are these people, then, at such a point

---

[14] At the time when this story was written, unemployed people often formed queues outside theatres (tickets could not then be booked in advance) long before they opened and then sold their places in the queue to people who wanted to see the performance—a practice that will play an important role in one of the later stories in the collection.

of deprivation that they cannot be scandalized by anything, and are ready to laugh at anything?"

But he hoped that the mockery would engender insults, for insults would render his friends more fervent, and that fervor would procure him sincere enemies among the others. Assembling his disciples, he began by telling them that it was necessary for the Son of Man to suffer a great deal and that he should be rejected by the Senators, by the Priests and by the Scribes, and that he should be put to death, like the false messiah known as Christ. In saying that, he had little faith in it himself, but he gave evidence of it, in order that it would be spread around.

Meanwhile, the Scribes to whom he continued giving sums of money were propagating his glory in the two worlds and the dailies, fulfilling the prophecy: "To the four corners of the Universe, Demons will advertise his coming."

A great number of imbecilities were therefore written about him, and Judas, who paid out money on his behalf, said to the Master: "At least you're content; roses have been spread in your honor, and palms shaken."

But his Master replied to him: "The eulogy of fools is more cruel than their scorn, for the insults of those who do not understand are inoffensive, while it is painful to see oneself admired because of ridiculous ideas that no one ought to be able to have."

In his great notoriety, Emanuel was anxious, for even the priests, in spite of his prodigies, had no thought of seeing them as miracles, nor of recognizing the Antichrist, and no one was moved to anger or fear.

It was then that the Messenger, who doubted his enemies almost as much as his friends, began to doubt himself, and thought, sadly: "When one routinely observes the futility of humans and their lives, one is close to the moment when it will be necessary to observe the futility of one's own life, one's own effort, and everything."

Then his Father came to his aid and permitted that a terrible plague fell upon the region. The Son cured all those who were rich enough to dare to summon him, and also a large number of those who were cared for in public places with Caesar's deniers.

And Herod the Tetrarch said: "Who is this man, then, about whom I have heard so much." And he wanted to see him.

When Herod received Emmanuel, he experienced a keen joy, and hoped that he would see him perform some miracle, but modesty forbade him to make such a request. However, he asked several questions, and Emmanuel replied to him politely. Throughout this time, Herod, imitated by his guardsmen, treated him with a good deal of deference, and before sending him away, and dressed him with a scarlet ribbon, which was a sign of honor reserved for chevaliers—and when his cross was given to him, he was thirty-three years old, like Christ.

Then the Messenger thought: "Shall I be increasingly lost among the multitude?"

Immediately, his Father, to excite him further, suggested to thirty-nine augurs assembled beneath the Cupola, who gave prizes for Virtue, to do well by choosing him as one of them. Emmanuel was astonished by it, because the people in question were accustomed to elect those who create, less readily than those who gaze upon creation. However, he crossed the river for the second time, cured a blind man near the Temple of Arts and went in; immediately, he was declared Immortal.

Now, his task being to die, he was discontented with this benefit, but he consoled himself with the thought that the title sometimes lacked the sanction that the future ought to grant it.

He resolved, however, to go to another country, where the souls would not be as new.

Because of that resolution, he agreed to accompany a man who promised him great wealth if he consented to follow him from city to city and show himself to people; the man was named Barnum and had come expressly for that purpose from the island of America. His disciples having desired to follow him, he departed with them, and many passengers embarked on the ship that carried them away.

On the evening of the fourth day, however, a turbulent wind rose furiously, and the waves invaded the ship, so that the vessel began to fill up. The merchants were terrified, for their goods and also their lives. But he was asleep in the poop and his disciples woke him up, saying: "Master, aren't you worried that we might perish?"

Having been thus awakened, he spoke authoritatively to the winds and said to the sea: "Shut up and calm down."

The wind ceased forthwith, and there was a great calm. Then, turning to those who had trembled, he asked: "Why were you afraid? Have you no faith?"

Then the leader of the toll-collectors and others were seized by astonishment and pity, and said to themselves: "Who is this man who imagines that he can command the wind and the sea? Poser!"

A banker who happened to be there remembers having heard stories of Jesus recounted, and declared with a smile: "We know that. It's old."

Emmanuel replied: "Know that nothing is new. If anything could be new, it would be false."

When he was on the other side of the sea, on the isle of the Americans, he traveled with his followers to numerous cities and as many theaters, repeating prodigies, evoking spirits, stopping the fall of stones, making rocks oscillate and springs gush forth, multiplying loaves of bread and professing doctrines—and his success was considerable. But he found the inhabitants of that country even more enclosed in matter and concern for wealth.

One day, when he was on the sea shore, he saw a man running toward him who was almost naked, because he usually lived in the mountains, howling and bruising himself with stones. And the man shouted in a loud voice: "I beg you not to torment me."

Whereupon Emmanuel said: "Unclean spirit, come out of that man."

Now, there was a large herd of swine passing by, on the hillside. The unclean spirits, having emerged, entered into the swine and the herd hurled itself impetuously into the sea, where it drowned. There were about two thousand of them. Those who were herding the swine fled, in order to carry the news to the city and throughout the countryside.

Then Simon Peter questioned him in these terms: "Why did you end a thousand existences in order to change one? Do the souls of a thousand pigs weigh less in the balance than a human soul? The swine might have been useful, since they would have been eaten, while that elector is no good for anything."

Emmanuel replied: "You have ears in order not to hear; understand that the thousand pigs do not belong to me, but that man is now mine."

Peter then said; "Do you think that he will be happier henceforth? You once made a vow never to cure a lunatic."

David went on: "It's true that I said that in my youth, but this is what is truer still: it is one thing to retain a pure idea, another to put it into action. A man who pursues a goal among human beings, if he wants to attain it, must sacrifice to the interests of his cause the interests of others and his own conscience."

As he was walking while he talked, he was hungry, and, perceiving a fig-tree in the distance, he went to see it, but only found a few leaves, because it was not the season for figs. He was discontented, however, because proud men do not like resistance, and speaking out, he proffered: "Let no one ever eat your fruit." And all those who were following him heard him, and the next day, the fig-tree was found to be withered all the way to the roots, which was reported to the farmer who cultivated it.

Then he and the man who owned the pigs conferred together and said: "It's necessary that we should be reimbursed, and that the judge should call us."

That is why Emmanuel was summoned to the Tribunal, and he rejoiced, thinking that the hour of his suffering had come and that his reign was about to commence.

That is why he loudly confessed the prodigies of which he was accused. But he was sentenced to pay three thousand talents in damages, as well as the tribute of expenses, and at the moment when he thought he would be tortured a little, or at least insulted by the porter and the sergeants, the senior judge said to him: "Go in peace."

Now, even though he had confessed his action and paid the entire sum, the scribes wrote that he was to be commended.

Then David, gripped by sadness, wanted to leave that country.

Having thus fulfilled the prophecy of Saint Ephrem[15] and visited the four corners of the Universe, he returned to Babylon. At that time the entire people was occupied with the election of Senators and did not notice his return, by which he was disappointed. He therefore decided to offer himself to the voters in order to recall attention to himself, and went to public meetings, where he spoke at length.

---

[15] As with Saint Methodius, the name of Saint Ephrem the Syrian—a prolific writer of hymns and homilies—was usurped by numerous later writers in order to give spurious authority to their petty and mostly bilious outpourings, including a prophetic "sermon" about the Antichrist and the end of the world. Nowadays, of course, it has become the most famous and most widely-available of his "writings," especially in America.

As it was already late, his disciples came to him and said: "This place is deserted, and it's getting late; send them away so they can take their nourishment."

He replied: "Give them something to eat yourselves."

Then he had bread, fish and meat distributed, and all those who were there were sated, and the carried away twelve baskets full of leftovers which were given to the little dogs. Now, those who had eaten numbered about five thousand, and David was elected.

When he appeared in the Senate, however, the others, in fear of a superior man who had come among them and who might therefore diminish them or guide them, were jealous, and cried: "Get out of here, for you have corrupted the electorate."

He replied: "If I have corrupted it with bread, you have corrupted it with words, which are the bread of the soul, for you have abused its lack of intelligence in telling parables and lies that have deceived it. And I have done for the hungry what you have not done, for I have given them bread without having promised it, and you have promised less useful things that you have not delivered."

Then he confounded them in their hypocrisy, but they decided that he was insulting the Senate and universal suffrage, and wanted to invalidate his election. And against him were said a great number of the things that please assemblies, and which are so effective because they are sonorous and devoid of reason; and everyone was content with them.

Then he rose to his feet and aid: "Imbecile, whose mind is satisfied with the emptiness of your words, what is your name?"

And a great voice replied: "My name is Legion."

Then, being on top of the Mountain, he told them this parable: "The State is like a chariot drawn by four horses, and the forces that draw it are the Ideal, Love, Truth and Justice; each of them is incarnate in a college of beings, and each of the four colleges represents one of the four virtues: the Priest is there for the Ideal, the Young Woman for Love, the Politician for Truth and the Magistrate for Justice, and that is the Chariot of God.

"But the Priest, instead of the ideal, is concerned with domination and wealth; he wants to lead the people, not in order that the people be well led, but in order to be their leader, so that he wants it in his own interest, not in the interests of all.

"The Young Woman, instead of purity, is concerned with elegance, which is a kind of debauchery, and instead of love, seeks advantageous marriages, which is a kind of prostitution.

"The Politician, no longer being the thinker anxious for social amelioration, has become the socialite crafting the amelioration of his power and his fortune.

"The Magistrate, who once rendered justice to all, having the audacity of virtue, and who more recently sold it to the highest bidder, having the audacity of crime, no longer renders it or sells it to anyone but himself—which is to say that he traffics in secret with his duty, and decides what it best for the progress of his career.

"And that is the Chariot of Satan."

Then, around him, the voices became indignant, while consciences remained untouched. In the midst of the tumult, the imitator of Christ thought with anguish about the son of God and meditated: "O Jesus, those who speak in your name are really the henchmen of my Father, and yet, they do not even work any longer for me."

Everyone, seeing that he had fallen silent with a sad expression, immediately assumed that he was afraid, and shouted louder.

But in a voice that was no longer of the earth and which rumbled, he proffered: "Men of egotism and lies, I shall throw you out of here, for this is my Father's house, and my name too is Legion. I am the Number! When I spoke of my right, you did not hear; when I speak of my strength, you will be obliged to hear!"

Having a heart full of disgust, he went down into the street, where the people were anxiously awaiting the council's decision, and confessed: "This is the house from which I have been expelled, because I said that you were being deceived." And the people gave him great ovations.

He added: "Follow me, and we shall expel the sellers!"

And all were of that opinion, and raced through the city, extolling Emmanuel and attacking the shops of the merchants; there was, therefore, a great tumult, and the centurions were too weak to resist the multitude, and he tetrarch sent guards and soldiers to arrest David.

At that moment, Emanuel shivered with joy and said: "I praise you, Father. Henceforth, your Son will be seated at the left hand of the power of God."

And, turning to his disciples: "Let him who has no sword sell his robe and buy a sword. For I tell you, the things that were predicted of me are about to arrive."

The he drew away, to the vicinity of a stone fountain, and thought—and when he came back, a troop surrounded him, in order to recognize him.

Those who were with him asked: "Lord, shall we strike with the sword?" And one of them struck a servant of the sovereign and cut off his right ear.

But Emmanuel said: "Stop!" And, having picked up the wounded man's ear, he healed him.

Then Judas, one of the twelve, but who was more intelligent than the others, realized that his master would not be condemned, and, thinking that he would be rewarded later for having given evidence of his fidelity in misfortunate, drew near to him in order to kiss him.

Immediately, the soldiers seized David and took him away.

And Peter, less subtle than Judas, followed at a distance; and when, on three occasions, men or women looked at him and said: "Are you a friend of those people?" he replied: "I'm not one of them, and I don't know who you're talking about."

Meanwhile, the people, digging up the paving stones, had raised ramparts in the middle of the street and, as a sign of revolution, planted blood-red flags. And the city was reminiscent of Sodom on the day of its punishment, for the houses of the rich went up in flames, and the stones of walls were hurled into the clouds, like the lava of a volcano.

And the disorder lasted two days, at the end of which all those who could be suspected of being poor or hungry had been put to the sword; their bodies were taken away in vast abattoir-carts, and as the carts were overfull, bloody feet hung down outside.

Emmanuel, however, had been well-treated by his guards, because he was important, and when the day of judgment arrived, the publicans, the rich and the merchants assembled in the Tribunal, which was crowded, and had the accused led before the Jury so that he might be interrogated.

Then Pilate, the chief judge, who knew that David was powerful and rich, said to the Jurors: "This man is presented to you as having incited the people to riot; and yet, having questioned him in our presence, I have not found him guilty of any of the crimes of which he is accused."

He spoke to the thus, having the desire to save David, and they thought as he did because David, being a Bourgeois, belonged to their race, was as rich as them and more powerful than them, and they had high hopes of him.

Now, a plebeian named Barabbas had been put in prison for the sedition that had occurred in the city, and as the Jurors, being property-owners, feared thieves, they cried: "We want Barabbas!"

Then Pilate pronounced that what they wanted should be done, and he released David and abandoned Barabbas to their will, with the result that the latter was led to execution.

Then Emmanuel went back to his sumptuous house, where he shut himself in, only taking with him Peter, James and John, and began to be gripped by fear and great agitation.

And he confessed to them: "My soul is full of sadness, even unto death."

But they tried to console him, saying: "Why are you weeping? Are you not free? Have you not escaped the danger? Do you not possess great renown and much wealth?"

He replied: "Humans! Do you not understand that what makes the wellbeing of multitudes is nothing but a cup of bitterness for a man who dreams of the beyond. Stay here and watch."

Having drawn away, he lay down on his bed and meditated:

"Behold my calvary, and its name is Impotence! O Christ, you came at the right time, but now it is too late, and you would suffer less than me; and in the luxury of my dwelling, I envy your cross, your crown and your nails."

Then he rebelled, crying: "O brutes, bellies without hearts or heads, do you not worship anything? Bow down to the Devil, then, since you no longer want God!"

In the end, having fallen asleep through weariness, he had a vision, and in that vision his Father descended toward him and said, in an angry voice:

"So this is all that you were able to do? You're sleeping in softness instead of going to die for my glory and our power. And yet you've come in the time of the humans that I've prepared for my reign."

And in his dream he replied: "Father, you have prepared them too well, and all faith is dead; the Idea now leaves them indifferent, and they do not kill one another because of it."

Now, in his dream he was continuing to moan when his disciples came in, crying: "Get up! People have come to congratulate you and to render to you what they owe you."

Then he got up and received them benevolently, and when someone said: "We thought you were dead," he replied: "I am resurrected!"

And the next day, he resumed his ordinary life, and was heaped with honors and riches, with the result that he married the daughter of a man who was powerful by reason of his fortune; he was not even deceived by that wife, but he had three sons by her and lived to be old.

And when he died, he was not damned, for God no longer existed.

THE END OF THE WORLD

Science had announced, in a precise fashion, that the end of the world would occur on the third of April of the last year of the Selenian Era, at five twenty-seven in the evening.

Humankind had been awaiting that date for a long time.

Already, in the first centuries of the Rational Era, which had succeeded the Christian Era, the hypothesis of the final cataclysm had been the object of problems and scientific reports, but 3748 years ago, the date and the conditions of the event had been established mathematically by Dr. Zacharie Furst.

I

The new epoch was revealed on the day when, in a solemn session of the seven Academies, that illustrious scientist had given his admirable lecture on "The Inequality of Satellite Movements and the Eccentricity of Orbits."

To begin with, the austere title of the work had not excited public curiosity overmuch; only a few young women of the highest society, who were interested in the progress of the human mind, had judged it worth listening to the session, which was to become memorable. In overwhelming heat, they fanned themselves discreetly during the lecture, sixty-three pages long, in which the professor, in a slow voice, linked up the series of arguments and algebraic equations.

From time to time, it happened that a lady accredited by her fine profile, her intelligence, her kind face, or even her gallant adventures, interrupted the rhythmic movement of her fan and immobilized her head, slightly tilted toward the shoulder in the attitude of a young chicken, in order to understand better. All of them then rivaled her in attentiveness, and listened to a sentence all the way to the end.

"You recall, Messieurs, that a monk named Galileo discovered, a few years after Jesus Christ, the principle of rotation; and the astrologer Newton almost immediately affirmed that the distance described by the moon during a short interval of time, in the direction of its radial vector, is equal to the height through which the moon would fall toward the Earth is the same time, if it were only obedient to the action of that planet supposed to extend as far as the moon and decreasing proportionately by the square of the distance."

The sentence having terminated, the white heads of the Academy and the blonde heads in the audience oscillated gently, in approval.

"What a terrible thing, dear Madame, that the moon is falling upon the Earth! Oh, they have no respect for anything, these scientists!"

The heat increased. In the semi-silence of the fall, bizarre words were heard flowing from the podium, which were lost in the hemicycle: "Inequality of the movements of satellites in latitude... Integration of differential equations... Perturbations over centuries..."

Then the attentive crowd sat there for a quarter of an hour without listening any longer. The scientist's voice became weary; at the beginning of each new paragraph, it inflated slightly, like a balloon blown up by a child, and went down again almost immediately. That voice had been speaking for at least fifty minutes when it stopped. The first part of the report was complete, but everyone only realized that on seeing the president shake his head. Discreet applause spread; people admired the gesture of the learned professor, who drank a few grams of water at that precise moment—and the voice, more forceful and almost authoritarian, resumed:

"Second chapter. In the movement of a point along any curve whatsoever, the centrifugal force is equal to the square of the velocity divided by the osculatory radius of the curve."

The women sensed that that must be an axiom, and indisputable—but the voice, instead of lowering, as usual, rose further, and one might have thought that it was pregnant with menace, as it added: "Thus, the centrifugal force will diminish if the velocity diminishes or if the osculatory radius increases."

That conclusion was too unintelligible not to be approved, and pronounced beneath a cupola, it could not fail to satisfy ears or brains that perceived the sound of the words without having grasped their meaning. But the effort of curiosity that the more sonorous sentence had caused to spring up in the auditorium was quickly renounced, for the doctor, in a more monotonous tone than ever, was already reading out a long table exclusively composed of figures, in which dates alternated with numbers. The scientist recited them by turns, with a feeble alteration of intonation, like the questions and answers in a dialogue: a date, a number; another date, another number; then, from time to time, a differential total—and the pages of the manuscript turned vainly beneath the fingers of the illustrious master, without the list of numbers and dates coming to an end.

That was the crux of the work, the doubly admirable result of experimental hard labor and the inventiveness of genius. That simple chapter established for the first time, with indisputable authority, the record of the decreases to which the mean movement in the rotation of the moon about its center of gravity had been subjected over a period of forty centuries. Now, as that movement is exactly equal to the mean movement of the revolution of the satellite around the Earth, it followed simultaneously from the aforementioned table that the real velocity of the satellite had decreased mathematically, and, in consequence, the centrifugal force along with it; but, the apparent velocity having remained constant, it was necessary, in the absence of any other hypothesis, to admit that the orbit was shrinking; and as the centrifugal force had not accelerated, by reason of that fact, the laws of celestial mechanics theoretically corroborated the astronomical observations, and the double conclusion imposed itself irrefutably: the moon is getting closer to the Earth and its mean movement diminishing in increasing proportions.

Thunderous applause, coming from the amphitheater where the Institut de Sciences was seated, greeted the end of the second chapter; the beautiful listeners also clapped their little hands enthusiastically, their delicate instinct advertising in the depths of the soul the grandeur of the things they had just heard.

The flutter of fans thus became even more discreet during the reading of the third chapter, for everyone in the audience, male and female, felt honor-bound not to miss anything in the report, or at least not to appear to have missed anything. They listened with keen concentration, with a more-than-indulgent deference, and the insolent respect that resembles the condescension of ineptitude toward thought.

The beginning, at any rate, was less arid. The scientist had anticipated the ovation merited by the conclusions of the second part, and his text responded to it. Modestly, he denied having invented anything or discovered anything. He attributed to others the glory of the theoretical principle, whose initial idea was lost in what is sometimes called the night of time. He had only resumed, in a better-informed epoch and with vastly-improved data, the work that Laplace had sketched out in the final ages of the Christian Era, in a century of ignorance in which, having nothing on which to operate his calculations but the incomplete observations furnished by Flamsteed, Bradley and Maskelyne,[16] he had nevertheless indicated the possibility of subsequently establishing a law of perturbations.

---

[16] John Flamsteed (1646-1719), James Bradley (1693-1762) and Nevil Maskelyne (1732-1811) all held the position of British Astronomer Royal, and as such, participated in a long continuous program of meticulous observations and measurements, made within the limitations of the optical instruments available to them—which were, indeed, insufficiently accurate for Pierre Laplace to make the desired calculation.

"And our sole merit," Furst said, "is that of being born sufficiently late to possess the elements permitting that law to be established."

People hastened to applaud, even though, in sum, if they had thought about it, protests would have been more appropriate than applause; and the mathematician continued.

The observations of the past thus having permitted a law to be posited, the law could, in its turn, reveal the future: the proportional decrease of the mean movement and the proportional shrinking of the orbit being given by the preceding table, it was sufficient to construct by analogy an analogous table to discover the lapse of time after which, by virtue of drawing nearer to the Earth, the satellite would end up entering the sphere of our attraction, properly speaking, combined with that of its mass.

The eminent Academician became very tired during the reading of that second table, which was relatively short, and his voice lacked amplitude when he came to conclude:

"Thus, before the end of the 3749th solar year, the spiral that is wrongly described by the name of the lunar ellipse will be transformed, under the direct action of gravity, into a new parabola, whose curve and duration remain to be studied."

An anxiety agitated among the females, for they had sensed the announcement, not of the end of the world, but of another chapter, and truly, at the present moment, they were expending as much zeal in desiring the end of that august tedium as they had put into being desirous of the honor of taking part in it.

The professor, warmly congratulated by his colleagues, shook hands and drank a little water. When everyone was in place and sitting down, he rose to his feet. "Fourth chapter. This is the last."

That favorable news restored the serenity of the elegant listeners.

"Study of the parabola." The astronomer coughed and continued: "Bodies attract one another in direct proportion to the squares of their masses."

A lady blushed, and coughed in her turn, in order to keep her composure. Several others smiled; licentiousness was beginning to claim its rights. Lewd comments were exchanged in low voices, murmured very close to ears, while the scientist cited the numbers corresponding to the masses of the Earth and the moon, their reciprocal attraction, and their new distance, in order to obtain the final term in the formula. He then studied the force and the rotational speed that the satellite would have at the given moment and, reintroducing the first number, constructed the parallelogram of forces, determined the parabola, and then calculated the acceleration, calculated the resistance, and finally fixed the duration corresponding to the course of the trajectory.

Assuredly, no one had taken the trouble to follow the equations that had succeeded one another thus, in letters and numbers, for the incompetent notabilities would have tried in vain, and for the scientists, the problem, now posed, was one of those of which it is customary to say: "To pose the question is to resolve it." They were, therefore, reflecting on the premises, neglecting the conclusion.

Among the lay persons, however, attention revived, terribly this time, when Professor Zacharie Furst, having solved his final equation and completed the division of time, concluded, calmly and in an ever-fainter voice: "In 3748 years, 93 days, 17 hours and 27 minutes, counting from the first of January next, the Moon, falling upon the Earth, will collide with our planet."

They had understood.

"Eh? What? The Moon?"

"What did he say?"

"What an impact!"

"It's impossible."

"The Moon!"

"From the first of January!"

"That's what he sad."

One strong mind dared to respond: "He's mad."

And already, a few colleagues were sadly expressing regret at seeing such a noble career terminated by a public act of aberration and dementia.

"He's lived one year too many."

"Ten years too many."

Some were mourning him, others admiring him; a few were smiling subtly, and no one knew whether their mockery was for the crowd or for the report; they did not know that themselves.

Furst sat down, exhausted, and mopped his brow; one of his pupils came to kiss his hand, and that caused several skeptics, covertly pointing their fingers, to smile again. However, when the dean of the Academy, Monsieur Boyer himself, who was the most decorated and most earnest of scientists, advanced with difficulty toward his old comrade and then, full of emotion, his face moist with tears, extend his tremulous arms toward the orator and hug him to his bosom, the amazed and enthused hall cheered the couple participating in that old men's embrace frantically, and belief set in.

Furst was great, forever; the Moon was going to fall on the Earth. They consented to it; they were proud to consent to it. It seemed to those human brains that the matter had been decided by the present session, and that, by attending the session, they had done it. As if making an award, they had just decreed—yes, voted in—a new principle, unforgettable for humankind. The end of a world? Get away! The end of *the* world! They deigned to consent to it, and their work was magnificent.

"But when, then?" asked frightened ladies.

"The first of January."

"This year?"

"My dear, that's in the past."

"Next year?"

"That's what I meant."

A very young member of the Institut reassured the group that he was honoring with his company. "On the first of January, we'll have another three thousand years and a few centuries to live."

They were relieved. No matter! They had had quite a fright. In spite the high temperature of the hall, they felt a little cold chill in their shoulders, and when they went out, they all raised their eyes toward the zenith from the top of the peristyle steps, in order to search for the formidable aerolith there, and to see it coming.

It was about five o'clock in the evening, and in a soft green-tinted sky, decorated with thin rosy clouds, they saw a slender, spare and slight crescent, as coquettish as a jewel, which seemed to be shaped in a subtle metal, mingled with gold and silver.

"There is it!"

"My God!"

It was as pretty as a young virgin, that gentle and blonde daylight moon; it seemed to be warm and smiling.

Prudently, one nervous woman clad in chestnut-brown silk opened an umbrella and ran to her carriage, into which she threw herself, and nestled in a corner, in the joy of having a refuge.

In the middle of the courtyard, the scientists were surrounded and assailed, and all the society people demanded a summary repetition of the report to which hardly anyone had listened. The journalists took notes. Furst was scarcely able to get across the courtyard, and people gazed with religious terror at the roll of paper that was sticking out of his coat pocket, as if the end of the world were within it. One pretty widow, who remained exuberant, shouted: "May I touch it, Master?"

People questioned one another.

"Well, what do you think?"

"It's admirable."

"Isn't it?"

"The report will be published, I suppose?"

"I want to read it again, for one misses so much at the first reading."

"It's admirable!"

They talked about it as they would a piece of music; for people in society, at that time, were not content, as they are today, to judge works of art without preliminary study; they also judged scientific works in the same way—which is, of course, just as legitimate.

Almost all of those distinguished individuals were dining in town that evening; they were even more distinguished then, and their importance was triumphant. They recounted and explained; they spoke in loud voices; people listened to them with lowered voices.

The next day, the newspapers summarized Furst's theory in brief and precise terms.

The excitement was considerable.

The opinion of the press was favorable. In the entire world, no popular paper dared neglect the reproduction of the noble professor's features; those that did not have his image invented it in haste. He appeared here with a long beard, there clean-shaven, thin or stout, young, old, blond, gray-haired; he had blue eyes and brown eyes, and all the appearances of which glory might dream. His work was commented on everywhere, approved of everywhere; his conclusions were indisputable and undisputed; the hundred academies of the world sent him delegates, and kings crosses; his own fatherland resolved to honor him.

That is why the parliament of the Europic Confederation unanimously voted him a day of approval, and when he died, his funeral expenses were paid by the Occidental Treasury. All the people swelled his cortege, for the scientist had acquired a popularity equal to that of a politician. Before dying, however, he had the joy of seeing his work affirmed to such a point that the social situation was transformed by it.

In those days, things were done quickly; four months after the Institut's session, a universal congress voted to reform of the calendar, and on the first of January of the following year a new age began for the world with the year 3749 of the Selenian Era. The human species, mathematically sure of the future, would henceforth count the years and days backwards, until the death of its planet.

II

Time had passed; it had almost run out. Another five years, and nothing would be left of that long-lived humankind.

Over 3744 years, atavism had accustomed human beings to the idea of that planetary funeral, and when the ultimate generation appeared, they had been habituated for centuries to dying on the appointed date.

They were not at all sad; on the contrary. The people of the day made merry—for not only did the imminence of the end give a renewed zest to life, but the anticipation of the cataclysm itself generated more joy than terror.

Humans, in fact, weary of enjoyments and discoveries, had seen too much, and in those ages when they was nothing left to conquer, the immortal appetite for novelty sought its nourishment in vain; human curiosity had become more anxious, and for hundreds of years, people had envied the happiness of the last-comers, who would witness the unique spectacle. Only they, among all humankind, would see what no one else would see. They were called "the Elect." In the minds of the last ancestors, they were comparable to the blessed individuals who, in the ancient religion of Moses, had been chosen by Jehovah to witness the advent of the One whom the Father had deigned to promise to his children. They were the fortunate race, of the moment when the definitive curiosity of humankind would be satisfied; a halo had awaited them for a long time; a kind of mysticism had developed in advance of them; they seemed sacred to their forebears.

The grandeur of those who are preparing themselves for death made them into enviable martyrs of a sort, establishing an atmosphere of piety around their persons. Thus blossomed the ultimate flowering of the human dream; and the final seed of a kind of deism, which death had once seemed to be, resumed stirring dully in the depths of that race devoid of mystery and priests, with the result that people thought about the end of the world as other civilizations had once thought about the Judgment of the resuscitated dead, and the Moon preoccupied the last-comers in much the same way that the gods had preoccupied the first.

The atheistic world had its god.[17]

What are gods, in fact, but immanent forces that poetry has ornamented with attributes? And what do they demand, if not the attention of our minds? Whether they are honored by sacrifices or prayers, they require that we think about them, since their divinity is composed of our worship—which is to say, our thought.

Thus, the Moon was a god, although that was unknown to its skeptical people, who, by its means, ultimately satisfied the need for the beyond they thought they had renounced. They adored the prophetic deity that science had permitted without being aware of the fact. It inhabited the heavens, like the others, but, better than the others, one could see it there by looking up.

Instead of the terror of dubious hope, however, the final aspect of terrestrial religion was certainty, anticipation and smiles. For what tortures the mind durably is doubt; certainty is only painful to begin with. It had been known for too long for the knowledge still to be painful.

Sibling to the grave fatalism that once proclaimed in the Orient; "It is written," a good-humored and slightly ironic fatalism murmured complacently: "It is formulated"—and the world lived on under the menace of the Moon, nonchalantly and effortlessly, like a great harem under the promises of the Sun. Since no one could escape the inexorable law, no one thought of praying to it; consequently, it had nothing to refuse,

---

[17] Although the noun *lune* is feminine, the author uses *dieu* rather than *déesse* in referring to its quasi-divine status, while retaining the feminine pronoun for grammatical reasons; clearly, therefore, the quasi-deity in question is conceived as essentially neuter, as I have represented it in translation.

and because of that, no longer seemed inexorable; it was, therefore, a god without rigor, one that had neither rites not symbols, about which one talked without eloquence, like the weather: a simple god, of which one could make fun without risking any punishment or offending its religion, since laughing at it was laughing at oneself and one's own death.

It was featured in ditties, and that bravado flattered vanity. It accepted everything and on fine nights, also smiled. It is inevitable that gods resemble their peoples; otherwise, they would not be gods.

But it continued, even so—like its predecessors—to be the administrator of justice who makes a mockery of suffering, for the starveling crushed in the street by a carriage-wheel could shout at the rich passenger: "You'll be disemboweled like everyone else!"

A lexicon of new proverbs came into being. The common people adopted mocking locutions and dicta. One said by way of welcome: "You're falling like the Moon in April." When one encountered a funeral cortege, one greeted it with: "There's another who won't see the end of the world." At interments, people talked about the impending inlunement.[18] Everyone repeated the remarks on the theme they deemed to be the cleverest; a few invented new jokes.

It was a matter of good taste to be witty about the matter, and above all to manifest no dread. Those people who, enjoying a placid temperament and being uninterested in everything, would have preferred to die peacefully in their beds at an unknown date, only admitted it at the end of a meal, with a hearty laugh, as if it were a joke, to hide their cowardice beneath their gaiety. But the pusillanimous were few in number, and anyone who expressed such a bizarre desire without laughing was immediately deemed to be an eccentric.

---

[18] This pun, in which *enterrement* is supplemented by the improvised *enlunement*, only survives the Anglicization of the terms in poor condition.

In the same way, old people hid their desire to live longer behind a desire to see the marvel—which, however, at their brutish age, scarcely tempted them any longer—and said while caressing their grandchildren's hair: "You'll see the end of the world."

With that hope so strongly accredited, those whose days had not been fortunate and to whom existence promised little lived as best they could, being patient and not seeking death voluntarily.

What do people need in order to support their tribulations? To have a goal! Humankind had but one goal: to see!

All weariness was comforted. People waited. The human race was like a crowd in a railway station hoping for the whistle of the departing train. To some, the interval seemed long, and they would gladly have advanced the hands of the clock to hasten the departure, but no one wanted to leave alone, and suicides were rare. They wanted to see! No one any longer killed themselves because their business had failed or because they had undertaken some shameful enterprise. Only occasional insensate individuals, racked by amorous chagrin, cried out in the solitude: "I don't give a damn about the moon!" Then they killed themselves abruptly, without reflection.

They were mourned with slight disdain; they were imbeciles for not having understood the sublime spectacle that was offered to them, and impolite toward the universe that had brought them to it.

"Since one is certain to die then, what's the point of killing oneself?"

One might have thought that their race was the first to possess the certainty of dying, because they were sure of dying on a fixed date.

Is it not an analogous sensation that permits us to talk about people condemned to death as if not all people were? The truth is that they are condemned at a precise date, and as long as the idea of death is not combined with the knowledge of the moment of its occurrence, we only half-comprehend the necessity of dying. The instinct of self-preservation forbids us to have a clear and precise notion of our end, so long as we cannot yet specify it, and that instinct, in giving us the desire to escape death even after death, has driven us to imagine the immortality of the soul.

In that age, however—alas!—science had put paid to that pretentious vanity a long time before; at the same stroke, all the attentive gods had vanished, and no one believed that the Eternal and the Absolute could possibly be interested in their interests or fantasies; no one was any longer unaware that general laws do not care about particular instances.

Henceforth, humans knew that they were no more than errant animals, kin to aphids: an infinitesimal force in the midst of a universe of forces.

Along with the flattering illusion of their importance, they had gradually lost the entire treasure of illusions that had flowed therefrom to enliven life. Reason had given them nothing in exchange for what it had taken away, for reason is not as benevolent as superior spirits, and average stupidity can only extract misery therefrom. The pasturage of the intelligent is the poison of the mediocre; truth nourishes the strong but, poorly digested by the weak, is nothing for them but a septic ferment that causes them to rot faster. The world does not take long to make errors of received verities! Since their pampering gods and their own immortality had been sent to the slaughterhouse, they had sent everything else the same way.

One thing having crumbled, everything crumbled; the edifice of conventions, customs and virtues is built in such a way that dislodging one stone disequilibrates all the rest. Error is the indispensable armor of minds; it is their breastplate, and that is what protects them; slicing through the errors, philosophy had stabbed the human soul. It did not even remember any longer having been led by aphorisms, illusions and superstitions; it almost required genius to comprehend the paradoxical book in which the history could be read of a species of people that had imagined Hell, Paradise and all the other myths.

The ideal was no more; only the real existed. No abstractions, things! Good, evil—what did those words signify? Humans had set down the burden of chimeras. They were tranquil, and lived in peace with the consciousness of their nonentity.

Thus widowed, the human soul had soon died, and one might have thought that, by way of revenge against the religions of old, the human animal would last longer than its soul.

Humans no longer affirmed anything, knowing that every affirmation is a lie. The Christian Era had decreed: "There is truth and falsehood," the Rational Era: "Everything is true." The people of the world's end said: "Everything is false."

They had learned from their ancestors the inanity of theories, the renewal of imbecility, the fluctuation of principles and nonsense; no idea merited more than any other that one might deign to proclaim it, and never again would a furious desire to prove something resuscitate enthusiasm. Ideas having become despicable, no one thought of dying, and more than they thought of living, for an idea. Who would have talked about serving a cause? Such naivety no longer raised its head. No one could pledge his faith, since faith no longer existed, and abnegation was henceforth a word devoid of meaning. Heroism had not retained the right to exist; because the principle of battling was dead, there were no more battles, and because there were no more battles, there was no more courage.

To sacrifice one's life for a duty, is it not necessary that there should be something there to admired us, even if it is only ourselves? And when the cult of absolute and abstract things has been exiled from our consciousness, we shall not even find in ourselves the necessary admirer.

Thus, those who clung to a duty were no longer to be found. People were no longer mad; that was the madness of the time.

By way of compensation, however, phraseology had lost a part of its rights; it seemed that stupidity had diminished, since it was less exploited.

Only old Republicans still repeated a few formulae relative to honor, but no one listened to them, much less argued with them, and even though everyone knew that they talked that way habitually, no one even paid their phrases the attention that intellectual juggling might merit.

The certainty of the end had eliminated from politics the party bent on reform. Economists were out of work; politicians no longer promised the masses anything, since they had no benefit to obtain by their promises. No one said: "What's new on the horizon?" anymore, because it as inevitably necessary to reply: "Nothing."

With all the other residues of primitive and so-long-inviolable barbarism, fatherlands had disappeared, and wars, and armies, and logically, military men; the noise of sabers and peace-time bravado was no longer heard in the streets; no one lived or died for his fatherland or motherland.

Those were benefits; they were not the only ones. The absence of duties having abolished virtues, the absence of virtues abolished hypocrisies; lies lasted longer, admittedly, but people lied in order to repair things, from day to day, and only a little; as for noble lies, they had been retired, and no one any longer tested, for the needs of vain grandeur, the limits of nature. Nature invited, and the law did not prohibit; it dared not and could not. What would conservative laws still have had to protect? "The world ends with us!" The brief duration of the future no longer imposed restraint; and, social interests no longer having to be consolidated to the detriment of individual interests, legal codes were softening day by day.

For is laws are only the means of consolidating societies, the constitution of societies are no longer the real objective, but merely the means of improving individual existence.

On the day when a collectivity no longer has a future, its laws no longer have any force because they no longer have any reason for existence; the individual will then march upon them and reclaim his animal rights, one after another, until they are all recovered.

As at the beginning of the ages, there was nothing but the individual. However, as it was still necessary, until the end, even in the interest of individuals, to protect certain primordial elements, such as life and property, a few precise and expert texts were retained, which continued to regulate the immediate relations of one being with another; for want to moral rules, they delimited right and duty. Both were simple: right was called enjoyment; duty consisted in not allowing oneself to be caught in the execution of what it was indispensable to consider as a fraud—a fraud, not a crime. In committing one of them, one did not render oneself guilty, since the notions of good and evil no longer existed, but one rendered oneself dangerous, since the notions of mine and yours had not been abolished. Someone who was arrested for having wanted to augment his own enjoyment at the expense of the enjoyment of others, was not shamed as a criminal but mourned as an impotent individual, mocked as an unskillful one; he was subject to restrain without incurring shame.

In spite of the universal demoralization, the great crimes of yore diminished. Hatred, which is a passion as well as a killjoy, was suppressed under both headings. There were few murders. By the same token, in the absence of long-term interests, people hardly ever poisoned their relatives. That was loading one's arms with awkward complications! For love of life, people even avoided stealing; theft might lead to imprisonment, that partial death, which was capable of becoming definitive, for prisons were more than ever comparable to cemeteries, since the condemned person entered a cell as if being buried alive in a tomb from which he would never emerge, and under whose debris he would be crushed.

Sometimes, however, bakers, butchers and grocers—and, in general, anyone who sold comestibles—were found in their shops with their throats cut or their skulls caved in. Some wretch, dying of hunger, had made the decision to steal a loaf of bread, and, in order not to die, to risk a penalty that would become death. So, when he saw that he was caught, he would kill the policeman, since the penalty would be no greater, just as, in order to avoid being pursued or recognized, he had killed the shopkeeper.

People did not like that; they avoided talking about it; such tales of misery were expelled from the joy, like excrement from a feast.

One day, however, the alarm was raised. Those who were not enjoying themselves enough attacked each other in the cities. Throats were cut for the last time. Then, everyone hastened to forget.

People did as little work as possible, and that was very little indeed; for centuries machines had been doing the work—but even they no longer produced much, now that there was no longer any reason to store products.

In the almost-empty schools, too—what was the point of learning?—no trouble was taken. The unfortunate children whose families had dumped them there refused to do any impositions, and treated the curriculum according to its merits, at last.

If no one worked any longer, they enjoyed themselves a great deal, and cheated one another. Not for love of gold—the metal that had sanctified calves in the times of Moses was no longer even respected; it retained a certain love, but a love without jealousy, which threw it out of doors and windows. No one collected wealth any more, as the bourgeoisie had once routinely done; on the contrary, they collected enjoyments, and for those they dispersed wealth. Gold had become what it ought to be, a powerful thing without its own power, the vector of life, nothing in itself and everything in its movement: the blood of the world, which nourishes if it circulates and corrupts if it clots.

Misers were admired, as anchorites of a sort; they were not understood. People with private incomes no longer existed, since the value of capital had disappeared with the possibility of prolonging its usage; thrift was dead, along with credit, no one lent money. Every resource was realized in order to be transformed into material for immediate expenditure, and all stocks and shares were obsolete, since there was nothing to enjoy but the present.

As for people who had wealth, they were fêted, as before. Where did they get it? People had better things to do than investigate anything. Everyone was too occupied with themselves to occupy themselves with others.

Ready to forgive anything, ready to approve anything, provided that he was allowed to share in everything, the individual offered liberty in return for condescension. "The more I allow, the more you will allow me." Without anyone doing anything for anyone else, in the general egotism, they nevertheless helped one another to satisfy their desires, since everyone tolerated everything that did not hinder the expansion of their own desires. As in a jostling holiday crowd, they exchanged favors. A perpetual commerce of indulgent camaraderie momentarily brought together those transient beings, who forgot almost immediately, so urgent had existence become.

Was it not necessary to hasten to live, when death was hastening to arrive?

Everyone felt the same; people were similar; an exuberant banality comprised society.

The approach of death, by exasperating animal nervous tension, had, admittedly, exaggerated in each individual the tendencies typical of his nature, but in that excessive promiscuity, it had exaggerated common tendencies most of all. Now, above the tastes that are personal to us, two laws more powerful than ourselves impose themselves on all beings, to give us the double duty of preserving the individual and preserving the species: two indefeasible instincts, to live and to procreate. That is why, everywhere, the instinct to live, when excited, becomes a fury to live, while the instinct to love becomes a madness of lust.

And quickly!

To enjoy what remains. To profit, since one is about to lose everything! To drain the cup, before it breaks! Every man for himself, and death for all!

Everyone raced to live. Urgency reigned. A new animal stirred upon the earth, facile, hurried and benevolent; an expansive and joyous being, devoid of cares, devoid of dread, devoid of prejudices; a being that lived in order to live, and had nothing else to do. Humankind had regressed into full-blown animality

Ordinary people only think when they are bored; boredom had been abolished, as a waste of time, and people no longer thought.

They felt.

Like the dog that minds its own business, like the birds that flutters its wings amid the foliage, like the fly that circles in a sunbeam, and like Horace, they felt that life is pleasant, that light is pretty, that everything is beautiful and that time is fleeting. When they opened their eyes in the morning, people were glad to be still there; for two pins they would have shouted "Thank God!" Oh, the good Moon, which was not about to fall that evening! They were like an adolescent to whom a girl has confessed yesterday that she loves him with all her heart and who, as soon as he wakes up, is looking forward to the promised hours. To work! The profession of human beings was joy, and hardly anyone was on strike. No one concealed anything; mystery is the sublime enemy of laughter; no one wanted the sublime. Joy for joy's sake! The fear of disaster did not trouble them—quite the opposite, since to think about imminent death was to think more of life.

"A pity, all the same, that it has to end!"

And quickly, they began again.

They slept little, because the hours were precious, and there was no need to husband their strength for old age.

They would even have liked to be in several places at once, in order that no pleasure should be monopolized by another, and if anyone in that world wept, it would only have been out of regret for not being ubiquitous. For pleasure, no one spared any difficulty, and the women of the time were able to affirm that an informed man is worth two.

People said: "Nothing matters, except the present moment." Everywhere, however, there was an effort of memory toward the past, of aspiration toward the future, to relive everything there was and to live all that would not be.

They dreamed of inventing new sensual experiences.

Thus, uniformly, all over the world, those people clad in their glad rags were rejoicing, clear-sighted, frivolous, and above all futile: entire cities cutting loose.

When an agile woman, her breasts thrust out, appeared at a street corner, saying "Where can I get it?" a passer-by, without stopping, followed her with a rapid gaze: "Perhaps I won't have time." There was much of it to be found, however, and the pleas did not last long. "You're beautiful." The woman smiled—and *voilà*. Often, they eyes sufficed to say everything, as they always have sufficed—but words no longer gave the lie to the gaze.

Things were simplified.

For nothing more resembles the general soul of a people than the fashion in which they conceive the act of love. Among all barbarians, it is natural, like drinking and eating; in over-civilized epochs, it becomes impure and mystical at the same time; to the atheists of the Selenian Era, it had lost any sacred character and become jovial, savant and nimble, devoid of majesty.

One invited a woman to intercourse as we issue invitations to dinner; one waited in a kissing-room,[19] next to a low divan, small tables being laden with elixirs and fruits; she arrived, ceremoniously or unceremoniously, and sat down politely. Well-brought-up men returned a visit, as after a meal.

---

[19] I have transcribed "kissing-room" exactly as it appears in the original. The French *baiser* [kiss] is often used euphemistically to refer to sexual intercourse, and the author might have assumed that the same convention held in England, although English has the advantage of Anglo-Saxon roots as well as French ones, and tends to approach such subjects in a blunter and more brutal fashion.

A bad century for the jealous! They were deceived at the drop of a hat. Fortunately, the jealous, like their brethren the miserly, were very hard to find. Nevertheless, in the wreckage of all the sentiments that had once encumbered love and hindered the course of it affairs, a little jealousy had survived; it went back, in fact, to instinctive, animal causes, absent from the other mystical imaginations added by the human species to the natural need for sex, and that powerful origin permitted it, like any other malady, still to manifest itself—but it was not considered to be anything more than a pathological symptom, an idiosyncrasy, whose manifestation was deplored, as if it were a matter of gout or asthma.

Couples scarcely cultivated it; the model household was one in which the husband assisted the wife's pleasures, and *vice versa*. No one was deceived and everyone was content.

Everyone loved as they wished.

Fathers, no longer having to save the dignity of their name, closed the eyes of honor, and virgins slept where they liked.

Incest was seen again, as in the world's infancy.

A few morose old men muttered: "In my time..." They were lying, though, and the other of the family imposed silence on them with an amiable word.

"Did you enjoy yourself, daughter?" What did a lost virginity matter? They were no longer sold in exchange for the plush situation offered by a good marriage. In what drawing-room would anyone pull a face at virginal high spirits? There were none of like that, and would soon be none at all.

What harm was there in introducing beings of unknown blood to a hearth? The hearth was about to be pulverized. Was there a devoted mother who would care about having it said that her child was a bastard? They all were, and the child would not live, any more than anyone else would.

No one, therefore, took the usual precautions for the sake of virtue, but solely to avoid being accidentally deprived of joy, deprived of life.

For the ugliest or the most hurried, specialist physicians kept studs populated by handsome males, and offered all the comforts of luxury in bathrooms or playrooms. Sensible mothers took their daughters to such places for reasons of prudence. Music and good manners were cultivated there.

It will easily be recognized that such license would be impossible as a social system, since human beings always want to go further than they do and can. But so what? The work did not have to be continued. The world was really and truly coming to an end, and it would perish even if the Moon did not fulfill its mission, for an excess of living had always caused peoples to perish; like consumptives and torches, they acquire on a frenzy of hot vitality at the moment when their fire is about to go out.

We would be wrong, however, to be too rancorous in regard the people who will live in that time. Not only were the present conditions inciting them to behave in that was, but they had received nothing from the past that encouraged them to behave in any other way. Atavism had prepared them. What shapes the convictions of a race and its social soul is not reason but habit. People reason far less than they feel. If it is true to say that mores are born of belief, it is necessary to admit that mores engender belief in their turn; morality is born of long custom, and indisputable things are merely things that are very old. A way of behaving, even if it is immoral, infallibly becomes respectable when it has served several successive ancestral generations.

No more than any other, this one had not surged forth abruptly; it had been adapted and developed, progressing and becoming refined, from generation to generation, to the extent that chastity finally became unnatural; sex became a function again; license was a right; the pleasure obtained therefrom appeared as a duty, because of the person who gave it; polygamy became necessary and fidelity ridiculous; incontinence, no longer being a vice, because a physical virtue.

People no longer gloried in escaping what the dogmas of the distant past had reproved under the name of human weaknesses, but they took honor in showing themselves capable of them, for carnal ecstasy ceased to be an act of weakness and became a feat of strength. Sensuality no longer reduced us to the level of the beasts but, on the contrary, raised us to the rank of humans; no one was ashamed of it, but proud, since it proved a capability. No one any longer scorned the body, the source of joys; it was almost venerated. Virtue was inverted; conventions were read from the other side of the coin, and the old immorality was moral.

The soul was defunct, as I have told you; no one was any longer occupied with it; the body was about to die; that as what concerned people.

Still, it is necessary to spell it out: these people were not, in sum, much less estimable than us. Virtue does not reside solely in the act, but, above all, in the intention that determines the act. To save her honor, Dorothea[20] defended herself against her valet; she had him thrown into a gulf in the Sierra, and that was an expression of virtue; if her foot had slipped on a pebble, the valet would have thrown Dorothea down, and that would have been a crime. Was it, therefore, up to the pebble, to decide whether the homicidal struggle was or was not praiseworthy? No, but although the result would always have been a murder, the intentions differed: one intention was acting in accordance with the laws of virtue, the other contrary to them. What makes the morality of an act is the intention, what forms the intention is the will; for the valid use of the will it is necessary to know why one desires something, and to know that, it is first necessary to reason in order to comprehend it.

Now, it is rare that ordinary people—concierges, generals, rentiers—try to understand themselves or to reason. The will tell you themselves that they act "quite naturally" and that

---

[20] I do not know which of many literary Dorotheas Haraucourt has in mind, although he obviously expected his contemporary readers to recognize the reference. It is not the Dorothea featured in *Don Quixote*, nor the one in Lope de Vega's eponymous play.

"it just comes to them." Personally, I even think that they're proud of it. They have honesty "in the blood." It's unconscious, isn't it? But true virtue is conscious. Whether that bourgeois honesty comes from education, atavism or race, it comes from outside the self; it is learned, and not understood; it does not belong to the person who exercises it, and since its exercise is devoid of intention, he has it as if he did not have it—which is to say that, with regard to pure morality, he has none. The sole virtue is to comprehend virtue, and there is no honest man, nor good man, nor wise man, who can be honest, wise and good without knowing why he is thus.

From which it follows that, in spite of appearances, we are no richer in morality than those reprobates of the Selenian Era, and that even if, in reality, we behave better, it is necessary to confess that, in truth, we are no more meritorious.

Similarly, we would be wrong to believe that those beings, because they will differ from us, are coarse and brutal. Too many centuries had refined them; furthermore, their function was to live pleasantly, and the majority achieved it. Their license was elegant. Humans had retained for sensuality the only delicacy that was still in him. Joy became over-subtle, like a theological matter. Pleasure was more than a fashion; it was a kind of worship.

Death being god, sensuality was religion, and sexual intercourse sang the mass.

And death—more than springtime, more than nests full of birdsong and clumps of lilacs shading grassy divans, more than fresh and inviting springs, more than the perfume of flowers and the warmth of oriental days, more than shadow itself—death cried: "Make love!"

Pious in their fashion, the last humans obeyed the last god and thus lived according to its law, with the result that that depraved world was, nevertheless, like a supreme temple, and its cupola was the sky, in which the real symbol of god was traveling mathematically.

Their death, from on high, watched them stir, and caressed them in advance with its white radiance. They admired that radiance on their hands; then they raised their heads, their gaze encountered the radiance. Death and the dying contemplated one another, face to face, without hatred, expectantly.

And quickly, they returned to living! It had its orbit, they had their joy. Quickly, to joy!

Only a few more weeks remained to live. The refined took care to contract a marriage *in extremis*, and betrothed themselves for the afternoon of the third of April, in order to flourish at the supreme moment.

Laughter made them feverish them, however. Anxiety aggravated the nerves. But still, over the entire surface of the globe, an enormous cry rose up, as long as an orgasmic cry and as poignant as a death-rattle: an immense cry of gratitude: "It's good! It's good!"

Human life blossomed, and all of its joys were realities.

Only the artist conjured up chimeras.

III

A painter, whose name will only be known to his contemporaries, lived in those days.

He was one of the most bizarre beings that one could imagine in his era: he ate and drank just enough to nourish himself; when music was played in his presence, he blinked his eyes or shielded them with his hand, and that was assuredly not to hear better; he went walking on his own, his hands behind his back, scarcely saying a word to those he met; he studied celebrations without involving himself in them; he undressed women severely, like a judge, and, even though he was still young and handsome, only took a congruent portion of love, for reasons of hygiene; he did not refuse his favors, but was not prodigal with them.

He was taken for an ascetic. To tell the truth, he was no more of one than anyone else, but he sought his sensualities within himself, and found them. Precisely because he was happy, he was believed to be sad—for society does not willingly imagine that what it considers to be joys can be no more than tedium for some, and the majority will always refuse to admit that intense pleasures can exist of which it is ignorant. It will smile on hearing that the voluptuousness of art is exactly analogous to the voluptuousness of love, that both have creation for an end, the one ecstasizing the mind as the other ecstasizes the flesh, and that they are the two forms of sexual intercourse.

In that quasi-divine intoxication of bearing within himself the male and female principles, and of fecundating himself, the hallucinated individual of whom we are speaking scorned the other pleasures; he locked himself away in his periods of work, as with an adored mistress; every new work was a virgin who gave herself to him; he contemplated her for a long time with the eyes of thought before daring to approach her, and stroked her timidly at first, as if he were afraid of frightening her; then came the first caresses, and the hectic nuptials in which the joy perpetuated itself to engender joy, for a long time, until the work was finished; it was then like an act of love that was concluded; the deliria of passion were succeeded by sympathetic indifference. But almost immediately, the haunting glimpse of some work excited once again the desire for imminent possessions, and a new engagement was made, and the marriage recommenced.

What was the fate subsequently reserved by opinion for the ardently cherished work? He hardly cared about that; when the loved one leaves us to descend into the street and prostitute herself to passers-by, whether she is a woman or a work of art, the promiscuities are nothing but disgrace and the frictions mere soiling; she is no longer ours; she is stained; she has gone; all the happiness she could give, we have taken, we have had it, the love is dead. Those who create to extract profit from the work and not to enjoy it immediately are false artists, comparable to false lovers who take a woman for the money she brings, or will bring, to them.

Perhaps, anyway, our hero was a bad painter; a passion for art is not always sufficient to bestow talent, and in the same way that there are sterile couples, there exist artists without works. In miserable minds, the germ of an idea prepares itself in the egg, and stirs dully, but the intercourse of art never fertilizes it; unisexual minds, incomplete powers, they strive to create, and give themselves the illusion of it, while engendering only death, and their work is like the cemetery of their thought.

It does not matter; they have loved, they have believed, hoped, desired, if only for a moment. It's good.

So, the person with whom we are concerned delighted himself in that love, and, thanks to it, found life so good that he regretted soon having to quit it.

As others around him felt vaguely sad as they watched a woman pass by whom they would perhaps never possess, he was grief-stricken in glimpsing a harmony that he would not have the leisure to transpose on to a canvas.

One morning, a sudden idea made him leap out of bed, and his heart beat forcefully.

The end of the world!

The expectation and obsession of preceding centuries took a special form in him: people were going to see a unique landscape, a prodigious landscape!

Elect among a race of the Elect, he could for his own joy, multiply by art the sensation promised to everyone. What artist, throughout the ages, had been favored as much as him, as happy as him?

He wept with tenderness, and perhaps with gratitude.

He got up in haste, and bought a newspaper in order to read the exact position of the Moon, which the papers indicated every day.

Where should he take up his position?

The encounter of the planet and its satellite was to take place in the Indies, at 81° of longitude and 7° of latitude, in the south of Ceylon: the eastern slope of the Perotallagalla[21]

---

[21] I have retained the original's spelling here, although modern atlases render the mountain's name as Piduruthalagala. Aristillus is actually a crater rather than a mountain, but because

would be struck by Mount Aristillus, situated north-east of the lunar Sahara designated by the name of Mare Serenitatis.

"That's where it's necessary to go."

He had four full months ahead of him, to transport himself to the locale and organize his installation.

Without delay, he assembled all his pecuniary credit, packed his apparatus and a few supplies, and then, leaving the door open so that others might take advantage of his house and what he was leaving therein, he departed.

He saw, to his annoyance, that pleasure trains, steamships and aerostats were leaving at every moment for the Island of the Impact, were the influx would be great. In fact, all those who were chaste by temperament, or tranquil, or sad; all the contemplators unamused by action; all the bored, nostalgic and gastralgic; all the impotent, and the old, and excessively thin women—all those who, for any reason whatsoever, were turning away from life—were heading out there in droves, to get a better view.

Then again, it was elegant, for it gave one the appearance of an intellectual, a stoic or an artist. With the result that a vile population abounded on that excessively narrow island; the countless hotels were overflowing with human being, especially on the mountains and the plateaux; people were keeping away from the sea and low-lying areas because of the formidable tide that would rise as the satellite approached.

These tourists were intent on the honor of being crushed first, if only a few seconds before the rest of the Terrans; it would have been truly stupid to get oneself drowned by a tidal wave an hour before the end of the world, and not see anything! Thus, people were choosing places, and everyone was busy organizing his last minute appropriately.

The artist installed himself for his last work.

---

many 19th century astronomers thought of the lunar craters as volcanic rather than impact craters, they often assumed that they were situated at the tops of mountains.

Almost at the summit of Perotallagalla, he had a cage of crystal and steel erected, on powerful foundations, orientated in such a way that the view extended toward the point on the horizon where the phenomenon was to be manifest. He had supervised the construction with a jealous and paternal curiosity, as if the thing was already an integral part of the work so cherished in advance; now he awaited the hour, frenetically, and as soon as the last night arrived, in the middle of which the dawn of death ought to rise from a new Orient, he headed for the cage.

He suppressed an urge to run. Never had life seemed so exquisite to him. He went in, full of an intoxication which spread a concentrated sensuality through his entire body from the heights of his mind; one might have thought that he was going into the bedroom of a long-desired spouse, a sort of temple where a mysterious and possessive love was about to bloom. Exhausted by the excitement of hope, his legs buckled; in order to rest, he sat down on a stool, his heart beating rapidly and his palette in his hand. Life was enraptured within him. Was he living more or less than a little while ago? He was a new man. He was rejuvenated, and felt as a child feels, but he was as weak as an old man. The blood flowed so powerfully within his arteries that he right hand trembled, to the point of jiggling on his knee.

"I won't be able to do it!"

He tried to place a dry brush at an exact point on the canvas, but he could not do it, his hand was shaking so persistently.

Then his joy became anxious, so much so that it resembled suffering.

He contemplated the forms around him without seeing them, with wide animal eyes; and because it was the hour when the beast no longer existed before the mind, it seemed, on the contrary, that the beast dwelt alone therein. He experienced an enormous lassitude in all his limbs, and, as if he had expended in the desire for his work all the strength that he would need to accomplish it, he was exhausted in advance by the imminent effort. Discouraged by having to furnish it for a second time, cowardly before the imminence, humble at not having been so earlier, and as mild as someone defeated, he waited.

But increasingly, his enthusiasm drained away, like fragments of a fresco peeling off; something naked and sad, something cold and ugly, a bleak misery, appeared beneath the ancient splendor, and all the décor of beautiful determination crumbled away gradually, to reveal to pride the shame of his impotence—and the human being saw himself as feeble as a human being.

At intervals, he turned his heavy gaze toward the summit of the Ocean, then toward his canvas, wondering what image and what hues were about to appear there. Then, all that trouble seemed to him to be futile and mad. He no longer understood. Was it not only yesterday, however, that he had delightedly established a sketch, so exact in its principal lines and initial planes, in the background of the picture, in order to reserve the larger part for the sky, the great sky, where the festival of light that no one had ever seen was about to be held?

In truth, he no longer understood.

Was it not only yesterday, however, that he had loved this expectation, with all his power and with all his life?

With a mechanical gesture, he tried once again to place his brush on the white canvas—but his arm fell back. He was no longer in love. Love was dead. But a part of him, perhaps out of habit, wanted him to stay even so, and to try again, until the end; that is why, in his soul, he experienced an anguish similar to that of the lover who prolongs the grip of possession when affection has gone. What was he doing there, instead of resting in peace?

In truth, he was no longer in love.

Then, he began to weep.

Abruptly, in a fit of anger, he threw his palette and brushes on the ground, and fled.

He was painfully ashamed of himself.

He had demanded more of himself than of a human being, and was only similar to all the rest, as impotent as all of them, unworthy, as much as any of them, of the supreme favor that had been granted to him of confronting the unique work.

He sat down on a mound on the plateau, to watch, like an ordinary man. Less than any other! For in being at odds with himself he was at odds with all of life, incapable of savoring anything.

In the grass, he saw an ant, which did not know, and felt superior to it.

Then he raised his head.

On the crest of the horizon, a light appeared.

"Already!"

A roseate mist had just scaled the rampart of the sea, and was swelling. Horizontally, a radiance appeared, scarcely perceptible at first, became sparkling in the mist, and quickly cut through it to spring into the depths of the sky, and turned red.

The artist contemplated it with astonishment, like a man beginning to remember.

He turned his head and, behind him, saw rainbows rounding out, each beneath the others, in a series of arcades. The summits brightened with carmine, florid and transparent.

He turned back to the lunar Orient.

Other rays had sprung forth—green, blue, violet, yellow—a thousand rays that radiated from the same center, ripping through the peace of the azure, spreading out to deploy the meteor of their prismatic fan through the resplendent half of the firmament; and those rays were moving, fleeing and returning, sliding through one another, exchanging their colors, living, rapid and furious: a sumptuousness of explosive harmonies agitating in the immense sheaf in which the multicolored waves were ascending and descending, scintillating all the while, streaming as if the fire of all the metals were rushing in torrents through dazzling space.

The sea, sparkling, reflected the enchantment of the sky.

The wind skimmed the warm earth, racing and whistling.

The man remained motionless, numb with admiration. There was a smile inside him, at his own negligibility. "Wouldn't one have to be made, to dream of setting that magic down on a sheet of fabric?"

Meanwhile, the hues thinned out, and the colors became lees defined, still vibrant and more tremulous than ever, and also more furtive, losing in precision what they gained in brightness. The lances of flame pressed together, and became more confused, and there was now a fluid sheet of brightness running from below to on high, paler and yet more brilliant than before.

At the zenith, four images of the Moon, gigantic and rubicund, were suspended like lanterns.

Then, from the point at which the mist had appeared shortly before, more hectic colors emerged; a red-gold incandescence burned at sea-level, slowly enlarged and thickened in the middle, and then designed the edge of a disk similar to that of the sun.

It was a deathrise.

The Moon rose swiftly. Human eyes had never seen the sun as vast; one might have believed the satellite half-emerged from the invisible when it had scarcely begun to surge forth; it hoisted itself up, and hoisted itself further, and its rutilant arc, ever larger, extended without limit over the fulgurant sea.

Finally, the monstrous ball disengaged itself entirely, and seemed to oscillate momentarily on the line of the Ocean, which became convex at that point.

The Moon began to climb.

It was as red as a winter sun.

Around it, the light sparkled, and bouquets of sparks sprang from the contours of the disk.

The deformed horizon swelled up; a liquid blister dilated above it and became rounder by the minute, reaching for the Moon. A terrible wind galloped from the mountain-tops. Long howls arrived from the sea. Lightning-bolts clattered in the limpid air. Clouds that seemed to come from nowhere were suddenly heaped up, dispersing as rapidly, without leaving traces in the sky.

Then the Moon became visible again, a little higher, always larger, with its girdle of sparks.

Bolides hurtled toward it, streaking the sky with a light more vivid than light. The air was whistling. Every brightness was noisy. The breath of the world swept thunder. A rumbling descended from the ether, a rumbling rose from the waves, another howled in the ravines, and the entire Earth was displayed in red, with heavy green shadows.

Suddenly, the painter ran to his cage and shut himself in.

The blister of the horizon had swollen further; waves like mountains exhausted themselves, to fall in a single mass; columns of water emerged from the sea, tilted or snaked toward the Moon and, dark on one side, dazzling on the other, precipitated themselves over the inundated plains and launched themselves forward to scale the mountains.

In haste, the man picked up his palette and his brushes.

The Moon no longer seemed to be advancing toward the zenith, but it was still swelling, like a balloon being blown up.

The artist worked.

Around him, the rocks were alive and the forms were sonorous. The stones were not rolling over one another; they were dancing, chasing one another and colliding with little blue sparks. The trees were taking flight. The wild beasts and reptiles, panic-stricken, were dragging themselves over the panting ground, and clinging to dislocated boulders. The island was a sea from which the highest mountain surged like an islet.

"Will I have time?"

Feverishly, he mixed the colors, searched for the shades, plastered hasty and anxious patches on the canvas.

The Moon, more enormous the closer it came, and more ardent, filled the entire height of the firmament, and came on, like a closing lid. Orange light seethed on its surface. The sky was flat and white, a creamy and lukewarm white, which was palpitating. On the ground, bright gleams stood out in sharp ridges, and the green dreariness of the shadows was bathed with red, as if a fiery vapor were shivering in their demi-hue.

"What time is it?"

A deafening racket was howling around the world, in which fire, air and water went insane with fury.

With each lightning-flash of the formidable tempest, he grasped furtive information, and reproduced it rapidly, from memory.

"Two twenty."

Everything cracked. The mountains crumbled. The cage vacillated on its steel crampons.

"No more than an hour!"

The circle of the Moon was still increasing.

The heat was suffocating.

"I won't get there!"

The sweat was running down his entire feverish body.

"It's too difficult!"

He was breathing effortfully; in his buzzing head, the blood was hammering the arteries and the inner surface of the cranium. His bloodshot eyes were closing; he could only make things out with difficulty.

But the brutal sketch was taking on an aspect of ardent and frantic life.

"A little more, just a little more!"

His clothes were burning his skin.

He did not hear the sound of a stone that had just collided with the crystal glass. He was enjoying himself. He made haste.

"Oh, that effervescence of tones, on the great disk!"

Through a crack, a gust of wind plunged into the cage. The canvas trembled.

He kept it steady with his left hand.

"Is it appropriate to sign it? Bah—it doesn't matter!"

He breathed. His heart leapt. Blood, summoned from without, sweated from his pores and ran along his fingers.

"To live for just another quarter of an hour!"

The steel of the crampons broke, but the cage remained upright.

For a brief moment, the Moon had been growing with a rapidity that seemed vertiginous. It melted. The base of its disk drew closer to the horizon, and the pyramid of water, striving to connect with the satellite, wagged a tempestuous cometary tail beneath it.

"Does the design need modifying?"

On the surface of the block, the orange tint of its fire was becoming more silvery with every passing moment.

"Do the shades need modifying?"

His tongue swelled up in his mouth.

With a sharp pain, he found the strength in his muscles to withdraw his agonized upper body slightly, in order to appreciate the effect of the ensemble.

"The green of the shadows isn't blue enough!"

He drew nearer to the easel, and raised his arm.

THE GORILLOID

I. Of Others

> The first day of the new year incites
> our minds to look into the future.
> Guy de l'Estang (1413)

Four thousand centuries have passed. The face of the world has changed, Our continent has been swallowed up by new seas; the glacial waters of the Pole descend as far as the shores of Africa. The only inhabitable regions girdle the globe between the two tropics. All our animal and vegetable species have been transformed during the Quinary period and the majority have ceased to exist. Humankind no longer exists.

On the other hand, several races of apes have been perfected, and among them, the Gorillas, having reached the highest degree of development, constitute the superior being. They live in societies, and their civilization, like their science, is highly advanced.

Now, on the 26.3 of the year 71.9.37, an extraordinary item of news spread, and for two lunes—the day then being thirty-six hours long—the newspapers everywhere have been discussing Professor Sffaty's discovery.

On an exploratory voyage to the North Pole, the illustrious scientist ventured into previously unknown regions. Having reached a latitude of 46°[22] he encountered a rocky archipelago of Secondary origin, where he wintered. On those islets he collected the fossil bones of vanished species, notably

---

[22] 46° is the approximate latitude of Mont Blanc, the highest peak in the Alps.

several skeletons of a previously unknown antediluvian ape, which presented strange resemblances to the Gorillas.

The professor even succeeded in capturing a live specimen of one of these "humans"—as he called the prehistoric animal in question.

The news of this event, initially treated with great suspicion, did not take long to spread, and immediately impassioned public opinion in spite of its scientific character. Violent polemics appeared in the newspapers, the question at stake being: Are Apes descended from Humans?

Politics and religion envenomed the debate, which promptly ceased to remain zoological.

A lecture by Professor Sffaty, advertised as being due to take place in the large lecture-hall of the Museum of Karysk, has brought together an enormous and select crowd. People have fought over tickets. Five hundred Gorillas of the noblest birth, the most illustrious apes in politics, finance and the various Institutes, have assembled in the hall, which has been crowded since the doors opened.

The building's surroundings are cluttered with a popular multitude, and one might believe that all Gorillakind is taking an interest, in its conscience and in its dignity, in the questions that are about to be treated in that solemn session.

The auditorium is unsettled; the adverse opinions of materialism and idealism are already manifest with a latent acrimony that the severity of the location is only just retaining within the bounds of decency. The police, affecting to fear a riot, have taken exceptional measures to ensure order in the hall and its surroundings.

While waiting for the lecture to begin, opera glasses are aimed at two twin tables that have been laden with bones.

The moment is approaching; the room is warming up.

Professor Sffaty finally appears.

Prolonged applause and a hostile tumult greet his entrance simultaneously.

He is rather pale but quite calm. His fine bearing and the dignity of his attitude end up holding sway. After only a quar-

ter of an hour, silence is almost reestablished, and the doctor can final make himself heard.

He speaks.

Messieurs,

Whatever humility imposes itself on the pioneers of Science, who habitually live in confrontation with the most sublime problems and incessantly observe the impotence of effort, I have the conviction today of seeing my tribulations and fatigues recompensed by a discovery of the most fundamental importance, and of presenting to you a document of the greatest possible interest to the history of our race, its origins and its future.

Sensation.

The newspapers of the entire world have already spoken to you about it, perhaps little too hastily. Perhaps too quickly, and perhaps also too categorically, in evaluating the character of this scientific revelation. Is it true as they claim, that I am bringing you our ancestor? In other words, is it true that Gorillas are descended from Humans? Messieurs, let us proceed less rapidly. Such a question is serious, and requires to be resolved as calmly as possible, by means of a very careful examination, with a precise method. That is why, before presenting the strange animal that will be the object of our study to you, it is first appropriate to look back, in order better to explain the conditions of its existence and the environment in which it has been able to manifest itself.

Various movements.

Have no fear, Mesdames; I shall keep this necessary preamble as brief as possible, in order not to irritate you by abusing your patience.

Smiles.

Messieurs, everything leads us to believe that the boreal regions, presently covered by an immense Ocean, were not always sunk beneath the glacial waters. We know, and no one any longer disputes it, that the polar zone was once much less extensive, and that in the first ages of the world, when the terrestrial globe knew no seasons, the average temperature at the poles was equal to that of the tropics, and certainly far superior to that which we enjoy today in our equatorial climes. That certainty has been acquired by Science.

However, the hypothesis, more contestable and more contested, of a vanished continent, which occupied that portion of our planet in the epoch when the zone of polar ice scarcely descended below the forty-second degree of north latitude, is another matter. Those problematic lands, which legend calls Europides, or Europe, would have spread out in the place where the ice of the Europic Ocean now extends, and the rare islands that we see, scattered over that vast sea, would simply be the summits of its highest mountains, still emerging to attest the previous existence of a continent that is no more.

Let us hasten to say that the existence of a continent is still no more than a hypothesis—a logical hypothesis, corroborated by all the notions of geology, but which has not, to date, been scientifically demonstrated by authentic vestiges, the only evidence that we can admit. For you can easily understand that it is permissible to say: 'The sea once covered the continent on which we reside, and has built us this fatherland—here are its traces!'—but it is less easy to go to study, at enormously profound submarine depths, the vestiges of an ancient terrestrial life. And although we observe experimentally that everywhere the land is, the sea was, we cannot establish by the same method that land surged forth where the sea hollows out—but we can at least suppose it, by analogy. Continents have their vicissitudes. No one is unaware that, since the creation of the globe, all the land presently visible and known, was by turns abandoned and repossessed, left once again by the sea that subsequently came to reoccupy it, and the successive layers of the terrestrial crust are here to certify this perpetual alternation.

A commencement of lassitude appears to be affecting the audience, whose members are utterly uninterested in geological considerations, and want to hear something else. Estimating that the preamble is too long, several ladies are shifting in

their seats and fanning themselves. The explorer pays no heed.
He continues calmly.

That a Europe, or Europides, existed is therefore proba-ble. One can even assert that, to some extent, the discovery of the Gorilloid that we have bought back is a further argument in favor of the thesis.

In fact, Messieurs, a constant harmony reigns in nature between all the various manifestations of life; animals and vegetables alike exist in a direct relationship with the envi-ronment they inhabit. You know that, and every one of you has been able to observe it many times over while taking walks. Species, in the animal kingdom as well as the vegeta-ble, corresponding to the climates of their respective regions, are appropriate to them, in a sense denouncing them. Regions that are damp or dry, cold or hot, elevated or low-lying, have their particular flora and fauna.

Now, that law of propriety is manifest in many other ef-fects, less familiar but no less logical; what is true for tem-peratures, altitudes or hygrometric conditions is also true for space: the proportions of extent exercise their influence on forms of life, and that influence imposes itself like that of any other ambient condition. The population of islands cannot and does not resemble that of continents; they have their own in-habitants and always will. Large herbivores correspond to abundant pasture; fast-moving animals such as deer, reindeer or horses suppose the deployment of large surfaces, without which they would not be able to live or develop normally— and, let us also say, without which they could not be born. A bird with a large wingspan is conclusive evidence of distance, as a fish is conclusive evidence of water.

If, therefore, we encounter, in insular locations, the fos-sils of species that I shall call continental, we can affirm with-out hesitation that the islands were formerly an integral part of a continent, from which they were separated by some cata-clysm.

Such is precisely the case with the Alpians that we have just explored. Our collection of fossils, gathered among the rocks of the boreal region, attests to the existence in those desolate regions of a once-prosperous continent. You can, at your leisure, examine these specimens of fossil bones, which the ice has conserved for us over several thousand centuries, and which will subsequently be classified at the Museum. But henceforth, and most of all, the strange simian that you will shortly contemplate, the last survivor of a world, will appear to you and cannot fail to appear to you, as the witness of a lost continent, and perhaps of a level of culture that seems to have been quite advanced, not only physically but also intellectually.

Movements. The explorer addresses a few whispered words to his assistant, who steps back. Prolonged agitation in the auditorium.

Before then...

Various movements Murmurs.

Messieurs, I understand your legitimate impatience, and it flatters me, as a proof of the powerful interest that you are kind enough to attach to my discovery, but the presentation of the Human cannot usefully be made if it is not preceded by an osteological examination of earlier specimens: the skeletons of yesterday, rather than the living specimen of today, will permit us to judge the degree of advancement reached by the race in the times of its prosperity. I shall pass over that study as rapidly as possible, in order to return to it in a future lecture, but it is impossible for me to omit it, however anxious I am to please you!

The professor steps back to the tables on which the fossils bones are placed.

Messieurs I tell you that the Gorilloids to which we have given the name Humans were not unconscious brutes. The dimensions of their skulls prove it, no less than the opening of the facial angle. Among all the animals species that are or have been alive, only one facial angle is as widely open: ours.

Various sensations. The scientist, his arm outstretched, lifts up a human skull and displays its profile triumphantly. His attitude, a trifle over-theatrical, is emphatic, and some

people seem inclined to consider it provocative; that impres-
sion is accentuated when the lecturer, turning to a blackboard
standing behind him, shows thereon the human angle and the
gorillan angle, which are identical. Pointing to them each in
turn he says:

Theirs, then; ours, now. It's the same.

Prolonged movements.

The dentition, analogous to ours, attests an omnivore; this mammal held itself, as we do, in a vertical position, only utilizing its hind limbs for walking; it was a bimane!

Sensations.

Finally, the presence of certain osseous apophyses, the detailed study of which I shall not impose upon you, undeniably proves the progressive atrophy of organs once possessed the first specimens of the species, but which gradually disappeared as the race as refined—such as, for example, the vestige of a caudal appendage, which the Human skeleton presents, as ours does.

Murmurs, protests.

The professor affects not to hear them, pauses briefly, and continues:

We therefore find ourselves, without a doubt, in the presence of an advanced civilized, albeit degenerate, species, which occupied, before ours, continents anterior to ours: a superior species like our own, perhaps capable of abstract thought, and perhaps having had arts and sciences like ours!

I shall have said everything about this point, Messieurs, when I have added to these summary remarks the assertion of one fact, and one only, which with doubtless seems to you rich in possible deductions: these bones have not been collected in a native state in the soul of the Quinary epoch, as were those of the animals we found; they were buried in tombs of carved stone. Humans buried their dead!

Prolonged sensation.

Thus, Messieurs, Humans lived in society. Furthermore, they built. An agglomeration of sand and calcareous matter, compressed between the stones of tombs, which serves to hold them together, clearly appears to be, not a natural product, but the work of an intentional fabrication. Thus, Humans possessed industries. Living in society—as proved by the association of the tombs—they were able to group their houses like their tombs, and constitute cities...don't laugh, Messieurs, I'm not affirming it yet, but I say that they could have: the hypotheses, although not demonstrated, is at least plausible, and logic authorizes it! When we have searched the sea-bed—and we will search the Europic Sea, where the cities are submerged, as I am convinced they are, for want of proof to the contrary—and have brought back into the light those miserable remains of a vanished epoch, of a doomed species, then, doubtless, you will no longer be laughing. The irony of incredulity—which is to say, of ignorance—will be forced to admit, with us, with reason, with common sense, that one art supposes all the arts, that the possibility of one renders all the others possible and necessary, if there is time enough to attain them, and that it is evidence of a retrograde mind, in no way noble but merely closed, in no way proud, but simply vain, to refuse to conceive the possibility of races that are, or once were, equal to ours.

Enthusiastic applause from some benches. Whistles. Protests. The applause is redoubled. Tumult.

The honor of Gorillakind...

New interruption. Animal cries. The professor makes as if to withdraw. In the face of that threat, calm is gradually reestablished.

Messieurs, I am not polemicizing here; I am practicing science. There are some who are scornful of my thinking, who have been able momentarily to attribute to me the malevolent intention of offending the susceptibilities of others. I respect all beliefs, in the desire to see mine respected in return, and I do not consider that the verities acquired regarding the evolution of animal species are incompatible with any notion of the divinity, or that they cast a slur on legally recognized religions. I repeat that I am not making a political point here...

Applause.

…and I deem that the honor of the Gorillan species cannot reside in a jealous exclusivism, but, on the contrary, in the glory of thinking and seeking the truth, whatever it may be, on any subject whatsoever.

Dogmas inform us that the World was created for us and for us alone. Let us leave the dogmas there, I shall not dispute them; but let us at least recognize that, if such a conviction has been able to arise in our minds, analogous minds might have had it before us, and might have it after us. Who knows what the Alpian Bimanes of whom these are the relics, the Humans, might have thought about these matters? Who knows whether this Gorilloid species might not have arrived at its full development, while our ancestors, still primitive, were living in the caves of the prehistoric age, and who can tell whether its members might have professed, in our regard, an exclusivism analogous to the one on which we now pride ourselves in our turn? Who can tell whether they might have had, like us, dogmas and gods, and faith in their immortal souls?

Gentlemen, let us not pass judgment on things unknown, for fear of making temeritous judgments. The beings I am showing you might have believed themselves to be great. They are no longer. Respect their ashes! A few thousand centuries ago, the creatures that I have discovered thought, loved, suffered and desired, but it now requires the science of another race merely to establish that they existed!

These beings, superior to all known animals, reigned over themselves and over the globe, in the distant epochs when the habitable portion of our planet had not yet been reduced to the intertropical zone. Their domain was vaster than ours, but perhaps their notion of good and evil was identical to ours. How did they disappear? The law of evolution that had fashioned them logically, degenerated them logically, and when environmental conditions ceased to be in harmony with the species' organism, they died out logically.

When, shortly, we compare these two skeletons with the survivor that you are going to see, you will comprehend the slow regression of a grandeur that has attenuated, a strength that is exhausted, a race that is on the brink of extinction.

Applause. The professor turns and makes a sign to his assistant, who receives his instructions and leaves the room. The session is suspended briefly. Animated dialogues in the hall.

The assistants return, carrying a sort of cubic cage on a stretcher, covered with a sheet; they deposit it on a large table next to the podium and hang a placard on it: DO NOT TOUCH.

Lively movement of curiosity. Silence is completely reestablished. Opera-glasses are aimed at the veiled cage. The professor approaches and slowly lifts the edge of the sheet. He leans toward the cage, shaking his head in an amicable manner, as if to reassure the captive beast.

He opens the door of the cage.

The Human appears.

On the invitation of the professor, who encourages it with a hand gesture, the Human crosses the threshold and advances across the table.

Cries of surprise, followed by words rapidly exchanged in low voices.

The Human is clad in an ample bearskin cloak. It measures about one meter ten. Its head, enormous and pale, is speckled—its face as well as his head—with sparse hairs, dirty white in color. The blinking eyes, which seem to be those of an albino, are protected by long white lashes. Its expression is one of fright. Its torso and limbs are invisible beneath the draped cloak.

The professor leans toward the specimen and gently, by means of gestures, invites it to take off its cloak. The animal is visibly reluctant. In spite of the specimen's resistance, the professor proceeds to undress it himself.

A further cry of astonishment goes up in the auditorium.

The Human is completely naked; its upper body is weak and flat, as if crushed, but the abdomen is swollen and sticks out. The arms, extraordinarily short, terminate in minuscule hands with spatulate fingers. The short and knock-kneed limbs have enormous attachments. The entire body, dull gray in color, is striated with white hairs similar to those on the face.

The Human, embarrassed under the gazes of the crowd, turns its head to the right and the left, anxiously, as if seeking a refuge.

The opera-glasses study it; the dialogues become more animated. In many places a scarcely-scientific laugher shakes the powerful shoulders of aristocratic Gorillas. The ladies, keenly amused by the examination of the grotesque little male, whisper among themselves. A few scientists, who have come on to the stage, touch the Human, open its mouth, tap it on the back, work its joints, and examine the texture of its skin and the nuances of its hair with magnifying glasses.

II. The Last Couple

When it is reckoned that scientific and worldly curiosity has had time to satisfy itself, Professor Sffaty asks for the stage to be cleared, and returns to the table on which the two fossilized human skeletons are laid. He stands behind it.

By his attitude, he makes it understood that he is going to speak Calm is gradually reestablished in the audience. The assistants shout: "Silence, please!"

People cough. They settle down.

The professor drinks some water.

The silence is complete.

The professor speaks:

A first glance was sufficient, Mesdames and Messieurs, for you to observe the evident kinship between this small creature and our race, and I ask for no more proof for that than your cry of surprise—but we shall return to that delicate question later.

The second observation that imposes itself is that of a singularly notable difference between this ultimate specimen of a species and the two fossil skeletons that you are about to

133

see, and which are themselves fundamentally different from one another.

Three individuals, three epochs! The first, four thousand centuries old...

Sensations.

...goes back to the Quaternary period, in the course of which Humans seem to have been the veritable monarchs of the globe. The second skeleton, much more recent, dates from the Quinary epoch; it is a specimen of degeneration, which marks a intermediate stage between the glorious human here to my right and the rebrutalized human here to my left, the last survivor.

I shall spare you, Mesdames, the eminently instructive comparative study of these three types. Merely note the fundamental uniformity of the three modes: the animal is one, always the same, but gulfs of time separate the three individuals; between them, the work of degeneration has taken effect. In the same way that the species, in the course of centuries, and by virtue of an uninterrupted series of transformations, was able to obtain the full development of its organs and faculties, and to raise itself to a highly advanced state of culture, so it was able—I will gladly say that it was obliged—in continuing along the same path, to overshoot the target, while it still believed itself to be following it; having already reached the summit, it was necessary for it to complete its journey and descend again, while it imagined itself to be still climbing because it never stopped marching!

Every organism has a limit of development, which it cannot surpass; when it has completed the sequence of its schema, it stops, and from then on, any further effort only accelerates the fatal and inevitable disorganization. The force that developed it becomes the force that disaggregates it; stone, subjected to too much pressure, crumbles; metal evaporates; a planet dissolves; a plant becomes etiolated; a species degenerates; a kingdom falls apart; a rope breaks! All power has an end; all expansion a term. That extreme of possible resistance is called the critical point.

Messieurs, the weakness of species is not being able to stop at the critical point; minerals cling to it better than plants, which transgress it less than animals; of all the last-named, the most intelligent are the most injurious to themselves, because the notion of their capability incites hem to employ their latent strength in a way that exceeds the norm; in attempting to live more, to live to excess, they kill themselves. Perhaps we should be led to conclude that the viability of races is in inverse proportion to the consciousness they have of themselves, and that consciousness of strength is a mortal peril for any being that possesses it.

What we can, at least, affirm as certain is that the state of perfection resides in Harmony; that alone regulates the world and engenders life; the equilibrium of forces constitutes perfect beauty, the only beauty, and also the indispensable condition of all existence. When one of the forces becomes excessive, the equilibrium is broken, and the work belongs henceforth to death. To desire to go beyond is to aspire to destruction; to surpass natural limits is to return to oblivion.

Where are the limits? Our Reason searches for them but does not know them; Art sometimes divines them, and Science sometimes defines them, but our certainties are restricted. We go on nevertheless, and effort towards the better sometimes leads us toward the worse, with the result that we often deteriorate that which was worth more before our coming, and history informs us that, in many reforms, our confidence in the hope of edifying that which might be merely ends up degrading that which was.

Repeated applause.

I am only speaking here, Messieurs, from an abstract point of view, and I beg you not to see allusions in my discourse that are not there. We are not examining, at present, the burning social questions of the gorilla species, but the past conditions of the human species, and I say that this bimane, once arrived at its most noble development—which is to say, the perfect equilibrium between its psychic strengths and its

135

physical strengths, was able to aspire to an exaggerated development thereof, and sought it to its own detriment.

An abuse of its thinking faculties, insufficiently equilibrated by the use of its muscular faculties, produced a cerebral hypertrophy concomitant with the atrophy of its limbs. Is it not permissible to suppose that this superior species, in the momentum of intellectual labor and nervous vibration, was unable to stop, and that it has deliberately killed itself, without wishing to comprehend, intoxicated as it was by the conquering power of its genius?

Such a conjecture, Messieurs, makes you smile in the face of this monster—and yet, comparative anatomy proposes this hypothesis to us, and even imposes it upon us. In fact, let us return to the skeleton of the Quaternary Human.

Professor Sffaty turns a handle, and the black velvet-topped table that bears the various parts of a human skeleton, fixed to it by metal supports, slowly tilts and presents it face to the audience.

Consider this being, its skull—what do we see? A large, solid case in exact proportion to the thoracic cage, with the limbs of locomotion and prehension. The human species is here in full bloom: it is Quaternary Humankind, the Human-King! To produce this majestic performance required centuries of selection, thousands of centuries. Now, let us compare it with this descendant of the penultimate hour, the child of the death-throes.

Turning another handle, he tilts the second table and presents the reconstituted bones of the Quinary Human.

This is the Quinary Human. Look: the skull has become ridiculously vast; the dorsal spine, crushed beneath that weight, which it can no longer hold high and straight, is bent. The ribs, which it draws backwards, retreat, and the torso becomes hollow. That retreat will naturally occasion a preeminence of the abdomen, which, no longer being maintained, swells and sags. But what it is necessary to note above all, Messieurs, is the condition of the upper and lower limbs, for they will furnish us with a precious indication, and will allow us an induction of a higher order.

The limbs, under that strengthless body, have weakened, become bowed, while we see the joints acquiring an excessive importance, still trying to maintain in equilibrium the fragile edifice of an animal on the brink of collapse—which is to say, ready to fall upon the ground from which it has progressively raised itself up. The arms are perhaps more significant still; their vigor and utility being no longer entertained by any exercise, they have become cachexic, reduced from one age to the next—and a gradual diminution of the muscles very probably preceded that shrinkage of the bones.

But what should we conclude from that, Messieurs, if not that the atrophy of the organs was consecutive to the disuse of their functions? The arms that are being lost, the legs that are becoming twisted, are limbs that are no longer being used, or are being used less and less. By contrast, the fingers, long, slender and nimble, give evidence of the frequent and subtle employment of the hand, exclusively devoted to delicate work and rapid gestures.

It is at this point, Messieurs, that I require all your attention. Two organs have developed to the detriment of the others: the brain and the hand. I shall be more precise: the brain and the fingers. Is it the case, therefore, that they alone were employed, all the rest having become useless? Is it the case that Humans, in their final period, were all thought and digitation? Is it the case that they had no need of anything else, and had begun to restrict the expenditure of their effort to a minimum? Is it the case that they had been able, by virtue of a long series of conquests, to tame natural forces, reducing them to the servitude of their slightest need, no longer having from then on, in order to produce movement, light, heat and death, to displace themselves on land or water and perhaps through the air, to move anything except their fingertips?

Sensation.

Messieurs, that power is frightening. Our scientists have not yet attained it, fortunately for us and our children, since it

137

precedes the end of everything. But it was logical, just as the denouement was. For what could become of such a being, after such an ascension?

At this point, Messieurs, I hear an objection that you have every right to make: the decline of Humankind, you will say, must have been slowed down for a long time by the profusion of imbeciles that doubtless existed in the human species and who prevented it from perishing. I confess, Messieurs, that the great utility of imbeciles to a race is incontestable, for they maintain a level of mediocrity that is opposed to the excess of mental development, and holds back its fatal consequences. I also agree that perhaps they might have saved the society, but the gods did not permit it; a terrible event undermined their beneficial endeavor.

What event?

Geology provides us with the answer.

Just as animals are alive and modifying themselves, the Earth, an enormous macrobe, has a life of its own, knowing nothing of the species pullulating on its surface. It too has its slow or abrupt transformations, for worlds, like us and more so than us, are subject to the law of perpetual becoming.

Suppose, therefore, that at the end of the Quinary Period—which is to say, when Humans reigned over everything, but only reigned by means of the brain and the fingers—that a cataclysm similar to those produced many times before, changed the face of our planet once again. Imagine the peoples—for we must believe in the existences of human peoples, human nations, human fatherlands—violently dispossessed of their empires, decimated and exiled, scattered in the wilderness of a new world. What then becomes of that series of groups which escaped the disaster? What will be the situation of those creatures delivered henceforth solely to the resources of individual capability, deprived of their science and their technology, their hands empty in the face of formidable nature, their arms disarmed before the laws of eternal life? Such beings, artificially constituted, capable of prospering by means of the mutual aid of the Society that they have organized artificially but incapable of existing by themselves, must perish.

Messieurs, that is exactly what happened; the supposition I requested of you is an established fact of the history of the heavenly body we inhabit: geology informs us of the upheaval that occurred at the end of the Quinary Epoch and brought it to a close. Human societies were abolished at a stroke. In effect, humans became extinct. The disappearance of that superb race thus presents itself as a normal consequence of its excessive development, and the marvel is not in seeing so much ability collapse in a single moment into a conclusive inability to live; on the contrary, it would have been astonishing if it had been able to prolong its existence and survive the shock that reduced it to primitive existence and its necessities.

That is why, Messieurs, the only surprising thing is seeing that some specimens, admittedly very rare, have been able to continue the species. The prodigy would seem inconceivable to us, in fact, if paleontology did not provide example of analogous survivals; indeed, the large cetaceans and the large pachyderms, not to mention the large reptiles—the whale, the elephant, the rhinoceros, the crocodile—had not completely disappeared in the time that we will call, if you will permit, the Reign of Humankind. We possess their fossils; those degenerate witnesses of the Quaternary and Tertiary epochs had therefore persisted for millions of years beyond their normal age, and humans were able to see those vestiges of another time, marvel at their proportions and their unusual forms, and be as astonished by them as we are by this human! In the same way, a few humans persisted in living when they had no right to do so, and have been able to survive into our era.

Evidently, the humans that survive no longer furnish us with an exact image of what humans were at the supreme moment of their cerebral hypertrophy—far from it! For you can easily understand that those degenerates, thrust back into the midst of natural forces and constrained by them to sustain a precarious struggle, had, by adaptation, to recover a few armaments and sensible attenuate the vices of their deformation. That is the probability indicated to us by reason; it is also a reality that anatomy demonstrates to us.

The individual that you see here, compared to the skeletons of its ancestors, is sufficient to prove that humankind, following the world's upheaval, was reanimalized. We have brought back another document that will make this comparative study easier, and permit us conclusions more clearly categorical. I am taking about a third skeleton: a modern skeleton, that of the female counterpart of the male you can see.

Sensation.

It was for us a capital regret that we were unable to collect in the living state this last human female. Its presence in our collections would doubtless have permitted us to obtain products whose rearing and consequent study would have been very curious. Unfortunately, in spite of our efforts to spare it, the poor beast was killed during the hunt.

Marked sensation.

We have dissected it with great care, and if I abstain from presenting that anatomical specimen to you, so precious for the demonstration of the hypothesis that I announced to you just now, it is, firstly, to avoid extending inordinately a lecture that is already long, and also out of a sense of compassion—for one day when, by chance, the male you see here perceived the bones of its companion in our laboratory, it showed us evidence of the most violent despair, uttering sobs that were almost gorillan, and I would reproach myself, Mesdames, for repeating that dolorous scene in front of you.

Disapproving murmurs. The professor pretends not to hear them. He drinks some water.

The murmurs accentuate, however; the crowd demands the spectacle of that dolor, about which they have been told while refusing to let them see it. The protests become increasingly violent, and Professor Sffaty resigns himself to having the skull, at least, of the female brought out.

The sign that he addresses to his assistants, understood by everyone, reestablishes calm; applause resounds.

The Human contemplates this frantic clamor with bewilderment. Solitary for centuries, it no longer has any notion of assemblies, and the noise frightens it. It turns its head, looking to the right and the left, seeking a means of escape.

Suddenly, it perceives the skull in the hands of an assistant. It recognizes it and, mad with fury, it runs to grab it. But the Gorilla raises its long arms above its head and the gnome, impotent, falls to its knees, extends its joined hands toward the skull of the last female human, and weeps.

Smiling, the Gorilla lowers its arms again. The Human takes possession of the cherished head and covers it with kisses. Its little shoulders are seen heaving with each sob.

An assistant takes the skull back and carries it away. The Human extends its arms toward the retreating relic.

The crowd applauds.

III. The Gorilloid

That moving scene, in exciting the nervous tension of the auditorium, had been well-designed to prepare a feverish welcome for Professor Sffaty's conclusions: anticipated conclusions, discounted by some, revolting to others, impatiently awaited by the combativeness of all.

Suddenly, a relative tranquility emerges throughout the hall; silence is gradually reestablished, and that very silence resembles an injunction finally to formulate those subversive conclusions, against which some are waiting to protest indignantly.

The lecturer, who senses that public preoccupation and is not at all apprehensive about it, collects himself momentarily before he resumes speaking. Then he extends his right hand, and in a firm but unprovocative voice, he says:

I would have finished, Messieurs, if it were not still necessary for me to touch upon, if only briefly, the thorniest part of this study, and to reach the conclusion you expect of us. I indicated it at the beginning of this talk, and public opinion, with adverse passions, has already asked the question. Are Gorillas descended from Humans?

Movements.

I am only too well aware that the hypothesis alone has raised indignant protests, and that we have been accused of attacking the self-respect of our race, which God created and fashioned in his own image. I am only too well aware of how difficult and scabrous the question is from social, religious and mundane viewpoints. Messieurs, from the scientific viewpoint, it is not; we study life in its multiform aspects, we study it without preconceptions and without fury, in order to extract, insofar as it is possible, the great laws that preside over the progression of beings. In any case, in order to reassure the most legitimate scruples. I will immediately tell you my personal and categorical response to the question posed:

No! Gorillas are not descended from Humans.

Various movements.

The reason is simple. Humans have disappeared, and we have just contemplated their ruination. Now, if they were truly our ancestors, they would still exist, since they would exist in us, by means of us, who would represent their perpetual life down here. So, since it pleases some people to consider that descendancy as a humiliation for us and an abasement of our dignity, let us discard the hypothesis, Messieurs. I consent to that, and I assert it.

But if we are not descended from Humans, does that mean that they and we are not descended from a common ancestor? If they are not our ancestors, does that mean that they are not our kin—elder brethren of a sort?

Agitation. Ironic laughter.

You would laugh even louder if I told you that once, in the Quaternary centuries, the human species was able to smile as you are doing, and become indignant, too, at the mere idea of a kinship with us! Then, it was radiant in all its glory, while we were still struggling in the limbo of animality, striving with great difficulty to bring forth our consciousness. It was doubtless scornful of us, refusing to recognize any link between itself and us, seeing us as nothing but beasts, and—who knows?—perhaps putting us in cages...

Laughter.

I'm joking, Messieurs. But if Humans were once able to contest the fraternity of the two races, and deny us because they doubted our perfectibility, we are able in our turn to reason in the same way, since intellectual ability presents itself to us as an accomplished fact. We have less right than them to deny the evident similarities, and the necessity of confessing that common characteristics engender common possibilities imposes itself even more forcefully upon us. Among the myriad species that exist or have existed, none is closer to ours. Time alone separates us. Like us, they have passed through the phases of their normal evolution, in parallel with us, but before us. They ascended more rapidly; they descended again sooner.

That ascent, Messieurs, we know about today; that branch of Simians, themselves the issue of Prosimians, which were born of Marsupials, eventually goes back, via the Proto-mammals all the way to the Dipneumona and the Gastraeads,[23] and the inferior Molllusks connect them with to the Zoo-phytes, the Algae and the original Protoplasma.

Undoubtedly, Messieurs, Humans protested, in their time, against such a humble origin, and did not want to admit that it was also the most noble, since the baseness of the ex-

---

[23] I have substituted the Latin *Dipneumona* for the text's *Dip-neusties*; implying possession of two sets or kinds of breathing apparatus, it has been applied to various animal groups, the one intended here probably being lungfishes, imagined as the ancestors of all land vertebrates. The obsolete term *Gastraead* referred to a hypothetical primitive organism similar in form to an embryonic gastrula: an aggregation of cells whose components have begun to differentiate, but still seems capable of assuming any mature form. It was a derivative of Ernst Haeckel's assertion that "ontogeny recapitulates phylogeny," which is only true in a very vague, quasi-metaphorical sense.

traction procures the laborious climb, and honors the climber. That they would be no more inclined than we are to consent to recognize that verity, is also probable. The pride of that advanced race must have been equal to ours, if not even more foolish, and we are entitled to credit any presumptuousness to beings whose skulls were able to acquire a form like this!

He takes the enormous skull of the Quinary Human in both hands, and holds it up before the crowd.

Who among us can say what dreams were hatched in there? Perhaps humans considered themselves, as we do, to be angelic, supraterrestrial creatures, who had nothing in common with the rest of life! Humans, before us, might perhaps have been able to believe that the world had been created for them, that a God was watching over them, that the stars shone in order to embellish their nights, and that their existence was the ultimate reason for everything! Perhaps they believed, like us, that they possessed within them the principle of an immortal soul!

Laughter.

That opinion amuses us today. Messieurs, and yet, grotesque as it appears to us when it is professed by others, we do not hesitate to renew it for our own usage.

Protests. Several ladies get up and leave.

Forgive me, I beg you, if it impossible for me not to point out the fundamental vice of the reasoning that opposes us. When we observe, for two branches of the same family, the same progress, is it not illogical to admit it for one and deny it for the other?

Animated protests. Tumult.

I see nothing diminishing for us in being the relatives of Humans, who were majestic in their epoch as we are in ours! I cannot see anything humiliating in the honor of having, like them, followed the route of progress.

Laughter and shouting. Violent protests. Someone whistles.

It is Pride that is manifest here, and I am addressing myself to Reason!

Pride doomed Humankind! Pride is the force that creates at the outset, and kills in the end! It drives those who pursue a task, and leads them astray when the task is finished! Pride in the work accomplished is called vanity!

Increasing tumult.

Is it certain that the highest are also the greatest, and that we are able to measure our work accurately? In the ages when Humans were infatuated with their power, building the cities and knowledge that have disappeared with them, modest corals were building a world and empires, which have triumphed over the sea and on which we live!

Bravo! Bravo!

Enough!

Bravo!

Why become irritated, Messieurs? Let us look around us more widely! Everything moves and works in fraternal nature! Nothing is stationary, and progress is incessant for all.

For progress is not, as some think, the exclusive prerogative of intelligent creatures; it is applicable to everything that lives; it is life in motion, and that is why nothing can slow it down or stop it. It moves, and it must move; it is irreducible and necessary, incessant in the divine order, like the great laws of universal gravitation, from which it follows and results, Messieurs, and it continues in us and around us, everywhere and simultaneously!

That is what traces the thread connecting groups and individuals, and we can follow it back, following with it, through the ages, through the species, the curve of unbreakable linkages by which the infinitely small and the infinitely great are connected! If you consent to comprehend the divine labor of Progress, follow it and trace it back, the curve that it has traced since the dawn of time, and you will see how it took hold of matter in order to extract from it, little by little, life in its innumerable forms, which it diversified and ramified, which it specialized and focused, separating each from the rest without ever detaching it! Follow it, and by means of the chain of evident filiations it will lead you without interruption to a conception of the common origin of the unique family!

Movement.

Brethren of aphids, but brethren also of stars, you will perceive the infinitesimal in relation to the immense, borne away together by the Law that regulates everything!

Then, Messieurs, the immense and the infinitesimal will seem to you to be equals, with regard to the infinite in which they move obediently. Then, too, you will conceive that the unanimous ascension of beings is identified with the circle of total movement, and that it is, if I might put it thus, the orbit of existence.

Then, finally, by virtue of having contemplated here the Humankind that Progress raised so high to drag down so low, we shall obtain a great enlightenment, and you will emerge from this enclosure, Messieurs, with the notion and the proof of an exceedingly important truth; for you will know that Progress is not a goal, in the narrow sense that our moralists understand, but, on the contrary, the very Force that raises us all from oblivion and leads us all back to it, with the same gentleness, the same certainty and the same means, in order to maintain universal, eternal, infinite life!

Repeated applause. Lively animation.

The professor, surrounded, receives congratulations. Groups press around the platform on which the Human is standing.

In the middle of that crowd, the animals shows signs of great nervous distress; its face is grimacing with tics and its eyes, rolling in their orbits, frequently turn toward the professor, from whom it seems to be imploring help.

In spite of the prohibition on the blackboard, hands reach out toward it, to stroke it. It utters shrill cries, and becomes more and more distressed.

At a signal from the professor, the assistants open the cage, in which the Human hurriedly takes refuge. It is seen crouching down at the back.

The keepers take it away.

A TRIP TO PARIS

I. Five Thousand Years

On the eighteenth of July 2745 of the Pi-pang Era, a date that corresponds precisely to the twelfth of July 6983 of the Christian Era, the poor fisherman who fulfilled the functions of the keeper of the electric lighthouse on the Butt Montmartre was surprised to see the Oceanian Aerotram, which very rarely headed into those deserted parts, appearing over the horizon.

He called his wife and she came out in a hurry, but he had no need to point anything out to her, because, as soon as she arrived on the threshold of the hut, she perceived the slender convoy of carriages, which was already close.

"Coming here, believe me!"

"To do what, silly woman?"

"Trip. City people, ideas. Where from, train?"

"Blue—Tahiti."

"Coming here, I tell you!"

Indeed, the train stopped at the foot of the lighthouse. The Parisian woman went swiftly back into the hut, to smooth her hair down over her forehead and put it up at the back, to cover her shoulders with a relatively new shawl, and to put brown shoes on her feet, which had been bare. With the hem of her short dress she rubbed her cheeks and her mouth in front of a shard of a mirror, in order to be beautiful, smiled at the image of her little turned-up nose, and came back at a run.

She reappeared just in time to see the city-dwellers get down from the carriages.

There were about a hundred people there, elegantly dressed, with the sober, stern, dull, uniform elegance that characterized the epoch and scarcely permitted the sexes to be distinguished. Out of deference, the Parisian woman dared not go closer in order to see better. Enviously, she watched her husband, who was heading toward the people, obliged as he was his professional duty. He spoke to them. The travelers were forming a semicircle around him, and seemed to be interrogating him. With an extended arm, he was apparently giving directions, toward the south and the west. The majority of the visitors were listening attentively, even advancing their heads to listen; a few, on the other hand, had moved away from the central group, standing to one side, and, standing on the platform of the lighthouse, they were contemplating the location with gestures similar to the fisherman's.

The Parisian woman, by way of imitation, also turned to look, but saw nothing except the usual landscape. The sea was tranquil and milky, almost devoid of waves, beneath a pale sky, and the water was beginning to go down, releasing the islands in the gulf, which were growing by degrees. Each of six was crowned with motionless bracken, from which emerged the brown roof of a small house the color of earth. Two sailing ships were edging across the bay, heading out to sea. Directly ahead, the sheer wall of the cliffs of Meudon reared up, as white as linen and plumed with fir-trees, closing the southern horizon, while the gulf extended eastwards toward the sands of the estuary. There, the bright green grasslands marked the place where the two rivers, the Seine and the Marne, opened into the sea. In places, in the far distance, between the hills of the continent, the silvery plates of ponds could be seen gleaming.

"What's to look at there?"

To help herself understand, the woman turned her head toward the foreigners again, and saw her man, who was coming back at a run.

"Who? Wanting what? From where?"

"From Tahiti. Left this morning. Trip. Scientists, they say."

"What, scientists?"

"Looking—things from past times, they say."

"What, you?"

"Escort, guide: islands, ruins, emperor, cemetery."

"Woman with?"

"Mingled, me think."

"Pretty women?"

"Similar, men similar."

"Me, what?"

"House!"

The Montmartean woman pulled a face, resentfully, but her man frowned threateningly, and she went back to the hut. He turned his back and walked along the strand. The coast was flat and low, garnished with shingle and flints. The fisherman put his boat into the water, got into it alone, and started rowing toward the isles. When he was some way off, the woman came out of the hut. In order not to be seen by her husband or anyone else, she crouched down and crawled through the bracken; she climbed up to the lighthouse in that fashion. When she was close enough to hear voices, she stopped. The sounds reached her distinctly, as is usually the case on the sea shore in calm weather, and she could make out all the words, for the Earth's inhabitants all spoke the same language, but most of the time she did not understand; the meaning of overly abstract locutions was unknown to her, and overly complicated syntax was not in accordance with her habit of coarse and abrupt speech.

Meanwhile, the man who seemed to be the guide or leader of the others, was speaking alone in the edge of the parapet; he expressed himself with pride, and articulated his speech clearly, as if he were very sure of not being mistaken, or as if his words were so precious that not a single one ought to be lost. At any rate, his companions were listening to him attentively, and the Parisian woman quickly realized that he must be the Scientist her man had mentioned, who was explaining things about long-gone times.

When she stopped to listen, the man was saying: "...to guide you here and to descend from the lighthouse, the culminating point, firstly in order to contemplate in its entirety the place where that city was deployed whose existence is revealed to us by history, which was called Paris. Others more qualified than me will explain and demonstrate the progressive phases of the geological processes that gradually led to the swallowing up of the city and its neighboring areas; I shall refer you, for that study, to two works by my eminent colleague Professor Taku: *Collapses and Exhaustions of the Land* and, more especially, *Submarine Europe*, in which he studies the transformations of this regions more specifically.

"The exact researches of geology, and the near-mathematical method that is applicable to it since the important discovery of Lois de Foho, have permitted our modern scientists to measure with precision the progress and the duration of the phenomenon that gradually suppressed this part of the old continent. Submarine explorers have confirmed by long exploration the exactitude of the phenomena that the laws affirm, and we thus know, without a doubt, that the ancient Parisian city, before being submerged, was distant from the sea for many centuries; its vanished glory goes back to that epoch.

"Four thousand years ago, a triangular province extended westwards of Paris, and its tip extended into the Ocean. The granitic island of Bretagne over which we passed today, not long ago, are the last vestiges of that near-isle, the eastern part of which, reaching all the way to Parisian soil, seems to have been one that a few historical documents mention, Normandy, still recognizable by the emersion of its Jurassic crests. Paris was then bathed by a large river, the Seine, or Séquane,[24] which traversed the breadth of the empire. The ignorance of those times seems to have been so profound, and their indifference so gross that for centuries, the gradual sinking of the ground went unnoticed, and even less was there any anxiety about the ultimate logical consequences deducible there-

---

[24] Grande Séquanaise was a French regions corresponding to one of the major divisions of Roman Gaul, covering the upper part of the Seine basin.

from—which is to say, the anticipation of the eventual inundation of the land.

"The capital was then, however, no more than twenty meters above sea level, and the sinking, whose rate is nowadays known to us, was progressing at seventy-eight centimeters per century. Already, as a futile warning, the pressure of the Ocean had drowned two neighboring regions. One of the two, which once continued Europe's occidental coast, was the Atlantis whose map—unknown to our predecessors—we have been able to reconstitute. The other, more recent in origin, extended to the north of Paris, connecting France to nascent England; the latter, from day to day, saw itself separated from the central plateau by a marine river that was known, poetically, as La Manche because of its long and narrow form, and which, more logically, because of its real action, was also called the English Channel.

"These terrains of the Tertiary Epoch, Messieurs, enjoyed a sad and brief fortune here; the last to appear, they were the first to disappear, and the sea, which yielded them up belatedly, soon retook possession of them. But those considerations draw us deep into the remoteness of the past, and do not, moreover, enter into our particular competence nor the curriculum of study for which we have gathered today, and which are to be the object of our field-trip. I am, in any case, only allowed to enter into geological questions in the most summary fashion, and to facilitate the comprehension of the natural causes that have collaborated, not only in the fall, but also in the disappearance of the once-celebrated peoples whose history will occupy our journey.

"Messieurs, Paris was here, beneath your feet; an excursion by boat in these shallow waters will soon procure you, if the weather remains good, the amusement of contemplating, on their bed of mud and silt, the rocky projections, now covered with algae and wrack that are, in reality, the ruins of that ancient city. It was vast, relatively, at least; the seven isles that we see rising from the waves were its seven hills. It filled that circle. But its population was not very numerous, for the number of citizens that inhabited it is estimated at scarcely two million. Compared to our modern cities, it was, therefore, little more than a village, and the importance that it was able to assume in the history of the world would be astonishing, if we did not bear in mind how much the conditions of existence have changed since then, and how different they were from ours.

"Spread out over the plain, the city was low-lying; its houses, measuring no more than twenty or thirty meters at the most, had no more than eight or ten stories, and its highest monuments only attained double that, being about sixty or seventy meters. Everything, moreover was built in the paleontic mode—which is to say, in stone—and that is what renders the study of its vestiges particularly interesting, very characteristic of the era that bears their name: the Age of Sculpted Stone."

The Parisian woman gradually lost interest in this discourse, unintelligible to her. The major effort of her attention became concentrated in the examination of the tourists and their clothing, especially in the discovery of the women who were doubtless to be found among them. She had little more success in that research than in the comprehension of scientific parlance; their torsos were rather indistinctly flat above dilated abdomens, their cheeks hairless or shaven, and generally pale and puffy, their foreheads broad and undecorated, their eyes hidden behind colorless or gray-tinted spectacles. Everything unified the types, and no slight visible nuance indicated any hint of coquetry.

Only the fisherwoman of the shore, who, in her primitive exile, had been able to continue to live in accordance with nature, conserved the instincts and aspects of womanhood. After she had examined the ladies of the Great Land for a long time though, she looked at herself, and, seeing how different she was from them—which is to say, from what she ought to be—she became ashamed of her garments, her bare hands, her uncovered neck and the breasts that swelled her bosom, and she was afraid, no longer of being caught out in her indiscretion, but of being seen in her grotesque ugliness.

At that precise moment, two or three travelers, taking advantage of a moment when the guide fell silent, came down the lighthouse steps. She thought that they were coming toward her, and got to her feet to flee. Only then did they notice her, and joyously uttered an appeal—and with extended arms, they pointed her out to the others. Quickly, she turned her back and, hugging the ground in order no longer to be visible, ran away through the bracken like a hunted beast. The sea breeze unfurled her hair behind her.

II. The Death-Throes

The professor advanced gravely to the edge of the parapet, and extended his arm in the direction of the gulf; the listeners grouped on the lighthouse's apron drew nearer in order to be better able to hear him.

"Messieurs, Paris stood here, but over these sinking lands the sea drew nearer, following, as it were, the course of the Séquanian river. The inhabitants of the capital that flourished five thousand years ago, two hundred kilometers from the Atlantic, saw the tides rising over the centuries that would ultimately engulf them. The city became a sea-port before conclusively sinking beneath the blue waters that now cover it.

"That final phase of Parisian life is not the one that will occupy us; the moral grandeur of the region and its historical importance had already diminished considerably when the continental city became a maritime city. Worldly preponderance had already passed to the other side of the globe, and from Europe, forsaken, old and diminished, which had, in its time, made history, the progress of civilization had transported the regency of world affairs to the southern continent of young America. One can, therefore, in a way, consider that the Era of the Yelloo, which succeeded the Christian Era and preceded ours, corresponded more or less to the era in which Paris, fallen from its former grandeur, became a port where few goods

153

were landed, a bathing station, a harbor of fishing boats rather than cargo vessels, its warehouses only serving a few miserable regions devoid of commerce or industry. Still fecund in fruits but sterile in humans—for, in the wake of Paris, all of Christian Europe was host to a race in decline, which, weary of having furnished its contingent of history, was dying out without having anything more to give.

"Messieurs, that end of a world is only interesting for us as the necessary and fatal conclusion that manifests itself when the time comes, and which must be noted simply to close the chapter, without dwelling on it any longer than it merits, or is appropriate.

"Let us pass on, therefore. The effectively living epoch is that of effort, and the effort of these people seems to have lasted two thousand years. A figure so considerable should not astonish us overmuch; the nations of those days subsisted much longer than ours. The human races, more clearly defined than they are today, still enjoyed a vital resistance that ulterior hybridization diminished significantly—for it is a physiological law that the crossing of species, in the animal realm as well as the human, produces by selection ingenious and refined products that are more delicate in both senses of the word, in their fragility as much as their grace, even more so in the products that are supreme, since nothing surpasses them in beauty, and because they are the final flowering of the race.

"Flowers without fruits! Their ephemeral splendor is a total, an end; races ripen in beauty, but that beauty is only a decadence, since reproductive anemia is their essential characteristic. Peoples that cross-breed are reaching their apogee and are, at the same time, on the eve of their decline. That is why, Messieurs, we see history increasing its pace at present, becoming more rapid as human promiscuity increases, and that is why a century or two is now sufficient to displace national supremacies whose evolution took ten or twenty centuries in an age when the peoples, divided into kingdoms and enclosed by frontiers, were ignorant of the rapidity of modern communications, which are convenient but humanicidal and genericidal.

"Europe suffered, in its time, the evil that is killing us today, and doubtless the sociologists of the Christian decadence were as anxious as ours are about a depopulation that nothing could avert, because it was physiological in nature, although they might have sought its causes in the economic order. For that reason, we shall see that Paris had to disappear before the other cities of Europe, and that this metropolis, for the same reason, was and had to be, in advance of all the others and more than all the others, flourishing, joyful and charming before dying—and that it died cheerfully, without knowing it, without having anticipated it, along with the entire race that populated its realm.

"It perished by virtue of being a center. Paris and France, or Gaul, was situated at an intersection, at the crossroads of Europe and in the path of the sun. All migrations passed through it: those from the east and the center on their usual route westwards, those from the south going northwards and those from the north heading southwards. Militarily, with armies or hordes, commercially, with products or conveyors of products, all the peoples passed through it, and it was subject, successively, to the bellicose or peaceful invasions of Romans and Germans, Scandinavians and the English, Africans and Cossacks, people from the Danube and the Urals. Each of them left its imprint, its blood.

That we know little about the history of these continual incursions is unimportant; although we lack historical documents to enlighten us as to the facts and their dates, we do at least have logic, which gives the hypotheses the value of certainty; an examination of the map demonstrates it itself that no human family could ever have been as mixed as that one, and less homogenous. This consideration implies others, by an analogous logic, for we must conclude that various atavisms were engendered in a that people with diverse aspirations, and that the multiplicity of psychic elements there occasioned the perpetual contact of incompatible needs and contradictory tendencies: an incessant discord in principles and desires.

"The contributions of nomadic or agricultural tribes, Aryans and Touranians, brachycephalics and dolichocephalics, the idealism of some and the realism of others, deposited at the outset and perennially resuscitated, must have provoked there, more than anywhere else, collisions and battles, a permanent state of civil war. The history of this land was surely turbulent, therefore, like that of Greece, and for identical reasons: full of abrupt gestures and unexpected decisions, of sudden bursts of energy and prompt collapses, of art and gaiety. Without a doubt, it was attractive to read about; without a doubt, too, those people were pretty to look at, endowed by all kinds of inheritance with all the virtues and all the vices, a synthesis of the world, a sum of human existence: humankind *par excellence*, or at least in its plenitude and in its multiformity.

"But, by virtue of the law, these hybrids could not last. While Germany, but England above all—of purer blood and, in consequence, more solid vitality—still resisted decline, they transplanted to America the last cutting of the Indo-European plant, where it was renovated, enriched, and extracted a renewal of its sap from virgin soil: the final one. The Anglo-Saxons of the New World took momentary possession of the globe, and, hybridizing in their turn, shining and dying in their turn, were shown the way to death by Gaul and Paris, and suffered the same fate. By a purely fortuitous coincidence, the land was drowned while its inhabitants became etiolated, and both returned to oblivion at the same time—or, to put it better, into the universal life that they had momentarily incarnated.

"What was then the world's adventure we now know better, the ages being closer at hand, and we need not insist upon it. None among us, Messieurs, is unaware that the regression of what was once called the white race corresponded noticeably with the progress of the yellow race, and that the increasing infertility of the one condemned it to death by reason of the fertility of the other. The invasion of the former by the latter was thus fatal and necessary; more than that, it was due. The Earth and the right to live on it belongs to those who are living, not those who are dying; when a race is finished, another takes it place.

"In the same way that the great reptiles of the Secondary Age had given way to the mammals of the Eocene and Pliocene, and those later on, to humankind, so the white race disappeared under the weight of the yellow, simply, naturally and in accordance with the Law. Europe, having reached its extreme point of civilization, attained it only to die immediately and become an Asiatic province; the triple military, commercial and industrial invasion stifled that anemic world, and the Christian Era, already virtually dead since the American reign, was ended definitively by the opening of the Yellean Era—which is to say, by the supremacy of the yellow race.

"The latter era was to last until our own began, and the same laws determined the same fate and the same end for it; the urgency and the right that had substituted Asia for Europe was to substitute Africa for Asia. The incomparable fecundity of the black race, impeded by eight or ten thousand years of continual massacres, had predestined it, from the very beginning, for the mastery of the world. It was unavoidable that there would come a day when the white and yellow races would cease slaughtering black people like livestock, and, more importantly, a day when they would cease to amuse themselves by slaughtering one another in battles or celebrations, by the hand of the executioner or that of the butcher.

"It is possible that, even in the Christian Era, farsighted physiologists perceived and revealed what the diplomats scarcely suspected: the future of the black people and their inevitable triumph. Our ancestors of that time, scarcely engaged with humanity and still so close to the mere anthropoid ape, were doubtless considered as inferior human beings, and consequently negligible; in reality, however, the opposite was the case, since they represented the future of humankind, a long-term investment: humans in the process of formation, a late-born race progressing toward its hour, black people followed their normal evolution over the course of centuries while white people, in a simultaneous process of chance, were in regression. Thus, our ancestors in Central Africa rose up the ranks of humankind while boastful Europe and overweening America were returning to their original oblivion.

"It was our good fortune that the end of Christianity had inaugurated a new mentality throughout the world, and that the religions of gods was succeeded by the religion of Humankind; philanthropic ideas of charity and pity, which were probably already inscribed in dogmas but not accepted into mores, then saw the light and showed is as brethren whom it was necessary to spare. Were not those very ideas, whose appearance is affirmed for us by the ancient legends of Sudan and Haiti, already an indication of the imminent death of the races of the West?

"The sentimentality of peoples is in direct proportion to their debility. Such a state of mind, when it becomes endemic, ought to be considered by science as a morbid symptom, attesting that a race, already neurotic, is entering its decline and headed for death. Quite touching to see, I admit, and very poetic to sing, that generous emotion of the heart might delight moralists and poets, but it frightens biologists who go back to the origins of vital manifestations, and who discover the profound evil beneath the superficial good.

"Messieurs, we owe our life to that ideological pity: the life that the white and yellow peoples allowed us was for them a new cause of death, for we precipitated their end in a bloody fashion. We have no remorse for that ingratitude. The species has but one duty, which is not that of gratitude but that of propagation; the right to live is primary, and, whatever utopians may say, the strong eliminate the weak and take their place, because that what nature intends; that is as true, and as inevitable, for the nations of a continent as for the grasses in a meadow, where the soil belongs by right to those which sow most seed.

"In any case, in order that we might more readily dispense with all gratitude, ancestral legends convey to us another fact that seems to testify to the perfidy employed in our regard. We ought to remember that, in spite of its humanitarian rhetoric, the white race was surreptitiously inclined to eliminate ours while affecting to protect it: a violent and sweet poison, all the more terrible because it attacked not merely the individual by also and especially the entire race, the very principles of life, was profusely distributed to our ancestors. They almost disappeared, burned by that fire-water, but their vital potential triumphed over the toxicity, and that was truly to the honor of humanity, since our premature suppression would only have slowed down the abolition of our predecessors, whose cycle was ended, and since, in our absence, no other race would have continued the august majesty of humankind on Earth—which, thanks to us, has lasted and will last a few more thousand years.

"Let us stop there; perhaps I have already prolonged this digression on our own genesis excessively, but it seemed to me to be appropriate, in the face of these ruins, first to explain how they were produced, in order that you can better understand how people lived here at the time of their splendor. That is what we shall examine together, in the course of a journey through the seven isles of Paris."

The professor paused, and his audience was astonished to see him smile at the conclusion of so severe a speech—but the scientist, in a more informal tone, added: "If you please, we're going to eat first."

That simplicity on the master's behalf charmed everyone, and the excursionists, smiling in their turn, sat down in a good mood on the cliff of Montmartre. Each one took a metal pill-box from a pocket, swallowed a few pills and drank water carried in sealed bottles, while watching from afar the fishing-boats that were coming toward them over the Paris Sea.

III. From the Top of the Butte

It was shortly after noon on a beautiful day in the year 6983 (the eighteenth of July, or the twelfth in the previous

159

calendar). The boats solicited by the sardine fisherman cast off one by one from the Parisian islands and the flotilla, traversing the gulf, headed for the lighthouse of Montmartre, where the Oceanian tourists awaited their arrival.

The eminent archeologist who was leading the scientific excursion judged that the moment had come to resume speaking.

"Messieurs, before proceeding methodically to visit this drowned city, let us get our bearings. Paris extends before us to the south, and we are at the northern extremity of the capital here. The Ocean stretches away to our right—which is to say, westwards—and the continental city, which gradually became a seaport, finally disappeared under the waves. The seven hills that swelled the city then became meager islets, which we see emerging.

"To the east is the Mont-de-Chaux, and to the north-west the public cemetery, the name of which is revealed to us by an inscription that we have now deciphered, the Père-Lachèze.[25]

"To the south-east is the necropolis of the Great Men, with the temple of the Grateful Fatherland.

"More directly to the south is the Isle of Senators and over there, to the south-west, the Isle of Valorous Warriors, or Mont Valeurien.[26]

---

[25] This slight perversion of the name of Père-Lachaise might be thought to make the second part of the name a little more reminiscent of *lâcheuse* [turncoat]. The distortion is not preserved in the only further reference, however. The "Mont-de-Chaux" is a corruption of the Buttes Chaumont.

[26] This reference is slightly puzzling, especially since we hear no more of this island, which is omitted from the tourists' itinerary without comment or explanation. *Valeur* can refer to paper money and such like as well as to bravery, so the name is probably a pun, but the present-day Bourse is south-south-east of Montmartre, and consultation of a modern map suggests that the professor is more likely to be pointing in the general direction of the present site of the Hôtel des Invalides

"Finally, to the west, is the Emperor's Isle, where the ruins are heaped of the most notorious monument that remains to us of that epoch. The examination of the sparse vestiges on these heights will permit us to study a vanished civilization chronologically, and to reconstitute the general lines of its history.

"Written documents, as you know, are rare, by reason of the methods of graphic reproduction then employed: paper, a sort of dried mud engraved in the dry state, but which soon returned to mud, was a invention injurious to human memory, their ideas, their philosophy, their history and their literature. Almost nothing has survived from those ages, which neverthe-less—we have proof of it—produced works worthy of so po-werful an empire and such a relatively advanced culture.

"Fortunately, stone, from these distant epochs as well as others more ancient still, provides us with more evidence than books; the lapidary document is the only one that lasts and preserves; let us honor it with our gratitude! That is what we are going to interrogate, and that is what will answer us, be resuscitating before us the soul of peoples who are no more. Let us listen to what it tells us, and watch emerging from the shores,[27] in response to the summons of our science, the suc-

---

or that of the Eiffel Tower; his next reference is obviously to the Arc de Triomphe, although that too is some way south of due west, viewed from the Butte de Montmartre. There is a suggestion in this that the axis of the Earths rotation has shifted somewhat, along with its magnetic poles, thus altering the directions indicated by the compass, but the evidence of-fered here is not altogether clear in that respect.

[27] The author's *grèves* [shores] creates an ideative link of sorts between the sandy shores of the Parisian islands and the sands of Egypt, from which the 19th and 20th centuries saw the sto-ry of a great civilization gradually emerge, but the word can also mean "stoppage;" Paris once had a Place de la Grève, marking the location where executions were carried out, al-though it was renamed the Place de l'Hôtel de Ville and the

161

cessive moments of a civilization that will file before our eyes and be translated for us by the irrefutable testimony of its art—petrified, if I might put it thus, in the gestures of its effort!

"When did that effort commence and how long did it last? I told you a little while ago that the number of centuries is not exactly know to us, but the approximately two thousand years that is attributed to the existence of French Gaul is subdivided for us into three quite distinct epochs, each of which is clearly characterized, and clearly defined by the type of its works and the influences that archeology discovers therein. The earliest, showing Roman influence, corresponds to the militaristic imperial epoch and constitutes the heroic age, the most glorious in the history and the most fecund in the arts. The second, showing Oriental influence, which becomes manifest at the beginning of the Republican period, and which gives us the commercial epoch, more civilized, more scientific, more practical but already exhausted. Finally, the third and last phase, of rural influence, consecutive to a return to nature, to the poverty of a fallen people, the ultimate expression of a race out of breath, but still trying to achieve something, the painful effort of which only ends in a realization as crude and primitive as itself. Modern art has conserved the ancient denomination of that moribund artistry: it is Gothic art.

"Let us cast a rapid eye over those three phases. The first emperor, Caesar, who conquered the Gauls, did not advance this far; the honor of discovering these distant regions and of transplanting Roman civilization here belonged to his successor Julian, who fully perceived the geographical importance of the crossroads and who, in order simultaneously to command the Gauls and the Germanes, England, the Hispanic and Iberian peninsulas, dreamed of transplanting the seat of the Empire here.

---

executions of the post-Revolutionary Terror took place in the Place de la République.

"The idea was ingenious and predestined to fortunate results, but still premature, It was only realized a little later, under the reign of Napo-Lion, who took up Julian's plans again and broke with the ancient metropolis, where he only left a high priest, the Pontiff; the latter then became the unique sovereign of Rome, and the all-conquering city became the capital of priests. That schism between the military and religious authorities, however, could not help giving rise to incessant conflicts, and we do, in fact, know that the struggle between the theocratic principle against the monarchic principle gave rise to countless fierce religious wars.

"Meanwhile, the emperor covered his new capital with temples and palaces, making it the center of the Western World; all wealth and genius flooded into it. The impulse was given; the work was colossal; it continued for a long time after the death of the celebrated tyrant. His dynasty, which continued his grandeur and his mission, lasted from the 6th to the 12th century, and only collapsed definitively in the wake of the famous wars of which Arabic legends have preserved the memory for us, and which brought the Orient and the Occident into collision, for the honor of their respective gods.

"Needless to say, in that skirmish of the soul, the Orient was triumphant. That formulation might be excessive, but at the very least, something in Europe died and something new was born. From their crusades in the land of light, the men of the mists brought back a new concept of life, of needs and tastes previously unknown, of doubts regarding their dogmas, of appetites for enjoyment. The races, in becoming more familiar with one another, also learned to be less scornful of one another, and exchanges began. The relationship continued, no longer bellicose but commercial, and the competition of products soon succeeded that of arms. International exhibitions closely followed the crusades. Existence became practical, and the world's soul became utilitarian; the gods, without being completely forgotten, nevertheless lost their prestige, as the princes lost their power; a conventional equality leveled the status of the citizens, and each one looked after his own interests; this was the Republican period, which lasted from the 12th to the 20th century.

"The third period opens thereafter, which is the Decadence; half a century suffices to transplant the regency of the world from Europe to America: a death-rattle, and the history of France is finished; that of Christianity is complete. That death-rattle only lasted two centuries.

"Messieurs, before passing on, let us examine what that religion had been, which was so influential on the mentality of thirty or forty Occidental generations. Have no fear—I shall not waste any of your time in the vain attempt to seek a definition of the divinity. The task is too arduous, full of perils and arbitrary for people of a race like ours, which, by virtue of atavism or cranial conformation, is deprived of the notion of the supernatural. People who can conceive of the idea of God, of miracles that oppose the normal functioning of universal laws, and a soul independent of the body, are too different from us for us to have any hope of reconstructing their state of mind, and the benefits they drew from it, with the aid of common sense and justice.

"Fine minds have gone astray on that dead-end path, and some—whose good faith it is not permissible for us to suspect, much less dare to accuse of joking—have even reached absurd conclusions. You are familiar with the most recent of them, which caused so much scandal. 'The god of the Christians,' he wrote, 'was a being with a human face, creator of the Earth and the heavens, but resident in the heavens, for whom, however, the innumerable worlds only existed as a decoration offered to human eyes. Concentrating his attention on our planet, that master occupied himself exclusively with human affairs; everyone expressed their personal and incompatible desires to him by means of a supplication called prayer, and he rewarded some with an everlasting felicity or punished others with an everlasting chastisement, for the soul is immortal.'

"The mere pronunciation of these hypotheses—or, rather, these fantasies or follies—is a gratuitous insult to intelligent beings, but it cannot be avoided. They provoked in the scientific world a reprobation of which you are not unaware, and there was unanimity in deploring the lapse of an old man who had dishonored his career with infantilisms unworthy of him and his glorious past. Let us not follow him into such wanderings. Fortunately for the human mind, the mythology of the Christians was quite different, and we now know, with certainty, at least its broad outlines. It is simultaneously simpler, and wiser, and also nobler.

"The Christians were idolaters who worshiped figures of stone or painted wood, but these figures represented ideas; their worship involved an innumerable polytheism: the gods and goddesses are represented therein with attributes whose meanings we do not know, the most common of which were a sword, a key, a book, a cross, a tower or a lizard, a skull, a sheet and a severed head. Above all, however, Messieurs, they worshiped the feminine principle, represented infinitely, on every wall and in every corner of their temples, by the image of a young woman carrying or suckling a child, a symbol of fecundity.

"In that goddess, depicted on all altars and always taking precedence, one cannot hesitate to recognize a transformation of Venus and Isis; her name, in any case, proves her parentage and her Hellenic origin; she is the *Chreiston*—the best of all[28]—and she gives her name to the ensemble of the myths over which she presides, to the entire religion. She is the Christ, the principle of life; facing her and against her is logically ranged the principle of death, represented with equal frequency by a dead man suspended from a cross, often merely by a simple cross.

All the tombs of the first and second epoch are decorated with this emblem, and it ornaments the threshold of every ne-

---

[28] The Greek *chreios* means "useful"—which, in a utilitarian society, would indeed be associated with the supreme virtue; just as, in a society beset by sexual neurosis, virginity would be esteemed as the best thing of all, especially (if paradoxically) in a mother.

cropolis. It funereal character is thus indisputable, even in the absence of a sculpted cadaver, and the two symbols explain one another; facing Fecundity, Death. There, in a sculptural formula, is the eternal antithesis, birth and death, the two forms of perpetual becoming, the two generators of universal existence, the double principle of constant renewal.

"Why that strange death and that cross, though? Science has been lost in conjectures for a long time. Finally, the significance of that typical detail has been revealed to us by a recent discovery: two frescoes found in an excavation in Naples represent two individuals who, without a doubt, can be identified with the crucified man. One is standing, against a column; his head in circled by brambles and an inscription comments: *Ecce Homo; this is the Man.*

"We are thus informed; the allegory become even clearer in the light of the second painting, in which the Man is walking, carrying a cross—his cross, by means of which he will soon die. We understand everything now: this creature drags through life the evil by which it will perish, its element of death; it is predestined to it and cannot avoid it; it even collaborates in its own demise, and prepares for it more than any other: to live is to work toward death. A subtle and poetic discovery of a reasoned fatalism! The Christians were fatalists, but scientifically, if I might put it thus, and spiritualists too, since the Man laden with his cross bears a crown on his head, like a king, but a crown of thorns, to signify simultaneously the glory and dolor of thought!

"You see, Messieurs, that these metaphysical conceptions are not at all worthy of scorn, and we are now very far from the bizarre definition of which I reminded you a little while ago, and of which I thought I ought to remind you again, in order that you might put your finger on the dangerous deviations to which imagination exposes us as soon as we fail to submit our hypotheses to the control of a strictly scientific method.

"Noble as these myths might have been, the people lost interest in them, as usually happens, and we must suppose that

martyrs. To remove any remaining hesitation, an enamel plaque found in the earth had revealed that a road going up the
side of the hill was named the Rue des Martyrs. This is what is
obvious: the people, with a word, were flagellating the odious
past, and avenging themselves, with that word, for the sufferings that tyranny had imposed on its victims, generations of
martyrs. Messieurs, the Bastille was here!

"You know that other etymologies have nevertheless
been proposed: Montmartre, or hill of Mars, because of the
citadel; Montmercre, or hill of Mercury, because of a temple
erected to the god of commerce, toward the end of the 19th
century. All these explanations are fantastic, and our enamel
plaque has demonstrated the fact. They do, however, share a
common characteristic that it is necessary to point out, which
is, in all three cases, an origin in the Roman language.

"For many centuries French Gaul was bilingual; its inscriptions prove it, some being in Latin and others in the indi-
genous dialect, the language of the conquerors and that of the
vanquished—which is to say that for a long time the conquering race constituted in these parts a definite caste: that aristo-
cracy, therefore, only consented to be dissolved into the autochthonous race at the beginning of the epoch in which it was
dispossessed of power, after the fall of the Bastille. From then
on, the language tended to become unified, and Latin, after
having been the official language of the empire, gradually
disappeared. Well before the end of the second period, the
inscriptions are all in the French language.

"This observation is of capital importance for us, for it
will permit us, with the chances of error reduced to a minimum, to attribute monuments to their respective eras."

The professor fell silent. Then he extended his arm toward the shore, to authorize his audience to descend, finally,
and board the boats. He walked with dignity, and the company
had soon invaded the boats cheerfully and installed themselves, laughing, on the badly-squared benches.

The flotilla got under way, and the thirteen boats advanced in convoy over the Gulf of Paris. The sea continued to

descend; the tourists, craning their necks over the side, leaned down in order to watch out for the abrupt appearance of the ruins that filed past on the sea bed. Rocky heaps, drowned in a green liquid light, stood out confusedly beneath the boats; the strokes of the oars left swirls of foam over the crumbled monuments, and the hulls soared where birds had once flown.

The excursion went straight from north to south, and on the archeologist's orders, they steered toward the Isle of the Great Men. That crossing of a calm sea, by means of a method of navigation that had fallen into disuse among civilized people, had the attraction of an oddity for the tourists, and the journey was joyful. The people who had climbed into the scientist's boat, however, obtained a supplementary lecture, for the learned individual was not fond of his own silence.

"You see," he said, "that these waters are shallow, but the depth increases as we approach the river. It was very wide and bordered by flat plains, which it covered with marshes. A large number of the houses had to be constructed on stilts, and the monuments of real importance took refuge on the higher ground, where the constituted Acropolises of a sort. It was like that, at least, during the early centuries, and it was only at the beginning of the Republican epoch that the river, dammed with quays—of which traces still exist—permitted temples and palaces to be built on its banks, some of which are known to us.

"The history of all peoples demonstrates to us, however, that colossal works are only ever inspired by religious faith or the pride of conquests; pragmatic ages are more economical with splendor, less concerned with beautiful works than good business. Republican monuments are, therefore, relatively rare, and those of the Decadence rarer still. Our divers have, however, discovered, in the very heart of the city, in the middle of the Seine, and enormous temple erected on an island served by numerous bridges; that chiseled mass, which can be considered as the prototype of the Decadence, presented all the characteristics of the bad taste typical of the 20th century.

"That was Gothic art in all its plenitude; you can judge that by the decorative fragments and statues removed from its portal, which are now in the Museum of Sumatra, where you have seen those bearded and impassive gods frozen in their hieratical poses, and that seated goddess presenting the infant: art without life, the end of art! The people, no longer comprehending their gods, no longer knew how to animate them. One wonders, with some commiseration, how, in our day, erudite men have been able, even for a moment, to see in those figures and ornamentations, simultaneously complicated and maladroit, the beginning rather than the end of art; it must surely be..."

Archeologists are usually pitiless in their treatment of other archeologists, and this one was about to mistreat his absent colleagues when his attention was attracted by the fishermen who, until then, had listened while rowing, but who had suddenly lifted their oars and stopped.

He interrogated them with his eyes. Then a Parisian pointed at the water with the end of his oar and declared: "Here, cathedral, Notre-Mère."

"Ah!" said the scientist. "We've arrived, it appears, above the temple I was talking about; it was consecrated, as that indigene had just told you, to the goddess of Fecundity, and the summits of its towers are visibly brushed by the present level of the sea. Is it appropriate to see, in that prodigious erection of stone, a survival of ithyphallic worship? Perhaps."

The Oceanians, leaning over the water, plunged their avid eyes into it; some of them thought they could make out, in the depths, plays of shadow and light, reliefs blurred as if in a dream, and they exclaimed: "I can see it!" But the professor, smiling and skeptical, gestured to the oarsmen, who pushed on southwards, departing toward the mountain of the Great Men.

"At the top," said the Master, "stood the temple of the Grateful Fatherland; its lines are grandiose; it was, along with the tomb of Napo-Lion, the most magnificent monument of Roman art in the Frankish capital."

171

They disembarked at the foot of the islet. The steps of the parvis, worn away by the erosion of tempests and dislocated by the fatigue of the ground, were still recognizable in places. The cylindrical bases of columns lay all around; the angles of the blocks were corroded by rain and the surfaces rusted by plaques of lichen; fragile blades of grass trembled in sheltered spots; a field of ferns was tangled in the area enclosed by the stumps, which filled everything. To the southeast, in order to receive the sunlight and shelter from squalls, two buildings had been constructed with the Panthéon's stones, and two small gardens attached to them cheered up the august tomb with flowers and vegetables.

The illustrious scientist wanted to walk along the encircling wall, before his students' eyes, and he led the way. He showed them the entrance to the underground passages, explained the affectation of the crypts, the nature of the sacrifices offered on such altars on every anniversary, and the touching worship of the French nation of its great men and their memory.

These words did not fail to provoke among the listeners a certain respectful emotion, of short duration. Afterwards, they embarked again. The boats, heading westwards, skirted the Isle of the Senators, which the low tide had completely uncovered.

"Tradition," said the master, "holds that this location was the site of some kind of forum, closed and covered, where the Council of Elders sat." With an ironic bonhomie, he added: "We have no objection to that, but there is no proof of the allegation, and nothing to confirm it—which is regrettable, for we cannot be content with these gratuitous hypotheses. For us, a hypothesis can only be the initiation of an investigation and not an affirmation; it is the point of departure, not the terminus that pleases laymen but saddens science—but science, soon or later, will do it justice. We shall encounter a further demonstration of that verity on the Emperor's Isle."

The oarsmen finally stopped on the sands of a rather extensive and gently sloping shore, at the top of which rocks were heaped up.

"Here it is," said the master.

They got down for a second time. At that moment, however, a young man, who had previously been very busy, and seemed to be the organizer or manager of the tour, came up to the professor and spoke to him mysteriously. The latter exhibited considerable surprise, and seemed a trifle vexed.

"We'll have to verify the fact," he said.

Everyone soon found out what the matter was: one of the excursionists had disappeared! A rapid investigation revealed that he had not taken a place, at any time, in any of the boats. The boatmen, fearing that they might be blamed for the disappearance, affirmed forcefully that they had, during each crossing, conveyed the same number of foreigners.

"He must have stayed at Montmartre, then, and we'll find him there for the departure."

"He's doubtless afraid of the sea."

"I saw him for the last time," said one lady, "when he was descending the cliff of the Bastille; it was at the moment when that native woman appeared in the bracken. Perhaps he followed her."

The idea of following a woman on the Butte de Montmartre seemed utterly absurd; that an amorously-inclined man might have sufficiently bad taste to offer himself to a Parisian woman was taking scientific exploration, devotion or curiosity too far; the entire company laughed at the eccentric's expense, and the shores of the Élysée resounded with laughter such as they had not heard for a long time.

"Ugh! A creature that eats dead fish and cooked roots!"

"The poor fellow can't have a subtle sense of smell!"

"What's his name? What does he do? Do any of you know?"

"He's an artist—a poet."

"That explains everything."

"Don't laugh," said the master, "and don't attract the attention of the lighthouse-keeper, who's already watching us. These men take umbrage, and he might think that we're mocking him."

"When we've done him the honor of recruiting him?"

"When he's being spared a chore?"

"Does one ever know, with these savages? It's not appropriate to judge them by the same standards as ourselves, nor to treat them lightly; ethnography claims that they're jealous."

"Jealous?"

This term of archaic psychology was unknown to several of them. The scientist had to explain that jealous was a sentiment once widespread in the Aryan races, and consisted of a sort of passionate irritability engendered by an exclusivism of possession. There again he had to explain; the word "possession" was unintelligible for civilized beings whose social relationships were based on the equality of the sexes and the absolute independence of every individual. The ladies listened with the greatest attention to the scientist's commentaries; they had difficulty understanding that a man of any epoch could have dared to claim ownership of a woman and considered someone else's body as something belonging to him.

"Bizarre! Anyway, look for yourselves and observe with your own eyes an example of hereditary survival." So saying, he pointed to one of the thirteen boats, which was drawing away over the gulf, heading northwards. "It's the man from the lighthouse; he heard us, and he's in a hurry. He's gone to find his wife and our companion, whom he'll probably attack."

"Very curious!"

"The poet was wrong, I think, to prefer sensational contingencies to the education of archaeology—but everyone to his taste. Let's go on, I beg you, for time's pressing."

Without giving any more thought to the eccentric, who was perhaps about to die, the tourists climbed the slope.

V. The Last Lover

The Oceanian tourists who were visiting the ruins of Paris on the eighteenth of July 6983 had descended from the boats in which thirteen Parisian fishermen had brought them to the Emperor's Isle. The eminent archeologist who was directing the scientific excursion only took a few steps and stopped. Everyone else stopped too.

"Before climbing the slope, Messieurs, let us turn around momentarily. Behind us stood the most beautiful of the djeri-ansrhai,[30] the one that Ramses II began and Ramses III completed, and which Napo-Lion brought back from the crusades. Four thousand years ago, the Parisians could still see that obelisk, four thousand years old, and we can see it again today, in the main square of Luxor, still intact and returned to proximity with its brother in front of the Chamber of Commerce. Stones travel, humans pass."

Having pronounced these solemn words, he resumed walking. The declivity of the ground was mild, and the tide had retreated a considerable distance; to reach the ruins heaped at the top of the islet the company had to walk for some time across uncovered sands, moistened by pools in which shrimps fled, and over slippery seaweeds. While they climbed the slope and a few stumbles made the little troop laugh, the professor continued his lesson:

"Note in passing, to our right and to our left, those two parallel rows of rocks clad in wrack; do they not seem to be following an authentic avenue? It is one, in fact; from above you will be better able to observe its rectitude and length; from the obelisk to the emperor's tomb, it measures no less than three thousand seven hundred cubits; for a long time, people were inclined to see it as a simple promenade, at the extremity of which a triumphal gate, or Arc de Triomphe, gaped unnecessarily. The illogicality of that opinion has now been dem-

---

[30] I have transcribed this word directly, being unable to discern any likely etymology.

onstrated; we know that there was a broad roadway here, bordered with tombs, reminiscent of the Appian Way, which climbed from the city to the capital mausoleum, which overlooked all the others from the summit of its hill. We even possess the names and ranks of the captains buried in two rows along the road leading to their leader's monument; the list is engraved on the lateral faces of the Caesarean tomb."

The travelers arrived at the top of the hill; as their approach, puffins took flight, screeching, from the midst of the rocks; a formless heap of stones stood there.

"Don't look for anything at your feet," said the master. "Nothing remains here any longer but the emotion of memory. Everything that survived is now in a place of safety, in the same Museum of Sumatra where you have doubtless admired the sublime masterpieces, the *Naked Young Warrior* and the *Winged Victory* that is carrying him, howling. Those magisterial sculptures decorated the immense cenotaph that was located here. I say 'cenotaph,' improperly but deliberately, for all the searches made to recover the body of the emperor have been and remain in vain. There is no need to be astonished by that; too many spades have dug here, over forty centuries, and the prey was too tempting for the scientists of all the ages or treasure-hunters.

"What is, in any case, more interesting for us, is the spirit of the works and the value of the art; without a doubt you have compared those imposing figures to the maladroit idols of the third period, about which we were talking a little while ago, and which are assembled in the next room. You have observed, or at least supposed, the gulf of time hollowed out between the great epoch of imperial art and it Gothic decadence. That interval was even longer than you probably think, and one detail furnishes the proof of it: the soldiers of the empire fought in the nude; sometimes a helmet and breastplate protected the head and torso of the leaders; this group informs us of that.

"By contrast, the individuals of the Gothic period, men or women, without exception, are all dressed in heavy clothing. The soldiers of the empire thus still participated in Greek and Roman fashions, while the Gothics were further away from them. Such a profound modification of mores implies a considerable duration, since it corresponds, and must correspond to an already sensible decline in temperature; and you can see, Messieurs, that ethnographic reasoning corroborates the assertions of archaeology here."

The scientist fell silent, then burst out laughing. "It must be recognized," he said, "that the Gothics weren't always wrong, for it's as well to cover up—the weather's getting chilly."

He buttoned his cloak, and everyone imitated him, laughing as he had, for the sea breeze was rising and the temperature lowering.

"The sea is rising again, Messieurs, and the tide commands; we need to return to Montmartre and our train, if we don't want to get back to Tahiti too late at night, for it's a long journey. We don't have time today to visit the north-eastern isle and its necropolis of the Père-de-la-Chaise, but we can console ourselves for that, since all the documents that have any value were collected, as they were here, and figure in our equatorial museums."

The tourists went back down the avenue. They had to squeeze into the boats, since one of them was missing, but the breeze permitted them to travel under sail, and the crossing was not as slow.

As they approached Montmartre, the company had the disagreeable surprise of perceiving the fisherman and his wife, tranquilly sitting on the threshold of their cabin, and chatting to the Oceanian poet who had stayed on their island. They had thought, and perhaps hoped, to find dead bodies and an extraordinary drama; the appetite for exceptional emotions was thus a trifle disappointed. For want of anything better, and at least to collect a few details, they headed toward the trio—but the Parisian, on seeing the company approaching, drew away and went up to the lighthouse.

177

"Well! You left us? The master gave us a superb lecture, and you missed a lot by not listening to it."

"Are you quite sure?"

"To come so far and only explore a woman!"

"I evoked while you listened; I've lived a love story four thousand years old."

The young women seemed the most enthusiastic to interrogate the lover; modesty, which is a social virtue and not at all natural, was at that time completely unknown, and physiological information could be requested or given without any constraint. The Oceanian related how the Parisian woman and he had gone to the shore, taken their clothes off and sunbathed, and coupled on the sand. The Montmartean confirmed the story, nodding her head.

"Woman, did you experience a satisfaction?"

"Two."

She was complimented. Her lover of an hour, invited to describe her, did so with praise and precision, indicating the particularities of her body and the proportions of everything, as freely as if he were describing the length of her hair or the dimensions of her mouth. He praised her exceedingly pale skin and the narrowness of her waist, but above all he lauded her abundant breasts.

"That," said the scientist, "is characteristic of women born in calcareous countries." He had just rejoined the circle, which had parted to give him passage.

Drawing nearer, then, he scientifically palpated the indigene's bosom and rump. He touched her skull and face, and, while instructing himself with his palms, he declared in a sententious voice: "Brachycephalic type, apparently, leucodermic and flavescent, leptorhinian, leptoprosopic—a veritable Celt."

They all wanted to inform themselves in the same fashion as the master; the Montmarteans woman let them do so without moving or speaking, and turning as commanded. Sometimes, however, the tickling of the hands made her squirm, with little squeals of infantile laughter.

They went up to the platform of the lighthouse. One of the more zealous administrators then thought it appropriate to express everyone's gratitude to the scientist. He did so gracefully, but his speech, probably prepared in advance, was not devoid of pomposity when he proclaimed, with gratitude and respect, the moving beauty of Archeological Science.

The master bowed and replied: "It is true, Monsieur, and you put it well, for that science is, among them all, the one that ought to move us, since it informs us as to human genesis and opens its arcana to us. When all the voices have fallen silent, it speaks! When the silence of oblivion has immured in darkness the secrets of races, their religions, their empires, it unseals the night of tombs, in to which the light enters with it! To it, the night confesses! At its touch, the dust of defunct centuries becomes warm again, living, and in the footprints that it sees there, its eye discovers the vestiges of souls, which is can read."

As he proffered these words, he extended his right arm over the city, and the amplitude of his oratorical gesture, tracing a semicircle in the air, took possession of the past.

Everyone applauded, and immediately headed for the carriages. The poet ran; behind him, the woman slowly climbed the hill. Already, the setting sun was making the facets of the waves sparkle.

When the Oceanians were installed in their carriages, the door closed hermetically without a sound, and everything became bleak again.

The Parisian woman was standing on the terrace, her dress flapping in the evening breeze.

Suddenly, the aerotram took off; a slender shadow ran over the waters, as rapid as black lightning. The air whistled. The woman watched the brown dot of the convoy diminish, in flight toward the horizon; almost immediately, it disappeared. One might have thought that it had penetrated into the sun.

She stood there, full of dreams, and contemplated the horizon. The sun disappeared in its turn. The red clouds were reflected in the sea, as if drowning in a golden bath in the place where Paris had been.

Then the silence became enormous, and gradually, everything sank into the shadows.

VI. In the Carriage

In the open sky, at a height of five hundred meters, the aerotram flew westwards. The Oceanian tourists who had come to visit the ruins of Paris on the eighteenth of July 6983, slightly tired by that day in the open air, installed themselves as best they could in the four wagons and wedged their hips into the seats. The warm temperature, after the sea breeze, the smoothness of the train, after the jolting of the boats, and the comfort of the seats, after the hardness of the benches and the fatigue of walking, were pleasant. In that physical voluptuousness, which crowned such a beautiful day s well, they exchanged words denuded of value but amiable:

"Charming excursion..."

"Very instructive..."

"Very interesting, those Parisians..."

"Like everything from the past!"

One joker, overjoyed to be returning, sang:

"Oh, let us flee these places
In which one feels so old!"

The travelers who found themselves in the professor's compartment, however, competed in eulogizing his lesson in archeology. The master, who was sitting directly opposite the poet, wanted to make it evident that he bore no resentment, and, while smiling, he spoke to the deserter from his course.

"Please explain one thing to me, Monsieur. Since the Montmartrean did not attack you when he caught you with his wife, why did he have to go back so quickly on learning about your...indiscretion?"

"In order, I think, to profit from it, by selling me these—and rather dearly, besides."

The poet took from his pocket a handful of *sous*, thin and corroded with oxide.

The man of science deigned to take this small change, which he spread over the palm of his hand with his middle finger. Then, not without disdain, he said: "Yes, French coins; there are many of them to be found in our country, which offers evidence that it was once a colony of that people."

He returned them to the poet, and added: "Vulgar bronze money, the most usual, the least rare—uninteresting coins."

"For you, Monsieur, but not for me, for they're the money of the poor, the most moving, since they were the hardest to earn, and have been worn away by the friction of all kinds of misery; they have more life and more soul. There's more humanity in an old copper sou than in a brand new louis d'or."

"Poet!" said a banker.

"Fantasist!" said the master.

"Truly, yes, Monsieur—like you."

The professor's hips jumped in the seat, as if a flea had bitten him. "Oh yes? Are you claiming, Monsieur, that archeological erudition and its classifications are merely vain poetry?"

"Poetry is never vain, Monsieur, since it invents and evokes, and its evocations enlarge the world for us, in parting the curtains of the unknown in the past or the future, not to mention the present! I therefore honor your poems as much as ours, or almost as much, for the only difference I can see between them, my dear master, resides in the fact that your imaginations speaks like a science that decrees truths, while ours is content to be an art that formulates dreams."

"Archeology is not a science?"

"No, Monsieur, and by definition, since it lacks conclusiveness; can you not see that the affirmations of that pretended science change at every moment, overturning one another? The truth of five years ago is no longer than of today, and yours, Monsieur, will perhaps be considered tomorrow as…as…"

"Don't bother to finish—I can guess."

"Thank you," said the young man, shaking the collection of old sous in his hand. "Without looking any further, are you sure that within a year, the numismatic theories of the engraver Swyams…?"

An expression of sad disdain became visible on the scientist's face, but the presumptuous rhymer continued regardless: "You know better than me, my dear Master, that the great artist in question, having assembled a very large collection of French medals and coins, has used them to draw up a system of chronology quite different from yours. Now, that new classification implies nothing less than a complete revision of all the notions currently professed by archeology with respect to France and its history."

The master's impatience was considerable; he made no attempt to hide it.

"A classification!" he cried. "You call that a classification, and you ask my opinion? It's simple: Swyams is an ignoramus, and his system is nonsense! What is he talking about, and what is he getting mixed up in? What does he know? Where does he come from? What preliminary studies has he made, in order to arrogate the right suddenly to formulate a theory and present a system? Thus, the best education serves no purpose, and the merest amateur, without any qualifications, can appoint himself our judge, to declare that we're progressing at hazard, if not in darkness, on shifting ground? Medals, dates! That's all very fine—but the evaluation that this ignoramus attributes to figures, unknown to him even more than they are to us, is he sure of it? When does his chronology commence—with the foundation of Rome, or of Paris? He neglects to tell us that. Why? Because he doesn't know! Well, young man, let a sculptor engrave medals, if he likes, and let him make a collection too, if it amuses him! But let him leave to scholars the care of classifying what he loves, and of drawing the conclusions therefrom that he is not equipped to deduce!"

The audience shared the master's opinion of artists who dare to offer an opinion in matters of art or the history of art, as if they were professionals. Nevertheless, that angry sermon had provoked a certain unease, and, to distract them, one tactful person suggested that they have supper.

The pillboxes reappeared; they were held out politely, everyone offering his neighbor one of the pills that he had brought, according to his own temperament and the needs of his hygiene.

"A little vanilla-flavored nitrate?"

"With pleasure."

"This peppered phosphate is tasty."

"I have a certain chlorate here, about which you must give me your opinion."

They sucked the pastilles, and drank frequent and brief sips of water from calibrated bottles that were being opened continually. A few people, with weaker stomachs, dissolved the salts in the water in their cups and drank the beverage.

One of the travelers reached for a button in the wall. "May I?"

"Please do—a little music is always pleasant."

Beneath the light pressure of the finger, a switch was activated, and the discreet harmonies of a distant orchestra slowly grew in volume in the carriage: a very simple system activated by the pressure of the air caused by the train's speed, which brought the musical apparatus into play, whose registers could be changed at will.

"Oh, we're not going very fast."

Indeed, the music was in a slow tempo.

"We ought, routinely, to be making fifteen ocles per cycle."

The Oceanian ocle was equivalent to a little more than ten meters, and the cycle represented half a second; the train thus covered our modern kilometer in about three seconds—which is to say, with a velocity approximately equal to the rotation of the Earth at that latitude; the distance traveled was thus fifteen degrees an hour, with the result that the train, heading westwards but veering slightly southwards, was assiduously following the setting sun, and the red star remained at the same height above the horizon. Twenty minutes after the departure from Montmartre, the carriages were passing over the Loire estuary.[31]

"Ah!" said a traveler who was leaning over the porthole in the floor, "we're leaving the continent now. The machine can pick up speed."

He was right; the musical tune accelerated its rhythm

"It's a long journey, all the same. There's a good deal of progress to be desired in the matter of locomotion."

"Imagine that, in our epoch, it still takes twelve hours to reach the antipodes."

"Ten hours!"

"You're right! You're getting off at Tahiti—I've got to go all the way to Tonga."

"Bah!" said one witty fellow. "What are you complaining about? You left at sunset and you'll be home by dusk."

"It's amusing," said a young woman, "to see that poor reddened star that can no longer succeed in setting."

"It's hot. Would it make you uncomfortable if we were to cool things down a little?"

"Not at all."

The indicator was lowered by a notch. At the front of each carriage, a reservoir of liquid air, 180 degrees below zero, emitted, between two stallium walls, a refrigerant quota that adjusted itself automatically to variations in speed and thus protected the material against the overheating produced by the friction of the external air. Similarly, the passengers

---

[31] Again, the directions indicated seem significantly askew if examined on a present-day map, lending credence to the suspicion—considerably strengthened by the evidence of this chapter—that the story's "west" is our south-west, by virtue of the planet axis having tilted in the interim.

were able, at will, to lower the interior temperature of the compartments. The evacuation of warm air was effected by a simple tap, which only had to be opened, as if one were opening a window.

"Land, to our left!"

"Ancient Spain. You might even be able to perceive, in the distance, the foothills of the Pyrenees."

"We'll be over the Azores in an hour."

"That's slow."

They arrived over the Azores. The conversations had languished. Several tourists were dozing. A few, having put their feet up on the seats, had lain down to sleep. Those who were still looking out of the portholes abandoned them, knowing that there would only be the sea extended beneath them for hours. With a last glance at the sun, still floating at the same height above a curvilinear horizon, they became drowsy in their turn.

Those who were sleeping badly observed, after five hours of travel, that they were skirting the Antilles, over which the sun was setting.

"In a moment, at Cape Gallinus, we'll be half way."

"Is that all?"

An hour after Martinique, they saw the isthmus of Panama, which they crossed in four minutes; an hour later, the Galapagos islands, where they changed hemisphere and summer abruptly became winter. No one felt any change, though, and again there was the sea, infinitely round and intimately bare.

The majority of the shutters had been closed over the portholes; for four hours, no one said another word.

Finally, the aerotrain stopped.

"Tahiti!"

They got off. The excursionists, stretching their limbs and rubbing their eyes, saw the red sun descending over a familiar landscape; in spite of their weariness, they smiled at it, in the exquisite sensation of coming home, where one belongs: for the people of that time, even though they were pale negroes, resembled us in many ways, and knew as well as we do

185

how to savor the pleasure of having finished with an unaccustomed pleasure.

A CHRISTMAS GIFT[32]

To begin with, I'll tell you who I am: I'm a cab-horse, but the gift of speech has just been granted to me, for one time only, and you're about to see in what extraordinary circumstances.

I was a handsome beast. You can take my word for that; I've never told a lie.. I couldn't have lied, since I couldn't talk, and I won't lie today, since Father Christmas has given me speech in order that I might tell the truth. He wants me to tell you about my adventure, and I'll tell it quite frankly, and explain everything without getting angry. My character is mild; I've never done any harm to anyone. I've always trotted as best I could, to keep people happy, because all goes well when people are happy.

Perhaps you've seen me in the street, and perhaps I've pulled you in my carriage, but you've never paid attention to me because passengers are never concerned with us. I had a very even trot and was always willing. I've received downpours on my back, I've traveled by night and on black ice, I've been very cold for hours on end, waiting at the stand in winter and I've been very hot in summer. When I was ill, I worked all the same, as you can imagine, but I had trouble getting under way. Then the whiplashes increased, and also the kicks, in the legs or the belly. I don't complain about that, since it's routine, and the man has a habit of beating me when he's annoyed about something.

---

[32] The French title, "Les Sabots de Noël" does not translate, because its ironic double meaning is lost. In 19th century France poor children left sabots (i.e., wooden shoes) to be filled with Christmas gifts, much as English children put up stockings, but *sabot*, as well as referring to crude human footwear, is also the term for a horse's hoof.

Then again, we notice things, and when I was going to be beaten I knew in advance, by the coachman's breath. When he breathed out a strong odor, having been drinking at the merchant's, I was sure to be hit. I didn't deserve it, but I didn't get annoyed about it, because men are probably obliged to beat horses when they've drunk that odor. I believe so; I was made to drink some one day, at the stand, for a joke, and it burned me so much I no longer recognized myself. I leapt about like a little imbecile, without knowing why, and attacked my vehicle—me, who's so reasonable! Then I understood that one does the opposite of what one wants when one had drunk that stuff.

Apart from that, my coachmen weren't bad. They gave me water, and food. I had one of them who stroked me with his hand, which gave me pleasure, and one who understood me, when I talked to him with my eyes.

All that's to establish that I don't have any complaints. I've even known happy days, at the beginning of my life, when I wasn't yet harnessed to a pine box. I have to do the hardest work when I have the least strength, but that's doubtless the way things have to be, since they always are.

I can't tell you how many winters and summers I've been a cab-horse; I can't count. I only know that it seems to have lasted a long time. It would have lasted longer, but the other night, when it was so icy, I was clumsy enough to slip at the exit of the theater. I broke a bone against the edge of the sidewalk. I was in a bad way; it was necessary to unhitch me, and to help me to get up again with kicks in the belly—as many as possible.

They saw my broken bone under the skin and said that I ought to be put down; when I heard that, I lost heart, because death is scary. When, after that, I was ordered to walk, I was sad, because I knew where I had to go, but that's the rule. I resigned myself to it; when one doesn't resign oneself it doesn't change anything, but one gets hit more. So I tried to walk, but I really couldn't, in spite of wanting to, and I fell again. Then I was dragged by the mouth to the edge of the road—in order that I wouldn't get in the way of the traffic, you understand—and the poor people had difficulty dragging me. I certainly wasn't fat, but I was heavy all the same, and more than I thought. I found that out when I scraped the pavement with my flank, and all my weight was hanging from my jaw. I even ripped my tongue, but that was my fault, because I was in so much pain that I wasn't careful of it and it got caught between my teeth.

After that, I waited on the ground. There were a lot of people around me, and I was choking a bit. Some of them felt sorry for me; others laughed, and there was a sort of little fête, in which big people uttered little cries because of the habit men have of tickling women if there's a bit of a crowd.

In the end, a cart arrived and I was hoisted on to it. I say goodbye to my poor old carriage, which I left there, and never saw again. We set off. A comrade was dragging me, head bowed, reflecting, and it made me envious, and I reflected too, and I remembered—and I arrived at the house where one dies.

I recognized it immediately; blood and death have an odor that we know well, we beasts, even when we've never smelled it, and I think that humans, in spite of their intelligence, don't have a sense of that frightful odor, because one sees them walking calmly in its midst when we're crazed to the point of being rendered stupid.

In the big courtyard into which I was taken I was greeted by men in bloody aprons, and they decided that I was going to be used in experiments. I was glad about that, because all I ask is to be useful, but more especially because my death would be delayed; that would be so much gained, and the experiments might last a long time. To be sure, I would have preferred finishing my short life in a less lugubrious place, but horses never have a choice.

I was taken right up to the house, and when I was taken out of the cart my halter was tied to a ring in the wall between a door and a window. Above the door there was a sign with words in big letters: VIVISECTION LABORATORY.

The window-sill was just at the height of my head, which I rested on it, because I was very tired. I could see into the room. I couldn't see very well at first, but then I saw more clearly. It was like a big butcher's shop, with a stone table all along the wall, and other tables in the middle of the room, and on all the tables a display of cadavers, which humans call meat, and which they buy to eat.

I turned my head away, because butchers' shops have always caused me a certain fear, and also repugnance, at the idea of a living animal that could put pieces of a dead animal in its mouth, and keep them inside it, carrying them around everywhere.

I looked elsewhere, hoping that someone would come and take me away. I was cold, because it was very frosty.

Finally, after a time, they remembered me, and I was glad when I was untied. To my great surprise, I was taken into the room; never in my life had I gone into a room.

As soon as I was across the threshold I found the odor of death very repulsive and, involuntarily, I tugged on my halter—but I obeyed immediately, because I always obeyed, knowing that it has to be that way, and not otherwise.

Then I was hitched to a very strange carriage, which had no wheels, and was made of large wooden beams, and whose shafts weren't in front of the carriage but in the middle. Girth-straps were put under my body and my feet were tied up, doubtless to prevent me from kicking—which seemed unnecessary to me, because I never kick—but I couldn't say so, and my new masters didn't know.

Afterwards, I felt myself being lifted off the ground, and I was suspended, held down by the straps on my feet, which hurt my broken bone a lot—but I couldn't tell them, and they didn't know.

I stayed in that position for a long time, and no one took any more notice of me, for a young man had just arrived, who seemed to be a stranger to the house, and the others were showing him everything and explaining things to him. They stopped in front of the pieces of meat, and I followed them with my eyes in order to occupy myself, so that I wouldn't feel the pain of my injury as much.

The dead beasts were much more numerous than I had thought, and of all sorts. There were rabbits, guinea-pigs, cats, birds, frogs and, most of all, dogs. There were all pinned down, displaying their insides through terrible openings, but they still had their skin.

Suddenly, I saw...

One piece of meat was alive!

It had just been detached. It was an entirely red animal, which had no more skin on its body, and which stood up on its four paws and began to walk, turning its head from right to left as if it were looking for a place to hide. It started to bark; then I realized that it was a dog. It barked very plaintively; the men were standing in a circle around it, examining it and reflecting, while a young gentleman, more cheerful than his comrades, laughed a lot as he looked at the dog. The dog looked at them, too, with very sad and fearful eyes. It went toward a corner, and they let it go, but it couldn't lie down, being too sensitive, so it stayed upright on its paws, which were trembling, and licked its red body. It was so frightful that I thought I had its skin instead of mine, and felt the stroke of its tongue, and forgot the pain of my broken bone.

But the butchers were no longer occupied with it. Walking from table to table, they examined the other tied-up beasts, explaining them to the stranger and touching them with shiny tools.

Then I realized that almost all those pieces of meat were also alive; one of them meowed frightfully as soon as they started poking it with the tools.

A young man said: "Personally, I always use cats to study the pain reflexes; cats have a more vibrant nervous system, and very subtle.

The stranger asked: "You don't anesthetize the subjects any more, then?"

"Are you mad? You have to have living nerves to study life; flesh that you put to sleep can't respond to you. I accept that curare is convenient to immobilize the animal, which becomes a block of wood—but sensitive wood, marvelously sensitive and perhaps even exasperated, although immobile and easy to carve."

"Do you use a lot of dogs?"

"No—four or five thousand a year."

They continued their walk, smoking their cigarettes, and invited the visitor to admire a poodle that had been emptying for weeks through a tap, and a large number on inventions and instruments: an apparatus for boiling rabbits alive, another for cooking them dry, entirely or partially, to a greater or lesser degree, more or less quickly and without losing sight of hem, and counting everything that can be counted.

When they arrived in front of me, I pulled on my girth-straps, in spite of all my reason, to try to run away. Then, they declared that it was necessary to get to work, because it was Christmas Eve, and they wouldn't be working the next day.

Then they held a discussion to decide what to do with me, and to share out my body.

The one who was in charge said that, in order to make the most of me, they ought to start with the less vital parts. They went to fetch their tools.

They checked my straps. Seven of them took aim at me, seated on stools or stood on trestles, and they all began at almost the same time.

Two of them, in front, cut my shins, and after having cut them, burned them.

Another said that he would be content to dissect the muscles of my tail, and did so.

The fourth cut into my lips and skinned an ear, while the fifth, at the rear, took the hoof off my left hind leg—but he made a mistake and went on to the right.

The last two opened up the leg to look at my broken bone inside, and joined the piece up by reaching inside me with their hands.

I can't say how much they hurt me, all together. I went stiff, but they didn't understand. With all my heart I begged them: "Pardon me... For pity's sake... Pardon me... Kill me quickly!" But they didn't understand, because horses can't talk. They had no suspicion of my torment, of course, and were acting without malice, and they weren't angry, because they were chatting to one another while they were making me suffer so much.

I was bleeding everywhere when they left for lunch.

I hoped to be dead by the time they came back, but I was still alive when they reappeared. There were only three of them.

They went back to work. Two of them sawed through the bone in my head, in a circle; they lifted it out like a lid and stood in front of me. All that I had endured until then was nothing compared with what I suffered when they shoved needles and pincers inside my head; they pulled everything about, slashed, crushed and twisted, announcing what they were about to do and naming parts of me that all had their names, and tied arteries with threads, cut nerves with blades and touched them with electricity, burned them with a red-hot iron, and stitched me up—and the pain ran through my whole body, and was so atrocious that I wasn't paying attention any longer when a young man crouched down and cut off my last two hooves, while smoking his pipe.

God of humans, what torture! Long, long, and neverending! What happened to me afterwards, I don't know; by dint of suffering, I no longer felt anything. I thought think that I died once, and that my gentlemen resuscitated me. They blew air into my throat with a tube and cried: "Bravo! It's working! We're reanimating it.

They rejoiced in seeing me revive, which proves that they aren't wicked. For myself, though, I just wanted to stay dead, and I would have said so if I could.

They were so happy to have brought me back to life that they danced around me chanting: "*Resurrexit...xit...xit...*!"

Then they loosened my straps to bring me down to the ground and see if I could stand on my four stumps, and they shouted politely:

"Giddy up, Cocotte!"

I tried to move my legs for obedience's sake, but they wouldn't budge any longer. I collapsed, and they had to haul me up into the air again with the straps.

Then, one of the young gentlemen declared that they'd done enough work, and that it was getting dark, and he proposed that they leave, and they talked about Christmas Eve. Then, the one who often laughed picked up my four hooves and arranged them in front of the stove, saying that he was getting them ready for Father Christmas, and his friends seemed delighted that he had said that—so delighted that they couldn't stop laughing.

Then they washed and left, and we stayed there, all the animals, in the dark. They could be heard breathing softly. Snow was falling outside. No one was touching me any longer, but all the sufferings of my day continued in unison, with so much force that I began to die again.

In the middle of the night, I was resuscitated again; the other pieces of meat were still breathing, and something inside the stove, which had gone out, was making a noise—but all I could see there were my four hooves.

Suddenly, an old man with a big white beard, who had toys in his arms, emerged from the stove. He looked at my four hooves for a long time; then he looked at me, and looked at all of us—and again he looked at my poor hooves, which had done so much walking, and he shook his head sadly.

Then I recognized Father Christmas, and he said to me: "I saw the hooves and I came, but I won't have come in vain, even though someone wanted to trick me. Yes, I'll leave you a gift, brave horse; I'll give you the gift of speech, and, before dying, you can tell your story, so that an animal can tell humans the truth."

The above revelations, published in a newspaper with a large circulation and immediately translated into several other languages, excited public opinion. It then became necessary to verify, as far as possible, the authenticity of the story. There was no possibility of interrogating the horse, for the poor animal, after the multiple tortures of its vivisection, had apparently found a deliverance and well-deserved rest in death.

Only one person could be usefully questioned: Father Christmas—but it isn't easy to catch up with the famous old man. After many false steps, whose futility proved discouraging, we were obliged to have recourse to recently-discovered methods for the materialization of specters. The effect was immediate; at our very first appeal, around midnight, Father Christmas condensed and became visible in front of the fireplace, a benevolent and melancholy phantom.

I hadn't seen him since my childhood; he still had his beard, just as white and as long, but he seemed to me considerably changed, not because forty years, added to centuries, had really aged him as much as they had aged me, but because the sentiment of a diminishing prestige had affected his morale; he seemed, by turns, weary, nervous and resentful. Such an attitude isn't rare among individuals who were once honored with popular credit but whose credit has waned; when the public cease to believe in them, their decline affects them, and I would not have been surprised if the excellent phantom, under the threat of his imminent end, had been following the common rule.

In order not to annoy him any further, I spoke to him with extreme deference.

"The charming memory I retain of your munificent visits, distant as they were, incites me to implore your well-known generosity once again. You're Father Christmas?"

"Yes."

"Did you really, a few days ago, grant speech to a cab-horse?"

"Yes."

"Would you consent to tell us what your objective was?"

"To abolish a evil by revealing it! I'm addressing adults, since children no longer deign to believe in me; soon, I'll no longer exist except as a myth of olden days; before disappearing, I want to render a service."

"That sentiment, which honors you, is worthy of you. Nevertheless, you're doing Science an injury, by discrediting it."

"Science! Who mentioned that? We're talking about innumerable and monstrous games, which have nothing in common with it but a lying label."

"You've been reproached nevertheless for having, by means of untimely revelations, hindered the labor of those who are seeking the truth, and whose valorous efforts are working for the relief of human miseries."

"I venerate all labor, I execrate all abuse! Now, among the abuses that dishonor society and soil the earth, none seems to me ore odious that that of strength torturing weakness, and torturing delightedly!"

"Honorable scientists, whose word cannot be held in doubt, affirm nevertheless that nothing of the sort happens in their establishments; that the operations they carry out are limited to the strict necessity of their task, and that all measures are taken to anesthetize the subject."

"They are speaking for themselves, and, about themselves, they're telling the truth—but they aren't speaking for others and don't answer for everyone! To be sure, I've seen heroes, and I've even seen saints, devoting their lives and their health magnificently to the search for secrets that Nature hides from humans, and their dream of lessening human misery is the most august dream of them all. But is it the case, because they exist, that others don't exist? Is it the case, because their ambition is generous, that the parody of their actions isn't vain and criminal?"

"I understand, but, allow me to tell you, in all sincerity, that you have been criticized for having permitted—for having wanted—a simple cab-horse, ignorant uneducated in such matters, to take presumption to the extent of speaking publicly about things it knows nothing about."

"Pain? It knows about that!"

"You have been reproached for having, in this circumstance lacked tact in believing, dramatizing in an unseemly and—how can I put it?—excessively precipitate and candid manner, and giving others to believe things that are not true.

"They are!"

"It is insufficient to affirm it; it's necessary to prove it."

"Say simply that it's necessary to see! Enter a veterinary school, as I do, by the chimney, or by the door, and you will see trepanning, tracheotomies, the placing of setons,[33] and twenty other operations that could and ought to be studied on dead animals, but are studied on living ones."

"I repeat that you are opposed by a formal denial, and that you cannot convince us if you are not precise, for you have been challenged to do so."

"Challenged?"

The old man jumped, and, rummaging in his pockets, he took out sheaves of paper which he leafed through feverishly. He repeated: "Challenged? Challenged?"

"The story of the horse is a pure fantasy of the imagination."

"Read, Monsieur, read this statement made under oath: 'A chestnut mare... The haunches open, the skin lacerated, scored with a red-hot iron, traversed by dozens of setons, tendons torn away, eyes gouged out... Amid laughter... Stood on its bloody feet to show the spectators present, occupied in lacerating seven other horses, all that human dexterity can produce without causing death.'"

"The flayed dog, a fantasy of the imagination?"

"Fantasy, yes, certainly, and imagination, yes, certainly, for it required both to invent and carry out that experiment of Professor X and Doctor Y, who have made it and reported it. As for that of Doctor Z, it consists of first trepanning the skull of a dog in order to plunge red-hot irons thereafter into its brain. But one such dog howled without respite, which proved

---

[33] A seton was any thin object inserted beneath the skin so as to provide an issue; the crude devices of that kind in use when the story was written have been considerably refined as their medical uses have become more commonplace.

that it was not anesthetized, and the operator mourned: 'We tried to keep it calm by beating it, but it cried even louder; it didn't understand the lesson; it was incorrigible.' Take note, Monsieur, that I am not making this up: I am quoting; I am reading!"

"The boiled beasts?"

"The text tells us: 'Boiled in their own blood,' and informs us that their temperature rises to 112°. We have others, on the other hand, that are plunged into boiling water in order to skin them alive, in order to discover how many days they can live thus. We also have a dog steeped in turpentine, set alight, and then put out and put under observation; we have one force-fed with stones, and others that I shall pass over, for, at the first glance, you have perceived, like me, the great interest that these experiments present for the enrichment of medical science. I do not contest that, Monsieur, and I do not want to get into that question, where my incompetence is an notorious as that of the horse—but you will concede in your turn that, to be legitimately authorized in such enterprises, one must at least give proof of special aptitude, and that these investigations of life and pain cannot be freely opened to the ingenuity of everyone."

"Scientists alone..."

"That's false! And for the second time, I tell you that these free investigations are currently undertaken in veterinary schools, where I have seen the unnecessary adorned by atrocity! Should I add that in one provincial Faculty, whose name I shall not speak, dogs are trained by the students to capture cats without killing them and bring them back to serve in laboratory experiments? It's the fashion, Monsieur. They are studying, those young people! They are zealous, and they have full latitude; they enter into the society, and the exercise of a privilege, new to them, is a charming temptation.

"Now, reflect on this, Monsieur—students, ordinarily, do not repeat their masters' experiments, and it is not customary for them, nor do they have the time, to verify, integrally and for themselves, the countless well-founded notions that

Science has generated; in botany, chemistry, physics, therapeutics, they accept; in physiology, they check! When they are informed that a specific remedy is effective against a specific disease, they believe it, but when they are told that a specific nerve reacts to a specific pain, they doubt it, or, at least, carry out experiments to make sure.

"Anatomical studies that could be carried out on cadavers, they sometimes carry out on living animals, for a change. Operations that a surgeon will never perform on a human and that a veterinary will never have occasion to attempt on a horse, like the resection of the hoof, are still carried out on living animals. Why? To accustom the neophyte to the spectacle of pain, and harden him! For that argument has been employed, and some have dared to maintain that medical education includes exercises in professional hardening!

"That, Monsieur, is a blasphemy! The physician goes out into the world as an apostle of pity; his true mission, if it is not always to cure, is at least to comfort, and how can he comfort those who suffer if he has killed pity in his own heart at the outset?"

"The theory of hardening..."

"Is sustained! I can cite the texts that preach it, and even texts in which monomaniacs extol the voluptuousness of the 'good vivisector.'"

"Allow me to believe that our students give little credit to these sadistic paradoxes."

"Legion are those who reprove them! Legion, more numerous still, are those who abstain from putting them into practice. I even know those who hold as sterile and barbaric the six lessons in physiology that the syllabus imposes on them. But there again I have no competence, and do not judge."

"You act wisely."

"I observe, and that is too much! I observe and I advertise. A tolerance exists; should it last? The facts I've recounted to you exist, licit and quotidian. Should they cease? Decide."

"If these practices were abolished, education would not suffer?"

"England and the United States have been able to forbid them without scientific decline."

"Your conclusion?"

"A piece of advice: that it is necessary to take care and not tempt people. Humans are not fundamentally perverse, I confess and I attest, but don't imagine, either, that civilization has expelled all cruel instincts from them. Instincts resurface, when their rebirth is provoked! Don't provoke them by offering them nourishment, and remember that if humans are superior to animals, by virtue of their souls, the soul of which you boast only possesses two nobilities: intelligence, conceded to a few; and pity, necessary to all!"

With these words, the phantom disaggregated into smoke, and my entreaties were unable to render him solid again.

He left via the chimney.

DOCTOR AUGUÉRAND'S DISCOVERY

I. Dr. Auguérand's Discovery

The affair was old. People hardly talked about it any-more except to laugh at it; even in scientific environments they only persisted in making it the subject of some joke. As for the newspapers, they never mentioned it any more, consi-dering the subject exhausted and monotonous. Society people, having once been passionately for or against, imitated the in-difference of the press. Professor Patrice Auguérand's bluff was gradually relegated to the category of old legends.

In fact, nineteen years had already passed since the loud publicity provoked by his discovery; the elixir of long life that he claimed to have found in 1922 had not yet immortalized anyone by 1941, and even Dr. Auguérand had got nothing out of it but numerous annoyances and notorious ridicule. It was generally regretted that a man of such ability had compro-mised the glory of his career by a fantasy unworthy of him, his character and his previous endeavors. No one understood why he had yielded to the temptation of facile advertisement and thrown his name into the streets; his high reputation in science, his considerable fortune and his declared taste for quiet pleasures ought, logically, to have kept him safe from any such adventure, which could not be explained either by a need for money or an appetite for popularity.

But so what? The most serious men have their weak-nesses. Besides, Monsieur Auguérand had paid for his, and had paid dearly; his moment of celebrity had been rapidly fol-lowed by universal derision. Under the pressure of jeers, and even catcalls, he had been obliged to abandon his positions of responsibility one by one—first his dean's chair, and then his chair in histology; in the meantime, he had renounced his clientele, or it had renounced him, and not one in eighteen years had been seen at sessions of the Académie de Médecine or those of the Institute.

"He's sulking," said some.

"He's ashamed," said others.

And everyone said: "He was wrong."

Whether it was out of vanity or resentment, sadness or rancor, the fact was that the old master lived alone. A bachelor with no family, having only distant relatives in the provinces, and cultivating no other friendships than that of the silent Thismonard, his inseparable companion, he lived a rather mysterious existence in his vast property at Neuilly. No one went in to the house except for tradesmen and the domestic staff, which was numerous but bizarre: all his servants were Chinese. He had doubtless been led to that organization by the increasing difficulty of finding tolerable domestics in France. He could at least, like so many others, have found French-speaking Chinese in the employment bureaux; on the contrary, he only admitted to his service Celestials ignorant of any European language, and it was even said that he had them come directly from Manchuria or Korea. A former professor from Canton served as both his interpreter and butler.

The staff in question never went out and talked even less.

It was known, however, that the professor had built three outhouses in the grounds of his house. One was minuscule, but constructed like a fortress or a prison, whose doors were reinforced with iron and windows furnished with bars; it was known as the laboratory. The second housed a veritable menagerie, in which the doctor kept animals of various species, mostly mammals. The third, large, well-lit and hygienic, fitted out like a sanitarium and provided with a garden, constituted a hospice. Poor old men were received there gratuitously, cared for with all expenses paid; their number was estimated at round thirty, and equity obliged one to believe that these hospitalized individuals did indeed receive good care, since the ministerial officers had never had occasion in eighteen years to go into the building to certify a death. In addition, the reports of sanitary inspectors unanimously attested to the perfect state of the premises and the people.

"What can be going on in there?" insinuated colleagues whose retrospective jealousy had not consented to disarm them.

Cattle, sheep and deer grazed the grass of the grounds. Neighbors who were too close or intolerant complained of hearing, during summer nights, the roaring of wild beasts and the croaking of frogs.

"He's gone mad, since that business!"

"Or at least obsessive."

"It's a scandal that, in this day and age, a madman is permitted to squander such sums lodging and nourishing dotards and animals, when millions of citizens have so much difficulty getting by."

"Only half a century ago, the poor died of hunger or cold; now, at least they have the right to a pittance and shelter."

"Which doesn't mean that aren't still rich people to be brought into line."

Things had reached this point of ironic or anodyne hostility when, on the fourteenth of July 1941—the anniversary of a date once famous but largely neglected now[34]—a twenty-line article appeared in an evening newspaper and reawakened attention.

Hazard, wrote the journalist, *is a great master. It procured us the surprise, this morning, of being in attendance at an unusual marriage, celebrated in the Maison Syndicale[35] of*

---

[34] The storming of the Bastille—the beginning of the Revolution of 1789.

[35] The Maison Syndicale in Central Paris became the central focus of trade union activity in Paris following the Courrières Mining Disaster of 1906, which caused and enormous scandal, having been not merely he worst such disaster in history but the first to be widely reported in the Press. It is not surprising that Haraucourt, writing so soon after the disaster, was in-

the twenty-seventh arrondissement in the Boulevard de Neuilly. Two inmates of the famous Dr. Auguérand were joined in legal matrimony. The husband had counted no less than seventy-one autumns and the wife admitted an almost equal number of springs. Bawdy, however, and replete, the ruddy-faced lady was more reminiscent of a Jordaens than a Velasquez;[36] she had the manner of an excessively young actress playing an excessively old role. After the sacramental words, the septuagenarian, clad in a suit with a mauve cravat, offered the sexagenarian an arm free of ankylosis, and the couple made their exit as one exits at twenty. Were they going to pick strawberries? One might believe so, and they gave one to think as much, so advantageous, even triumphant, were the expressions that they were both exhibiting. Smiles, which were not mocking, greeted them as they crossed the thresholds, and there was even a certain amount of applause, when Dr. Auguérand, a witness to the marriage, appeared behind them. Is that couple, perhaps, the result of his work, emerged from his test-tubes? A serious advertisement, then, for the elixir of life?

One final sentence, which we ask permission not to reproduce, indulged in wordplay and risked a joke that the press and public of 1940 will not find inadmissible.

No more was required. On the morning of the fifteenth of July on, reporters hastened to the Villa Auguérand and solicited interviews with the professor or his associates. The Chinese porter greeted them with speech reminiscent of birdsong, but whose syllables were so musical and unintelligible were that they were sufficient to bar any passage. The journalists persisted in vain; they were forced to restrict themselves to vague depictions of the outbuildings, and the very vagueness

---

clined to suggest that similar institutions might take over the functions of the local mairies in future.

[36] The Flemish master Jacob Jordaens (1593-1678) and the Spanish court painter Diego Velasquez (1599-166) represented rival schools of portrait painting, the former being less formal and arguably more robust.

of their descriptions leant the abode a renewal of mystery. All afternoon, airplanes circled over the grounds, trying to discover some scientific or intimate detail.

The doctor had become enigmatic again, and his affairs interesting, at least for two or three days. He was in demand again, but he remained inaccessible. The reporters who came in the evening, like those of the morning, heard nothing but chirping from Chinese lips. For want of anything better, they invented. One of them overstepped the mark; the claimed to have observed the married couple by night, passing before their open window in an aircraft, and furnished an exaggerated account of them; one of his colleagues riposted with diametrically opposed, and even more sensational, affirmations. Polemic ensued. Then, people wanted to know, at any price; the public ear demanded the truth.

It got it.

It got it via the voice of the faithful Thismonard, to whom one journalist had the idea of paying a visit. The confidant replied, in substance:

"There's no reason why I shouldn't talk to you. If my glorious friend has kept himself in seclusion for such a long time it's not, as some have said, because of a sentiment of rancor or ruffled pride. He doesn't deign either to complain or to reproach anyone. People have laughed at his discovery, but far from taking offense, he deems that people have a right— almost a duty—to doubt; the benefit that it brings to humankind is too considerable for it to be welcomed without a measure of the skepticism that is elementary prudence. Besides, I have nothing to say that you don't already know; there is no essential modification to be made to the declarations of 1922.

"At that time, Auguérand's discovery was conclusive and total, and had been for ten years. But ten years added to a life is not sufficient to demonstrate that one can prolong the normal duration of life; a Macrobian fact can only be proven by the lapse of time. That is why Auguérand wanted time to

205

go by. The Macrobians[37] that he is able to present today will bring you thirty years of experience, not the ten that they were able to do when you talked about them for the first time. We would have liked to wait for another ten years, but if the academies estimate that the present figure suffices and permits them to repent, my friend Patrice asks no more than to reserve a god welcome for them. As soon as they have formulated the desire, he will assign them a date and receive them. You can print that."

Interrogated as to the nature of the results obtained, Monsieur Thismonard replied:

"In order to be conclusive, our experiments had to be carried out, and have been carried out, not only on human beings but on various animal species, especially mammals, which furnish us with specimens exhibiting varying degrees of vital resistance, and have served in consequence for us to draw up comparative tables from which the conclusion emerges that we can triple the duration of life. For example, rodents, such as hares, rats or rabbits, live for an average of four years; we maintain them for twelve. Bulls rarely surpass their fifteenth year; we can take them to thirty-two, and even to fifty by maintaining them in a state of virginity.

"As regards the human species, one cannot be ambitious for such a large augmentation for them. Indeed, if we compare humans with other species, the proportional calculation of the three phases of growth, maturity and senility lead us to conclude that people, reaching puberty at sixteen, ought normally live for a hundred and ten or a hundred and twenty years; you know that they don't last as long, in spite of the promise that they have at the moment of puberty; thus, they wear them-

---

[37] The Macrobians were a people described by Herodotus, perhaps somewhat fancifully, who allegedly lived in the Somalian peninsula during the first millennium B.C. According to the historian they were not merely the tallest and most handsome of humans but had mastered the secret of longevity, enjoying an average lifespan of 120 years.

selves out more rapidly. Proportionally, thy exhaust their vital resistance more rapidly than other animals do.

"Why and in what way? Evidently, by virtue of the one thing that distinguishes them from other species: the soul, the idealists will tell you; the nervous system, the materialists will say: their passionate and intellectual expenditure. In consequence, we do not hope, save in exceptional cases and curiosities, to produce Macrobians three hundred years old, but we are certain of being easily able to prolong the useful period of a human existence—which is to say, their physical and intellectual virility—until the hundred and tenth year. It will be even easier to take subjects who expend less—imbeciles and the chaste—to a hundred and fifty. I confess to you that that is not our aim; we attain it by virtue of the logic of the situation, without having wanted it.

"We are not philanthropists, in the outdated meaning that past generations attached to the word; we think in the same way as our time, which is utilitarian, practical and socially economical; the 20th century no longer has to entertain unproductive consumers, useless mouths and impotent limbs; we do not render youth to decrepit individuals, because, on the one hand, we do not have the ability, and, on the other hand, we do not care to. To conserve for society, for social cooperation, robust strength, by doubling it and perhaps tripling it—that is what is important to us, and that is what we are realizing. You can print that."

The journalist did not hesitate to do so; he would have said more if he had been given the means. He concluded by declaring that Academy and the Faculty, thus given the means to verify, and, if necessary, to rectify their premature judgment of 1922, had a duty to inform themselves fully on a question of universal interest, to enlighten the country and the world, and, if there was a need, to make honorable amends for their initial errors.

The learned bodies were reluctant to suffer the humiliation of soliciting an audience with an independent scholar who had severed all connections with them, but public opinion, which had scarcely deigned to mock the inventor a few days before, had abruptly turned around. Millions of people, renewing the hope of prolonging their lives, even for half a century, demanded the truth. Imposing processions passed through the streets of Paris; a few disturbances occurred.

The minister sent the official scientists an invitation that was as good as a command. A committee of inquiry was appointed. On the twenty-second of July, it expressed to Dr. Auguérand, by letter, the desire to hear his communications regarding the cases of longevity he had observed. An appointment was made, for nine o'clock in the morning on the twenty-fourth of July, for the designated committee-members to present themselves at the villa in Neuilly.

II. A Memorable Meeting

On the twenty-fourth of July, the committee members delegated by the Académie des Sciences, the Académie de Médecine and the Faculté presented themselves at the door of the establishment that popular parlance was already designating by a famous abbreviation, the AC: the Auguérand Clinic.

In spite of the care that the scientists had taken not to divulge the time of this visit, no one in Paris was unaware of it. An enormous crowd gathered at the edge of the city. In the first row, the reporters were waiting, recognizable by their automatic telegraph apparatus. The members of the crowd, visibly nervous and impatient, argued among themselves—but it was worse when the delegates got out of their cars. Immediately, an almost hostile agitation was manifest in the first rows, and the people at the back, braver because they were less visible, sounded anonymous whistle-blasts.

To tell the truth, for nine days, opinion had scarcely been favorable to the representatives of official science, who were caught in a dilemma.

"If Dr. Auguérand really did discover a means of tripling human life thirty years before, you're guilty of having rejected it out of paltry jealousy, thus depriving us of such a benefit. If, on the contrary, he's merely a charlatan and visionary, you made the mistake of not cutting short the deceptive hopes that he put into people's minds. In either case, your duty is to be sure, and you're sinning by negligence, you whom we pay to know what we don't know, on our behalf!"

The door closed on the dear masters. Three representatives of the press accompanied them in order to telegraph the news in the course of the session. The great dailies, speculating on public curiosity, and counting on the worldwide publicity that the event promised, had installed their Hertzian transmission apparatus on the threshold of the city and the paper's headquarters, in such a way that here and there, in Paris, London and Berlin as soon as at Neuilly itself, the crowd would be able to read, in white letter projected on black screens, the details of the communications made by the inventor and a summary of the technical discussions. New York would receive the cable only a few minutes later.

A quarter of an hour went by, seeming very long. Suddenly, the sound of an electric bell provoked a movement of heads and shoulders in the front rows, with a murmur that gradually propagated to more distant ranks. A reporter raised his hand toward the screen and switched on the receiver; binoculars were aimed. The dispatch appeared.

9.45. Reception at door of house. Exchange of civilities. Cold courtesy. Reserve on both sides. Dr. Auguérand seems confident, but devoid of arrogance. To his left, his faithful friend Thismonard, is smiling with a triumphant air that authorizes every hope. Committee members introduced into a vast, severe and glacial room where seats are arranged in a semicircle. Chinese domestics standing at all exits, barring the passage of anyone wanting to wander around the building. The doctor, with his back to the old 19th century fireplace, prepares to make a preliminary speech. Session open.

This initial telegram only furnished few elements to the commentators; they concentrated, however, on the phrase relating to Monsieur Thismonard, whose triumphant attitude "authorized ever hope." That was sufficient to create a current of opinion, still indecisive but already favorable, so strong was the desire to see the conquest confirmed. That was why the disillusionment was sharp, even violent, when, ten minutes later, the second dispatch was inscribed:

Auguérand speaks, explains his system. I do not prolong human life, he says. The expression is inexact, unscientific to the highest degree. I have never said any such thing. It is madness to pretend that one can reform the laws of nature; by the very fact that they are laws, they must be recognized as fixed, logical and immutable. Science can only aspire to understand them, to penetrate the secret of their functioning, so long mysterious, and to discover the conditions of their best return.

The street greeted this preamble with a sequence of whistles, which immediately announced total defeat; from the start, Auguérand's failure was proclaimed definitive; the egotistical hopes of the world, resuscitated for a week, were about to be dashed for the second time. In Berlin and New York the consternation was profound; instantaneously, share prices fell on the Bourse. But in Paris and London, outbursts of laughter covered the disappointment.

Professor Auguérand continued:

"Life is a perpetual resistance to death. In a great many animal species, however, individuals, yielding to the solicitations of instincts that corrupt them, have progressively rendered the race in a less resistant condition. Thus, one can say that they have voluntarily restricted the duration of life, since that diminution of the duration is the mediate consequence of a dissipation to which they consent.

"Death is the total of millions and millions of partial, successive deaths that beings accept or impose on themselves without being aware of it; very few animals live out their normal lifespan; the human species is, with a very marked prominence, the one that deteriorates the most rapidly of all. Why? Because humans abuse their strength more than the others. The comfort and relative security of their material existence have been able to provide relative compensation for the prejudice caused by an excessive expense, but that purely negative attenuation of harm is incapable of compensating for the effects of positive vice.

"The logical remedy, the only one that could bring the human animal back to maximum longevity, would consist of returning the abuser to the simplest conditions of nature, from which, on the contrary, humans are increasingly removing themselves. But that remedy is illusory, because humankind would refuse its application, and will refuse it even more forcefully the more social organization augments the possibilities of existence.

"Thus, common sense obliges us to anticipate that the maximum duration of human life, already briefer today than it was twenty thousand years ago, will be further reduced in generations to come—and since the logical remedy is logically impracticable, we shall be forced, Messieurs, to have recourse to accommodations. In other words, if we cannot prevent humans from ruining themselves incessantly and without respite, let us try to ameliorate the effects of those repeated ruinations whose total is premature death."

Further booing welcomed this theoretical verbiage, incomprehensible to some, devoid of surprise for others, which was displayed on the screens like a categorical confession of impotence or a bluff ill-concealed by the words. The impression on the street was, moreover, only a reflection of that of the scientists.

Indeed, at that moment Dr. W. Letigre made the observation, not without irony, that the task in question was merely that of the most elementary medicine. The silent Touposcoff, in his customary fashion, went to the window, looked out over the garden and took out his watch to signify that he was wasting precious time. Professor Axilo was studying the ceiling through his platinum-rimmed spectacles and tugging his filamentous beard.

Monsieur Sigismund Ricardos of the Académie des Sciences Morales et Politiques, a statistician, took advantage of the interruption to recall that one of the 19th century precursors of the then-embryonic science of statistics had already noted the influence that mode of life exercises on the relative duration of existence; in that epoch, he said, the two categories of subjects attaining the most advanced ages were ecclesiastics and agriculturalists; by contrast, artists, writers, advocates and physicians were at the bottom of the scale of vital resistance.[38]

"From these statistics and others," Letigre added, "our predecessors felt able to conclude that excessive nervous strain, duplicated in sensual and intellectual forms, provokes the maximum exhaustion, and that alimentary intoxication, the effective cause of atherosclerosis, is secondarily manifest as a generator of precocious senility. Thus, love less, think less, eat less, and you will live longer."

General hilarity underlined this sally. The faithful Thismonard smiled with his imperturbable confidence.

Auguérand replied: "Thank you, Messieurs, for recalling observations that rejuvenate me in my turn, since they evoke the memory of my beginnings, the point of departure of the labors that were to lead me to the double discovery of which I have the honor of informing you today."

On reading this, an immense clamor went up from the exasperated crowd.

"Enough!"

---

[38] Haraucourt's "precursor" of statistical science is evidently fictitious, given that the actual 19th century French pioneer of this kind of analysis, Jacques Bertillon, continuing the work of his father Alphonse, found a diametrically opposite result with respect to the clergy, proving that, along with bachelors in general, they died younger, on average, than married men—from which he concluded that celibacy reduces life-expectancy. The English social scientist Herbert Spencer (a confirmed bachelor) interpreted the figures in a different way, suggesting that the cause and effect were the other way around: that sickly individuals unlikely to live long were more liable to be rejected as potential marriage partners, often having no recourse but to go into the priesthood.

"Down with Auguérand!"

"Enough!"[39]

"Basta!"

"Bravo Letigre!"

"Genuch!"

"Hurrah for Touposcoff!"

"Down with Thismonard!"

"Enough!"

The noise of the howling city-dwellers reached the hall. The Academicians, feeling that they had the support of pubic opinions, became restless in their seats. Several members, following Touposcoff's example, got up to go. Thismonard, motionless beside the fireplace, listened to the racket and seemed delighted. A pantogram[40] announced this confident attitude to the street. The indignant cries redoubled in volume. This time, however, the manifestation fell flat, for Auguérand had just extended his right arm in a gesture of appeasement, and he resumed speaking in a tranquil manner.

Then, on the black screen, they read:

Auguérand says: "Messieurs, I have simply found a means of recovering the quotidian losses, and, in consequence, of attenuating the resulting degradation. By the dimi-

---

[39] This exclamation is rendered in English, the previous one—and the next—having been a translation of "Assez!"

[40] The word *pantogramme* [pantogram] is probably improvised from *pantographe* [pantograph], a mechanical copying device. Haraucourt might have known that a device for copying images telegraphically had been patented in 1843 by the Scottish inventor Alexander Bain, and that a giant version of it built by Giovanni Caselli had sent a message from Paris to Amiens in 1856, displayed on a big screen like the one featured here. Bain's telegraph system, potentially the best and most versatile of all the candidates for 19th century development, would probably have integrated such a system eventually but it was ruthlessly annihilated by Samuel Morse, who would brook no competition.

nution of these partial deaths, I delay by as much the term of their total—which is to say, definitive death. I confessed to you just now that I cannot prolong life, but I can restore it very nearly to its normal duration, which had progressively diminished. In that way, not only can I extend the term of individual existence, but I can maintain subjects in their useful maturity for a number of years that varies between double and triple the present figures."

Sensation in the learned assembly. Thismond inspects the audience, beaming. Everyone is on their feet. Precipitate dialogues in low voices.

Touposcoff, surrounded, says slowly: "He's making fun of people!"

Legrand-Gauthier, very somber, but known for not exhibiting any hostility to anyone, poses a question: "If I understand correctly, my dear colleague, it's a matter of a double therapeutic treatment of the nervous and circulatory systems?"

Auguérand replies: "Exactly, my dear colleague. With your permission, we'll go together to examine the evidence that I feel duty-bound to submit to your competence."

General movement. Thismonard heads for the exit and leads the way.

This dispatch, so abruptly affirmative after the disappointment of the preceding communications, disconcerted the public. Was it a joke? The inventor, by his own confession, could not prolong life, but could nevertheless double or triple it? Many did not understand. A few sensed that the master had wanted, by playing with words, to unmask his adversaries and increase their discomfort. Others saw in his language, not a contradiction but a legitimate distinction and the mark of a scientific mind.

For the immense majority, however, which is simplistic, one fact stood out above all others: Auguérand can triple human life!" On the boulevards of Paris, in London, Berlin and New York, the news spread like lightning.

"Is it proven?"

"Not yet."

"He's introducing the committee to the subjects on which he's been experimenting for thirty years."

"By noon, we'll know."

Bets were made in London and New York. Already, Auguérand, discredited a few moments before, was being laid at evens.

Stock exchanges rose everywhere.

III. The Macrobians

Third pantogram, posted at 10.30 a.m.:

Thismonard leads the committee members to the menagerie, as if Auguérand does not deign to present these preparatory examples himself. On the way, the cicerone explains that short-lived animals have been very precious for the study of the cure, its procedure and effects, since they alone permitted the demonstration, within a lapse of thirty years, of tripled existences. The cages are maintained with a curious concern for hygiene and quietude. It has been observed, in fact, that the proximity of carnivores is sufficient to abridge the lives of prey species, by reason of the nervous expense occasioned in the latter by the presence of potential peril; same observation in respect of males lodged in proximity with females. All the cages are equipped with a card recording the animal's pedigree, its date of birth, its diet, and the average duration of life of an individual of the species.

Let us cite in passing:

Cats, mean duration, 16 years; typical obtained, 32 years; maximum, 46 years.

Cows, mean duration, 20 years; typical obtained, 52 years.

Bulls, mean duration, 15 years; typical obtained, 32 and 34 years, with trimestrial heifer; bullock, 45 years.

Hares, 4 years, attaining 12.

Rabbits, duration 4 years; impossible to extend beyond 8 (irreducible lasciviousness).

215

Dogs, ordinary duration 20 to 24 years; impossible to extend beyond 45 (cynicism).

Deer, maximum duration, 40 years; impossible to extend beyond 90 (annual excess of genetic instinct).

Rats, 4 years, attainment 12.

Pigs, 20 years; typical obtained 50, reaching 60 (undeserved reputation; much more chaste than namesakes of the human species).

Horses, duration 35, present specimens 60; still increasing.

Etc.

The complete official list will be published in due course.

This paragraph of the pantogram provoked mediocre applause; it only excited the Animal Protection Society, which had become very influential in 1941, and aged spinsters. As for the mass of the public, it was somewhat hesitant to conclude a perfect similarity between citizens and animals.

It is also necessary to remark that advantages so clearly marked in favor of chastity and even continence, were of a nature to cool the enthusiasm of French people; several men cheerfully declared their hostility to a cure that required so great a sacrifice as an initial premium; many women did not hesitate to give them loud support. To this criticism, moderate spirits objected that it would be permissible for anyone not to triple a lifespan by privation, but simply to double it while not depriving oneself of anything. Shopkeepers seemed full of confidence. Nevertheless, by a rather typical particularity, a sharp discontentment was manifest in Marseilles; the Cannebière declared that the very principal of such medication was an attack on the liberty of love, and the Bourse fell, while Stock Exchanges continued to rise elsewhere—notably in London and New York, where the premium attributed to good morals could not fail to obtain official approval.

Fourth pantogram, posted at 11.20:

Victory! Triumph! Doubt seems to be no longer permissible. Auguérand leads the committee into the human sanitarium. Thirty-three surprising subjects, men and women, all armed with their duly certified documents. The comparison of birth certificates with the present appearance of the individuals presents unimaginable contrasts.

M. Léonard Latude (the groom of 14 July), 71 years old, looks about 45.

The widowed Mme. Mathillat (the bride), 69, scarcely looks 38.

Marguerite Bouldeboul, 83, looks 60.

M. Alexis Perlot, 76, certainly doesn't look 50.

Mlle. Andréa Froussotte, 56, looks 30.

Her daughter Jeanne, similarly unmarried, 30, seems 22. Etc.

The complete official list will be published in due course.

The subjects were interrogated by the committee members; the Demoiselles Froussotte were ausculated. They male subjects registered their strength with the dynamometer. In the hydrotherapy room, Alexis Perlot, completely naked, lifted weights.

The committee, visibly impressed, maintained reservations nevertheless that might have been deemed excessive. Legrand-Gauthier finally broke the silence and, in a slow but categorical voice, affirmed his amazement. Touposcoff objected that the concordance of cases, while establishing a presumption in favor of the theory, could not be considered as scientifically conclusive. Letigre declared himself satisfied.

Thimonard made the observation at this point that the results obtained were far from representing the maximum possible, since the treatment had only produced its effects from the date that the subjects had begun to follow it. (Scientific hilarity.) All that it had been possible to accomplish was to maintain them at that age, without rejuvenating them. The quinquagenarians had remained quinquagenarians.

"A subject who is submitted to the cure in his thirtieth year conserves the vigor of his maturity, in all its forms, for a half a century."

Touposcoff asked whether continence was indispensable to the efficacy of the treatment.

Thismonard reassured him in these terms: "Absolute chastity being unnatural, it is inadmissible, nor even supposable, that it will be necessary, much less indispensable. Only moderation is required; in this as in all things, *in media stat virtues*—virtue resides in the median.

"The exact median?"

"No, the just median."[41]

An evident relaxation had been established for several minutes. The famous Professor Graunerr, who had not said a word thus far, nor given any sign of approval or disapproval, took the floor authoritatively and addressed the assembly.

"Out of devotion for science," he said, "I am ready to run the risks of the treatment personally."

"That heroism, my dear master," Thismonard replied, "will reward you, albeit belatedly."

This riposte provoked malicious remarks. It was, in fact, well known that Professor Graunerr would reach the age of retirement in 1942; several candidates were already canvassing support for the eventual acquisition of his chair. His maintenance of his responsibilities would produce numerous disappointments among his colleagues.

The beginning of the pantogram reporting all this had given the masses as profound emotional shock, but the end was give a poor welcome. The public was unanimous in criticizing the journalist who was mingling details of excessively particular interest with the great questions of general interest. The intrusion of such petty matters was judged inappropriate and utterly unwarranted.

---

[41] This old joke refers to the longstanding French political principle of the *juste milieu*, which refers to a fair compromise rather than an exact partition, as the phrase could also be construed. I have employed "median" rather than "middle" or "mean" because the text has already established a principle of statistical pedantry that mathematically-minded readers will doubtless appreciate.

"What do individual egotistical concerns matter in a debate in which the future of humankind is at stake?"

People scarcely suspected then the importance of the two remarks made by Messieurs Graunerr and Thismonard, nor the formidable conflict that had just been inaugurated, unknown even to the interlocutors. People were only to comprehend subsequently the social gravity of the problem unexpectedly posed upon the world. For the moment, the joyful emotion of the conquest took precedence over all other considerations. The eleven-twenty pantogram left no room for doubt; the cause was won for Dr. Auguérand, and also for humankind.

Half an hour later, all the peoples of the Earth were publishing the enormous news:

Human life can be extended!

At midday, the Bourse registered the highest rise of the century. The antipodes, where it was the middle of the night, and where dispatches were anxiously awaited, celebrated the event with sudden and general illuminations.

The following pantogram, dated ten past noon, related that the session was concluding with a visit to the laboratories.

The inventor presented his two elixirs. Their employment was very simple: once a week, three drops in a glass of water, taken on an empty stomach. The price of manufacture was virtually negligible—one franc fifty a liter. M. Sigismond Ricardos of the Académie des Sciences Morales, immediately calculated that at five centigrams a drop and 156 drops per person per year, one liter would be sufficient for the annual treatment of 128 individuals—which would require, for each one, a total expenditure on ten centimes a year.

Interrogated as to his intentions relative to the sale price of the product, the doctor declared that he had no intention of indulging in commerce. He would deliver his formula to the International Codex, but only on the expiration of the thirtieth year that he had assigned to the interval of its study—which is to say, in five months time. Until the first of January 1942, in order to avoid chemical analyses and counterfeiting, he would keep the secret of his formulae, and no quantity of elixir, however small, would leave his house. In the meantime all the people who so desired could present themselves at the clinic in Neuilly; a dispensary would be installed for their use in the villa's garden, and glasses of water would be provided free of charge for immediate consumption. It was recommended in the strictest possible fashion that no more than one glass per week be taken; the abuse of the treatment might present serious dangers.

The committee declared itself sufficiently enlightened. Professor Graunerr, having not eaten, asked to begin the treatment immediately. Dr. Auguérand poured him three drops of the yellow elixir. Graunerr raised his glass solemnly and, saluting the learned company with his gaze, he said: "I drink to the future of science"

"And to yours," replied one voice.

Smiles. Applause. The session ended. The committee was to reconvene at the Institut at three o'clock, to render its definitive verdict, which was henceforth not in doubt. Auguérand received warm congratulations; he showed the delegates out. There was an exchange of civilities—which, this time, were cordial and frank.

When the gate of the grounds opened to let the committee members out, a thunderous ovation acclaimed Auguérand, who immediately retreated.

In Paris and various other capitals, the disinterest of the inventor gave rise to the enthusiasm of some, the anxiety of others and the surprise of all; it was too abnormal a circumstance not to cause astonishment in an essentially practical epoch in which every invention represented a capital and every enterprise a business affair. That excess of generosity doubtless concealed some secret plan? It remained incontestable, nevertheless, that the benefit of the discovery would be accessible to all, rich and poor, without distinction. Henceforth, everyone, save for accident or disease, would have the means, or at least the hope, of remaining on Earth for a hundred and fifty or two hundred years. Human genius had finally conquered Duration, as it had previously conquered Space.

"Hurrah for Auguérand!"

The day was not to go by without alarm, however. At four o'clock, while the committee was in session at the Institut, a cablegram arrived from Chicago addressed to the doctor, which announced the formation of a company to exploit his discovery, and offered him twenty million dollars for the purchase of the patent. The different services of the daily press were then so meticulously organized that five newspapers received copies of the dispatch before the original had reached its destination. The boulevards were informed at the same time as the doctor.

What would he decide, in the face of such a strong temptation?

At five o'clock, it was learned that he had refused.

At five forty, the committee rendered its formal judgment, attesting to the reality of the results obtained by the treatment and only maintaining reservations with the regard to the chemical composition of the elixirs, unknown from then until the following first of January.

At five fifty, the representative of a London-based company, outbidding the American one, offered Auguérand eight million pounds sterling, equivalent to two hundred million francs.

The doctor's second refusal caused delirious enthusiasm in the world's population. In every language, people were glad to recognize in that noble gesture the proverbial disinterest of the French character, which had not degenerated at all.

Everywhere, successive editions of newspapers were printed. Every city saw agitation in its streets; the houses were empty, factories abandoned, work suspended. Old men, who were greeted with acclamations as they passed by, displayed faces radiant with joy, as if the discovery were only relevant to their decrepitude, although they would obtain less profit from it than anyone else.

Then, suddenly, upon that universal exuberance, that triumphant certainty, the great evening newspapers fell like an icy shroud. Reason had just spoken—too late, as always. An impression like that of a sleeper awaking from a crazy dream abruptly disconcerted the still-hallucinated minds. An immense malaise enveloped the terrestrial globe. In the depths of all human pupils, an anxiety emerged. The name of Graunerr was bandied about, leaving behind it a wake of anguish. Young faces became somber, and the old men were seen hastily returning home...

IV. Make Way for the Young!

It is necessary to confess that the movement began in France, in a light-hearted manner; is that country, where it is said that everything ends up in songs, one might say that everything begins in caricatures, which are pictorial songs.

The first to appear was the one by *Pal*, at six-thirty. It represented Professor Graunerr, in a toga and bonnet, standing on his doctoral chair, with one hand raising a cup from which he was about to drink, and the other blessing, with three drops, the crowd of candidates laying siege to his position. A few were reaching out with clawed fingers toward the desired placement, while others, probably touched by the benediction, were fleeting with dolorous expression. The caption read: "I'm drinking to my future!"

The second caricature, by *Témoin*, appeared in the cinema at six fifty; it depicted a thin old man, decrepit and doddery, in the countryside, who threw his spade away in despair and lay down in a furrow, as if to die of exhaustion there; he got up immediately, with great difficulty, and went up a hill to a thatched cottage, and the scene shifted to the interior of the house. Like a dying man opening his own tomb, the old man opened the door and came in; from a chest he took a bag of copper coins, emptied it on to the table and counted his treasure weeping. His three sons arrived, followed by their three wives and kids. The old man divided his money into three piles; he was put to bed and the bed surrounded, while they waited for him to die. But then the door opened again, and Mephistopheles appeared, wearing Auguérand's face; three drops of the elixir, and he moribund was standing up, cured and valiant. Then the drama:

"Give me back my money!"

The sons hesitated, the daughters-in-law protested, lecturing their men and preaching resistance. The rejuvenated old man took hold of his staff furiously and, alone against all of them, forced his heirs to give in one by one; all sent away, they went out cursing, while the little children, between the legs of the grown-ups, shook their fists at their grandfather. And the old man picked up his spade to go back to the field.

"You shan't have my land!"

In the next act, the children had grown up and become men, fathers to their own children, whom they watched grow up and multiply, to the extent that the cottage filled up with successive generations, too numerous for its restricted size, where they were crushed, choking, against the walls. They had all drunk the elixir, and no one was dying any longer—not even the lusty ancestor, who was driven by vital exuberance to be excessively familiar in corners with his own descendants, in conformity with the ancient laws of incest.

Finally, a saucepan was placed on the table, and the ancestor got ready to distribute the meal to his hungry family. He plunged a ladle into the enormous vessel and brought out the only potato, which everyone was expecting, and everyone could see; having taken it between his thumb and forefinger, he raised it up in front of his face, as a priest does with the host in order to present it to the faithful, and gobbled it up.

The piece was entitled: *The Last Communion*.

There was no laughter; everyone understood its economic message. In any case, if they had not understood, the editorial in the *Judgment Public* arrived just in time to make it precise; it appeared at exactly seven o'clock. It said

It's decided, then. The date is memorable in the auspices of stupidity. Today, the twenty-fifth of July 1941, a benefactor of humanity, who naively imagines himself such, has endowed the world with a previously-unknown scourge, the worst of all those that science and history have recorded thus far: social

223

plethora! How can it be that public common sense was not able, from the first moment, to see through this terrifying utopia? With a disconcerting candor, people have welcomed Dr. Auguérand's success and the demonstration of his discovery; it is done; the triumph is complete; we shall all live for a hundred and fifty to two hundred years! Which is to say that five, six, seven or even eight simultaneous generations will be competing for the jobs and food that are hardly sufficient for two or three.

No one has understood that, by virtue of this fact alone, we shall be abruptly reduced to the necessities of primitive barbarism, to the bloody struggle that once hurled our ancestors against one another, all the more determined to destroy those who are nearest to them, on the same continent, in the same province, in the same village and in the same family, competitors for the same wealth. We had succeeded, after two hundred centuries of murder and two centuries of philosophy, in putting an end to war, at least for a while. You are reestablishing it with a joyful hearts, more ferocious than it was before, more necessary than it was before, armed with the formidable means that progress has given it, and without mercy, because victory or defeat will be a matter of life or death for every people.

By multiplying us to excess, you have are condemning us to kill one another! Abortion and infanticide, which were crimes, will become duties. If you do not succeed, by means of international laws, in restricting the fecundity of women, there will no longer be any security on the planet, which will run red with indispensable murder. And how can you arrive at diplomatic agreement, what police will monitor you and suppress the increase in population among neighboring people, desirous as they will be to develop their numerical superiority—a desire and effort that will tend logically to mutual annihilation?

The *Drapeau Rouge*, the organ of the moderates, struck the same note:

In what animal species do you observe the coexistence of eight generations? You are returning to us, you say, the initial number of our years? All right; we'll take your word for it. But do not take the inference that you are restoring the natural order, for you are, on the contrary exiting from it, since that order is no longer what it was in the earliest days of the race. Then, the small number of humans permitted them to live much longer, which was possible but has ceased to be. Where do you see the available space? Are you going to populate Saturn, or would you prefer to conquer the planet Mars?

To triple the duration of the individual is to triple the number of individuals; two thirds will be in excess; as soon as you add them it will be necessary to get rid of them. How? Many by violence and the rest by disease. For that natural law, which you claim to be in error, will bring order to the fantasies of science and reestablish the equilibrium disrupted by your actions. Your benefit is only theoretical; the harm you do will be real. The dead will perhaps not be the same individuals, and they will die differently, but just as many will die, for our proportional disappearance is demanded by the economy of nature as well as political economy. Increases in poverty, disease and hatred, international wars, domestic crimes—that is what you are bringing us; that is your birthday gift! There is every reason to be proud of it. Thank you, Dr. Auguérand!

The *Balai* published an even more violent article, whose title alone is enough to convey its tenor: *Let's kill the old!* That deliberately excessive cynical piece obtained less credit but further disturbed the anxious minds of old people. A few thought it wise to declare, at the family dinner, that they had no intention of taking the treatment. Very rarely was any credence given to these assertions—which were, in any case, never sincere, for all those who made them had simultaneously made secret plans to visit to the dispensary at Neuilly the following morning.

Let us hasten to add that families could be found, in fairly considerable numbers, in which worthy individuals rejoined

225

in the idea of conserving the authors of their days and nights for longer, along with the delights or annoyances that those days and nights involved.

The evening was marked by a certain effervescence in the brasseries of the Latin Quarter. Professor Graunerr was roundly abused there, especially among medical students, who were more directly interested. There was much comment on *Pal*'s caricature; according to all the evidence, the movements in high places delayed by maintenance of a pontiff and others who would soon follow his example would produce stasis in all the echelons of the medical hierarchy, and the slowness of promotion could only be further accentuated henceforth. The younger generations foresaw themselves treading water interminably, condemned to vegetate indefinitely...

By eleven o'clock that night, the opinion had become unanimous; the name of Graunerr was no longer spoken without the accompaniment of insulting epithets and substantives borrowed from zoology. At that very moment, a summons to a meeting launched by the president of IASUE (the International Association of Students and University Employees) was circulated through the cafés, inviting the comrades to gather in the great hall of the Maison Syndicale at midnight to discuss what action to take.

An immense procession immediately formed, under the rallying cry: "Down with Graunerr!" When the file attempted to cross the bridges, it was driven back by the police; a rather hectic skirmish ensued, but without any serious incidents. At midnight, the streets suddenly emptied, the students having gone to the Maison. The meeting lasted more than three hours; numerous speeches were made there, all hostile to the reform. The president's oration was cheered:

"To hell with living longer! To succeed—that's what matters!"

A motion was passed demanding that a delegation be sent immediately to the Ministry of Information, in order to present the grievances of the young and to demand the pure and simple maintenance of the rules presently in place for the retirement of teaching staff.

"What about the private clientele? Will you have a law to constrain them from continuing to going to the old men for as long as they survive? You'll be competing with their glory, won't you?"

Consternation followed this interjection, then a clamor: "Down with the old men!"—soon followed by "Death to the old men!"

For ten minutes the agitation was extreme; in the overheated room, faces and brains were congested with anger; without discussion, a motion was adopted setting up an action committee to organize a demonstration that same morning at the Auguérand Institute. The agenda was suspended without the session closing; the students went *en masse* to gather at the villa in Neuilly, preceded by a red and gold corporative banner bearing the motto: *Make way for the young!*

The reassembly was fixed for nine o'clock, in front of the Fontaine Michel.

For the rest of the night there was calm in the streets, if not in minds—for the world of the schools was not the only one to become agitated, and there were soon multiple proofs of the fact. Shortly before daybreak, the violet placards of the anarchist faction were displayed on the walls: *The bourgeois are perpetuating themselves!* Paraphrasing the article in the *Balai*, the leader of the proletariat urged the faubourgs to open revolt against the intrusion of this new abuse, of which the poor would bear the brunt, as always.

"It is with your lives that they will increase theirs! In prolonging your existence, they are prolonging your misery, in order to exploit it for longer! They're insulting you with illusory benefits and underhanded promises! Don't let them get away with it! Break the fratricidal dream of the exploiters in the egg!"

The *Cloche d'ébène*, a free newspaper was distributed by the thousand at factory gates; it announced for the afternoon a challenge to Clément Boeuf: "We summon the government to

227

declare, yes or no, whether it intends to introduce disturbance into the social order and introduce to the peace of the world a ferment of individual and national hatreds."

Thus France, which had once preceded other nations in the path of adventurous reform, and which had now become pragmatic, the old France of epics, was reduced to preaching prudence and dogmatizing about egotism! At least it must be recognized that in that, as in everything else, it went from one extreme to the other and remained faithful to its character, if not its program, since it was ready to put the brake on innovators with the same passion with which, previously, it had given them free rein.

Immediately, Germany took the opposite stance to the thesis sustained here; the official press declared that all progress must be welcomed, under pain of obscurantism, and that, if it brought difficulties in application or secondary inconveniences resulting from side-effects of the principal benefit, that was no reason to reject it, but rather toward the problems off by remedies that remained to be found and would be found.

"France is wrong; it ought to be proud of its brainchild and of the progress that, once again, is emerging therefrom!"

Was Germany sincere and truly disinterested? Was it not trying, by flattering our proverbial vanity, to bring about a reversal of French opinion? Did its affectation of liberalism not conceal the already-nascent hope of further increasing, in favor of the Germanic lands, their numerical superiority, and of finally crushing us?

The *Cloche d'ébène* affirmed it: "We will not be duped by the Alboche!"

The idea caught on; after two hours, the supporters of Auguérand and his method were deemed to be affiliated to the interests of Germany; they were the *Alboche*. By contrast, the adversaries of longevity inevitably became the promoters of national defense; they were the *Frangins*.

Once again, two parties were born and constituted, furiously irreducible, as is fitting as soon as it is a matter of life and death. And the sun rose, radiantly, in the clear sky on the day of the twenty-sixth of July, which would decide the fate of future humankinds...

V. Alboches and Frangins

Thus, the question had unexpectedly become political and national, and two irreducible parties had formed on the night of the twenty-fifth and twenty-sixth of July: those who thought in the German fashion and wanted to prolong life, the Alboches; and those who thought along the French lines and claimed, in rejecting Auguérand's invention, to be maintaining the fraternity between individuals and peoples, the Frangins. The struggle commence with the day. Within the first hour, in fact, it became known that the Syndicate of State Functionaries, Employees and Workers had called a general strike for the day of the twenty-sixth; that it was demanding the strict application of the rules to all the title-holders of administrative offices who reached the age-limit; that it was demanding from the minister an immediate formal undertaking not to effect in future any prolongation of employment capable of hindering due advancement—under threat, in case of resistance, of continuing the strike until the petitioners received satisfaction.

All public services came to a stop: the mail, refuse collection, transport and the innumerable monopolies. Paris was about to be deprived on bread by the administration, of vegetables and fish by the railways, of meat by the abattoirs, of the greater part of its vehicles, of light—and, in consequence, of theaters. Food prices shot up instantaneously. Departing trains remained in the stations; the others stopped mid-route; no French steamship lifted anchor, but several made ports of call wherever they happened to be, awaiting telegraphic instructions from the Syndicate.

At seven o'clock it became known that the UOLS (Union of Officers on Land and Sea) had joined the protest.

The government panicked. A hastily-convened Council of Ministers affirmed that the demands were legitimate and the acquired rights were to be respected; they saved face by say-ing that Dr. Auguérand's discovery was too recent and too uncertain in its range to permit the introduction of any modifi-cation whatsoever to the laws and decrees relating to various age limits.

"Very well—but what then?"

"Then people will live, thanks to the elixir, but will no longer have a means of living? At sixty years, a third of life, people would have interminable days before them—twice as many as behind—but no bread for those years, and no right to earn their bread? Is that logical? Is it just? Is it even possible?"

The Minister had thought, by reaching an agreement, that he was begetting himself out of a major embarrassment, but he had merely ended up creating a new one. The adversaries of reform were certainly not soothed, for they mistrusted official promises, and they had a strong suspicion that the Minister had not found a solution to a difficult problem, but had merely displaced it, and even aggravated it further.

As for those who wanted to take advantage of the dis-covery and get their hands on the treatment while it was free, their number had probably only diminished in a minuscule proportion, but their serenity, and most of all they joy, was significantly corroded. One was obliged to suppose that they uncertainty of material existence would deter a good third of those future appetites; their number scarcely counted any te-nacious partisans save for the sick, who would not consent to give in, valetudinarians who were rubbing along, the rich who had their bread guaranteed and petty pensioners who were content with very little.

"Them again! Will it be necessary, for another century, to pay the pensions of those useless creatures? What a burden for the Treasury—what an ever-increasing burden! It will end in bankruptcy, and in the meantime, an increase in taxes will be unavoidable to nourish these still-healthy idlers to whom the right to work will be refused!"

Thus, the drinkers of the elixir became social parasites, and the responsible government found itself driven, by the very urgency of matters, to dread the reform, to fear its budgetary consequences, and, in consequence, to oppose it in principle.

"To Hell with Auguérand! The animal has backed us into a fine corner!"

The Treasury Minister, a fellow possessed of a subtle intelligence, proposed that the affair be gently put to sleep.

"Difficulties of this sort," he said, "seem new, but aren't. Our situation is analogous to that of any government confronted with an innovator whose discovery threatens to disrupt the established equilibrium and the adopted harmony. There aren't two ways of governing, but only one that's good; a little more difficult today than before, but it's still the only one: roll the client over to safeguard the moment. History can therefore point us in the direction of the remedy for our situation. It's identical to that of the Church in confrontation with Galileo, another genius who proposed an inconvenient truth. It's important to obtain a retraction of that truth. Do we lack the coercive mans that our predecessors possessed? You possess others. If Auguérand is disinterested, it will be more expensive, that's all, and it will certainly be less expensive than adopting his system.

"If we can't buy the doctor, let's buy his judges; let's address ourselves to the technical committee and extract a second report from them, full of restrictions. The mistake was not thinking of this plan yesterday, when it would have been less costly; a graver mistake, I regret to say, was the official dinner offered to the inventor by the President of the Republic. We're pressed for time, but we can still repair the situation. The note issued by the council this morning constitutes excellent preparation for this retreat.

"The declaration we need to obtain from the committee members is this: 'The public has drawn exaggerated conclusions from our report; Dr. Auguérand's discovery is real, but it does not have the enormous scope that has been credited to it; it seems to be able, in truth, to increase life by a few years, but it is important to be wary of the excess of philanthropy that

will draw opinion to admit too rapidly that which is insufficiently demonstrated.'

"One point, that's all. As to what this declaration will
cost us, don't worry about it; I'll find the necessary funds. The
question, returned for further study, will become akin to that
of Galileo in a quarter of a century: our successors will untan-
gle it."

The Minister of Police accepted the mission of handling
the negotiations; he did, in fact, hold various information of a
highly confidential character relating to some of the honorable
committee members, excellent strings that permitted him the
hope of acquiring a prompt acquiescence to the administration's desires.

The president was the first to be summoned. Professor
Graunerr promised to renounce the treatment, ostensibly, and
only to continue it under the title of a scientific experiment, *in
anima nobili*.[42] On Axilo, there was leverage via Russia, and
on Touposcoff via the princes, and on Letigre via the ladies.
But Legrand-Gauthier as seized, as soon as the subject was
broached, by an indignation of Corneillian proportions.

"Auguérand is a man of genius! His discovery is an immense benefit! You won't stifle it like this!"

He threatened to reveal the plot to Thismonard. He could
only be reduced to silence by a charge of indecent behavior
motivated by the complaint of a neighbor; he would have to be
released the following day, in recognition of the fact that he
had merely put his nose to her window, but a respite of twen-
ty-four hours was sufficient to liquidate an affair of State.

While these maneuvers kept the corridors of officialdom
busy, the streets went crazy.

At eight thirty-seven Thimonard arrived, breathless, at
the Neuilly clinic; he exploded into the doctor's study and
threw a stack of newspapers on to the desk.

---

[42] Moved by nobility.

"Oof! What a crowd! It took me three hours to get here, and I wouldn't have managed it if I hadn't had the idea of going round via Suresnes."

"Are there that many people?"

"Fantastic! You've taken precautions?"

"I think so, we've made arrangements as best we could,"

"I'm pleased to see you so calm. You're ready for anything, then?"

"Damn it! You're asking too much of me; I've made the best dispositions I can, and it wasn't easy. When I got back from the Élysée last night after the banquet, I got down to business. I worked all night. We have six dispensaries, and enough elixir for two thousand people, or thereabouts. For the first day, you'll admit that that isn't bad. Tomorrow, we'll do better."

"What's that you say? Tomorrow! Who's talking about tomorrow? It's a matter of today; there might not be a tomorrow. Have you read the papers?"

"I haven't had time."

"So you don't know anything about what's happening in Paris?"

"No. What?"

"Rioting, perhaps a revolution."

"Bah—in honor of what saint?"

"You, you fool."

"Me?"

"Listen to the street, you Archimedes. Can't you hear that, in the street?"

"Last night, I saw the unemployed forming a queue outside the gate, doubtless in the hope of selling their place to some well-off bourgeois; they exchanged a few revolver shots to punctuate the darkness.

"Don't laugh! It's not the time. Hurry up and understand. All Paris is up in arms. A general strike has been declared. They don't want the elixir, they don't want longevity, and they don't want you!"

"What?"

233

"You're a public enemy, a disturber of the universe—and as if that weren't enough, you're a national peril, an agent of Germany, an Alboche! The tricolor rosette is a rallying call against you. It's patriotic to detest you. That's where we are! It's a tight spot!"

The inventor slowly extended a hand toward the newspapers.

"Yes," said the other, "look at them, for your edification—but time's pressing."

Auguérand unfolded a paper and scanned it, skeptical at first, then stupefied, reading headlines or odd sentences at hazard, his eyes wide.

Suddenly, he blushed with shame. "Oh, Thismonard! The youth of the schools?"

"That's where the movement began."

"The workers too?"

"You're working to exploit them."

"And the civil servants! The army!"

"You're hindering promotion."

"They're losing their heads. Someone's leading this campaign. Who? My colleagues?"

"No one. It's happening all by itself."

"Come on, come on...I don't understand. It's pure madness."

"Madness? Wisdom? Even I've started to wonder who's right—you or them."

Auguérand let himself fall into an armchair. "Fifty years I've worked, and worked for them...for you know, my friend, to what aim I've worked doggedly, and that I didn't want either they money or their applause. You've seen me at work, you've followed my thinking every day and my lifelong efforts. To become in the end...what? An evildoer!"

"That's what you are! Your discovery is inconvenient for the immense majority of individual interests; thus, it is being suppressed—and you'll suffer the same fate, if you resist."

"Ah! Their justice..."

"That's not the question, or not yet. They will talk about justice over your coffin and in books. In the meantime, hold your nerve, be worthy of yourself! For the moment, it's a matter of warding off the blow. They're marching on Neuilly. At this moment, the students are setting out, banner at the head."

Auguérand screwed up the newspaper, threw it on the floor.

"Be bold, Patrice! I like you better that way—you're more like yourself."

"You said that they're marching on Neuilly."

"To demonstrate, nothing more—but don't trust that; there are too many of them. Many men united have need of brutal gestures. Expect trouble!"

"A handful of loudmouths, in sum..."

"Hundreds of thousands!"

"But the police..."

"General strike: no police. Besides, the government won't compromise itself for you."

"The President and his Ministers seemed delighted yesterday evening—even to excess, for their eulogies almost overwhelmed me."

"Yesterday! The wind has changed. They've let you go. You're the Alboche. Anyway, what could the brigands of the Sûreté do against such an avalanche? It would need the army—which has joined the strike. You can no longer expect anyone. You're on your own."

"That will scarcely change me..."

"What is going to change is the situation. Here it is— listen carefully. The queue of the unemployed extends as far as the Porte Maillot. There, it's a crush—a barrage of humans and wheels. All the carriages in Paris are cluttering the Étoile and the twelve avenues. The provinces are arriving by car and airplane. The whole field at the airport is white with wings. Fortunately, the Metro, the Tube[43] and the Telegraph have

---

[43] The system of Pneumatic Tube Transport invented by William Murdoch, which propelled small packages contained in

stopped. Fortunately, too, the students have set off too late; they won't be able to catch up with you. All that's in our favor."

"And everyone's against me—everyone?"

"No, my friend, but it comes to the same thing. Think about it. You have on your side, in the crowd, the poor old people who took candor as far as getting up at dawn to come to the fountain; they'll be mocked, abused, knocked down, trampled underfoot; they'll make a carpet of them. Against you, you have the unemployed, who won't be able to sell their places because no one can get to them any longer: discontent, followed by fury. They'll want to console themselves with a drop of elixir, and if you don't open the gates, they'll climb over. Dilemma: gate, or pillage."

"Good..."

"There remain those who are coming from behind, three-quarters of whom are your enemies. Their principled hostility won't prevent every one of them, individually, from carrying away a liter of existence under his arm, two if he can. Thus, they'll come in through the open breach like the rest and pillage what remains, if anything does remain—which seems improbable."

"Improbable." Auguérand took out his watch. "Seven minutes to," he said.

"You distribution of elixir is advertised for nine o'clock. "In ten minutes, the grounds will be invaded."

"Just so," said the inventor. "In ten minutes."

---

capsules, was more extensively developed in Paris, from 1866 onwards, than anywhere else. In actuality, it survived for some years after 1941, not being finally abandoned until 1984, but its importance had been declining throughout the 20th century.

VI. The Tragic Morning

There was amazement all over the world when people learned about France's attitude. Since midnight, the telegraph had launched the disconcerting news all the way to the antipodes: *Paris opposes the adoption of longevity*. At first, people hesitated to believe it, and when certainty imposed itself, they could hardly comprehend it. Then the successive dispatches brought the arguments against the Macrobians.

The arguments obtained, in the main, scant success; people were glad to find an opportunity to observe once again the stubbornly paradoxical character of the French mind, and almost everywhere they mocked our incoherence. The United States of North America, which still practiced tyranny and where people counted for very little, were almost alone in thinking like us. The English on the contrary, with their marked respect for the individual, came out strongly in favor of the liberty that everyone ought to have to live or not to live, at their own risk. Spain and voluptuous South America could ask for no more than to enjoy blissful existence for as long as possible, and rejected the worrying problems with the flick of a fan. Italy, where so many races are hybridized, hesitated and was divided. But black Africans persisted in dancing with joy in honor of Auguérand. The people of the Far East, imbued with respect for their ancestors, were religiously indignant that anyone might refuse the prolongation of old age. The Panslavists, strong in numbers and rich in space, even more than the Pangermanists, had sound reasons for adopting a system that would increase their importance. In brief, with the exception of the United States and a few northern Italian provinces, the concert of world opinion condemned us, in order to align themselves with the German theory: "Let us first welcome the benefit, and we shall deal with the difficulties it will provoke."

That was very easy to say, but not to do.

"France is her own mistress; Auguérand is in France, and his formula also. Who will insure humankind against the perils of Parisian bluntness? There is everything to fear from the impulsive mob, for which the head of a scientist is of no more account than that of a king, and which will raze a clinic even more readily than a Bastille."

This hypothesis—which, moreover, was not lacking in plausibility—inevitably gave rise to an immediate question: "Is it tolerable that the caprice of Paris should deprive humankind of a conquest that belongs to everyone?"

Thus posed, the question admitted but one answer: "No!"

Everyone was unanimous on this point. Even in the United States opinion was against us; in spite of their administrative despotism, they professed too fervent a worship with regard to inventions to consent to a crime against such a precious godsend.

"But how can we obviate the evil that is in preparation? Declare war on France? Send aircraft armed with bombs over Paris? They'll arrive too late. Paris has the means to respond; their victory would be uncertain; their advent would exasperate the capital and the worst excesses would be even more to be feared. Demand that the government protect the inventor and save his discovery? If the government cedes to the injunction of the powers, popular fury will turn against it and overturn it before it can act."

The morning telegrams aggravated the anxiety; with the day, the apprehensions of the night became a reality. When the magnitude of the agitation in the Schools and the Faubourgs became known, when news spread of the defection of the administrative services and that—more serious—of the police, and when accounts were read of the ever-increasing rush of the people toward Neuilly, a bleak discouragement disturbed minds everywhere. It was, however, of short duration almost everywhere; Negroes, Muslims and the Chinese were able to resign themselves by virtue of religious habit or innate philosophy. The others rose up in revolt.

"Paris is in possession of the life of the world, and will not hand it over!"

Consciences waxed indignant against the abuse of power; the bankruptcy of a delightful hope irritated two billion disappointed egotisms; the Auguérand discovery appeared more precious as the risk of being deprived of it increased. The philanthropy of a scientist who would deliver his formula to the human family gratuitously rendered more odious the exaction of a people who were taking possession of something that belonged to everyone in order to destroy it. From the depths of steppes and the slopes of mountains, from every country that the sun scorches or neglects, a long murmur rose up, and, as in the times of barbarian migrations, the eyes of races, charged with wrathful envy, turned toward the garden of France, where people lived in comfort and were never content.

In the majority of financial centers, Stock Exchanges registered considerable falls. In various places, our residents and colonists were insulted, their businesses boycotted, and some were pillaged. In Ohio, the populace lynched and revolverized three negroes, in the capacity of French citizens, and thus responsible.

These local measures were far from sufficient. It became urgently imperative to give a more solid satisfaction to world opinion. Governments provided it without delay, on the initiative of the Pangermanlich Republik; at eight o'clock in the morning, Berlin convened a telephonic Diplomatic Congress for eight thirty. The session did not open until eight thirty-three, however; the delay was due to France, which was expected, but did not appear—not because the French Republic was refusing to talk to the other powers, but simply because the general strike, by shutting down the power stations, isolated our ministries, even though the ambassadors maintained Hertzian communication with their respective governments and particular individuals, more favored than those in power, still benefited from automatic correspondence.

In spite of the precautions normally surrounding these kinds of conferences and protecting them against the curiosity of reportage—precautions that had been increased for such a grave circumstance—the secret got out. As the measures of prudence had been exceptional, the hypotheses they provoked were no less exaggerated; the fact that the diplomats were trying to hide served to prove what the whistle-blowers were able to suppose.

By eight forty a still-vague rumor of unknown origin was circulating in Paris, and at eight forty-seven the *Balai* posted a categorical pantogram: *Comminatory injunction of the powers; they are taking Auguérand under their protection.*

Immediately, the *Drapeau Rouge* replied with another pantogram: *Ministry refuses to take part in Berlin Congress.*

Paris became indignant at the first, and cheered the second, erroneous though it was. The two parties created a national solidarity in the face of the foreigner, legitimated it and necessitated it; the people and the government were marching in convoy for once. If the intrusion of the foreigner lent the demonstration a patriotic character, the adhesion of the government conferred a legitimacy upon it; henceforth, all action would be licit, as an expression of national pride, and the disorder itself, implicitly approved by the authorities, became equivalent to order, or even better, being summary and more rapid.

People did not reason in respect of these things; they felt them; a psychic electric current united the crowd. A shameful anxiety ran through the sparse Auguérandists, who began to doubt that they were right, and were dissolved even more than before in the great wave. At the same time, an enormous clamor rose up on the long hill that extends from the Étoile to the Seine: "Vive la France! Down with the Alboches!"

At the same moment, too, by a sort of telegraphic repercussion, the world learned this news: *The Parisian rioters are invading the villa at Neuilly.*

There was nothing to it, however. The most determined, the most impatient and, above all, the nearest, were now hesitating to risk the adventure. Some were even giving up, and trying to get away.

In fact, at eight fifty, the *Balai* had displayed a new pantogram in Neuilly, formulated in scarcely reassuring terms: *The Direct Action Committee informs citizens that they will be risking the most serious dangers if they penetrate the Macro-bians' residence.*

No one was unaware that the Committee made it a point of honor never to issue vain threats; thus, they were going to take action.

"They're going to blow it up!" The Clinic's butler, on duty at the door, ran to advise his master. He found him in the drawing-room, in company with Thismonad.

The doctor replied calmly: "That's all right. Warn the sanatorium; it has to be evacuated. Then come back."

"Shall we open the gates at nine o'clock?"

"No."

"What if they climb over?"

"Let them—and take care of yourself."

A more furious howl thundered outside: "Down with the Alboche! Death to the Alboches!"

"Monsieur hears that?"

Without further response, Auguérand went to the window and placed a hand on the handle. The butler withdrew.

The pitiless Thismonard was only able to respect his friend's meditation for twenty seconds. "You're looking at the trees for the last time? Bid them farewell, my friend—and the lawn where the young octogenarian deer are dancing, and the grass that your cows have been grazing for a third of a century, in order to inform you of the means of being like a God, you who wanted to give human beings as much as God had given them. Go and see the flasks and alembics, before they're smashed! Go and inspect the sanatorium and make a tour of the menagerie for one last time, while their stones are still standing. Let's go pat an adieu on the withers of the beautiful beasts and the hands of the brave people that you've rejuvenated out there in the depths of the park. If you want, we can release the tiger, as its brethren will be coming in..."

Auguérand cracked the knuckle of his middle finger against his palm. "You're annoying me with your infantile lyricism. Shut up."

Thismonard was only susceptible in favor of his great man. He shut up. But his mutism was not to last long; to occupy himself, he immediately consulted his watch—and shook his head, for the hand had rotated; then he went to the barometer, which he started tapping with his fingernail, and shook his head again.

"That's the only thing that can save us! The artillery of a downpour is the most effective against a mob…but the imbecile's rising!"

Auguérand did not hear him. Rigid at the window, pale in the green-tinted light that was falling toward him from the treetops, his features set, his hand still resting on the handle, he was staring at the curtain of foliage veiling the gate to the grounds, and his lips were moving feverishly in silent speech.

"You resemble a pilot who can hear a storm coming, but can't see anything…"

With these words, as if his remark had revealed the evidence of a verity that he had formulated without comprehending it, Thismonard saw himself in exactly the same situation as a shipwreck-victim on a reef in mid-ocean. In that house, besieged by a human tempest, there was against him—against the two of them—the monstrous force, rumbling there behind the foliage, ready to mount its assault, of a still-invisible rising tidal wave, which was about to appear, with its surf of red faces, in the gaps in the verdure: the anonymous wave of a hundred thousand angers. Death, without a doubt.

Clearly, with prescience that beasts possess, his flesh perceived the approach of death, and in the depths of his being a magnetic certainty notified him of the supreme moment. Of his artificial cheerfulness and his energy, nothing now remained; an animal fear numbed his muscles. In order to be less alone, he wanted to draw nearer to the other, and he observed that his legs were trembling.

"Oh, no!" he said. "Not that way!"

With a vigorous effort, he shook his soul and went to the window.

"Well? Have you decided?"

The inventor did not move; his tall figure seemed petrified.

"Wake up!"

Already, Thismonard was raising a hand to bring it down on Auguérand's shoulder, but his gesture remained suspended, for he had just perceived on the master's impassive profile a tear, which ran through the grooves of his wrinkles, and thought he was seeing a statue weep. Before that august dolor of the imagination, before those tears of the mind, he became aware of his pettiness, and the indignity of bestial fears. What was the death of the flesh compared with such a calvary, in which the work was about to perish in the person of the man who had brought it into the world, and knew what he had brought?

Thismonard took a step back, seized by respectful pity; the marble that he saw weeping was no longer his friend, but took on a symbolic majesty, like an outraged Christ: genius divining itself through insults and ingratitude.

VII. The End of a Dream

At that moment, above the human rumor, a metallic bell rang, clear and firm, like an alarm bell in the midst of a tempest.

"Nine o'clock!" said Thimonard.

They only heard the first stroke, greeted with a acclamation that drowned out all the rest.

"It's now..."

Only then did the inventor turn his head toward the confidant of his work, and say: "Do you believe that it's necessary?"

"What?"

"To punish them."

Horrified, Thismonard understood. The demigod was holding the life of the world in his hand and weighing it. That immobility, which a superficial examination had taken for dejection, was the sternness of the judge before which the world had been summoned, and was hesitating over his own verdict! Had he shed the two tears still shining on his face for humankind, before the condemnation, or over the work, before its abolition?

"Oh, Master, you're thinking...of..."

"I'm thinking about it."

Since the clock had chimed, the unemployed, with an imperious rhythm, were intoning the appeal: "El-ix-ir! El-ix-ir!"

"You want to?" Thismonard continued. "You could?"

"I no longer know where duty lies. I no longer know what my rights are."

Suddenly, an immense clamor of triumph drowned out all articulate voices.

"Are they climbing over?" Thismonard asked.

But Auguérand pointed at the sky. The other raised his eyes sand uttered an exclamation. The Direct Action Committee's airplane was arriving over the villa, the yellow letters DA on its violet wings: an enormous butterfly of death floating on the wind of menace.

"Quickly! The caltrops!"

Thismonard raced to the handle controlling the blades lying in the grass, which were stood upright at night in order to prevent nocturnal landings; the meadow was covered with lances.

Auguérand slowly raised both hands, in a despairing gesture that might have been a blessing or a curse.

"They wanted it..." He let his arms fall back, then, forcefully: "Come on!"

"The DA have seen the blades. They're turning."

"Their presence is protecting us. No one dares come in while they're here, for fear of bombs. They're giving us time. Come quickly."

"Where?"

"The laboratory."

"You're decided?"

They cross the room. As they reached the door, a tele-phone bell brought them to a halt."

"Should we answer it?"

"What good would it do?"

"Let me listen. One never knows. I'll catch up with you..."

"As you wish. I'll give you thirty seconds."

"Hello...? Hello...? Yes, the Clinic... No, it's Thismo-nard, his friend... Him? Impossible—busy... As if to him...who's speaking?"

Framed in the doorway, Auguérand waited. Thismo-nard's face, leaning over the apparatus, expanded and red-dened. His eyes, illuminated with joy, were raised to extend toward the door a gaze like that of a dog wanting to impart some good news to its master.

"I'll pass to your message, Monsieur l'Ambassadeur. Please wait. Patrice!"

"Speak quickly."

"The German Ambassador, by order of the Congress, of-fers you shelter with the benefit of diplomatic immunity. I addition, the Pangermanliche informs you confidentially that it is disposed to adopt your system for itself: honors, an annual pension or immediate capital, name your figure. The ambassa-dor's aircraft is on its way to pick you up. Your response?"

"That which another Frenchman made at Waterloo. Get lost."[44]

---

[44] I have translated "Vas-y," accurately enough, as "Get lost," but the dialogue makes it clear that this is a euphemism, and that we are actually dealing with what 19th century French literary parlance called "the word of Cambronne"—i.e. some-thing unprintable. When General Cambronne's command was surrounded at Waterloo and invited to surrender, he refused, and the rumor was swiftly put about that he had replied: "The guards do not surrender; they die!" It was closely followed by a counter-rumor alleging that what he had actually said was "Merde!"—which can be translated, in the appropriate con-

"Patrice..."

"Get lost, I tell you."

"Think about it! Cambronne survived the battle, but our fate is sealed, I can feel it—it's the end! Patrice, think of your work, which would be saved..."

"To serve what end? Hatred! He's just admitted it—they'll use me against people, and I've worked for people. They're perverting it. So much the worse for them."

"You're speaking in anger..."

"In complete discouragement. What you're going to tell them translates my whole thought; I can't put it any more exactly. Go on."

"Patrice, we'll die badly...."

"I've lived well."

"Irrevocable, Patrice?"

"Yes."

"Let the future judge, them and you!"

"Let them judge us, since I'm judging. Hurry up and join me."

Auguérand went out. Slowly, Thismonard returned to the apparatus, initially with a plaintive expression.

"Well, perhaps he's right." He shrugged one shoulder. "Bah!" Then, with a devil-may-care gesture, he gripped the receiver "Hello...? Monsieur l'Ambassador...?

Perfectly: I've transmitted your proposals to the doctor. His response...yes, well, his response: that of Cambronne, Monsieur l'Ambassador. My respects."

He hung up, and then burst out laughing in the corridor, as he galloped in pursuit of his friend. On the front steps of the

---

text, as "Fuck off!" rather than the literal "Shit!" French writers frustrated by not being allowed to represent speech as Frenchmen actually spoke, led by Victor Hugo, began referring to "the word of Cambronne" whenever they wanted to signal to the reader that an obscenity of that kind had been uttered.

246

building, however, he recoiled under the pressure of the almighty din coming from the street.

"The laughing's over, now."

To reach the laboratory it was necessary to cross half the park; having slid momentarily through the bushes, the pathway went around the lawn in the open. Thismonard, still running full tilt, went into the shade of the trees; his pace caused him to collide with flies that were trying to buzz amid the human racket.

"My word! They don't seem to suspect that they're hearing the vibration of a unique moment in the history of the world. They're circling around, as they did yesterday, as they will tomorrow…uh! Tomorrow? Their arbor won't be so comfortable tomorrow."

At the edge of the wood he perceived the doctor, fifty paces ahead, hastening along the uncovered pathway. Almost immediately, he heard the roar of an engine, and a shadow passed close by. Twenty meters from the ground, the Direct Action airplane, coming back after describing a horizontal circle, was now heading for the laboratory. Two human silhouettes were profiles between its wings; one as holding a rigid object, a staff or a rifle, which dipped. A detonation, as sharp as the crack of a whip, clicked imperceptibly in the din, and then a second.

Thismonard saw Auguérand throw his arms wide, in an attitude of crucifixion, and fall to his knees on the threshold of the laboratory. He raced forward, paying no heed to the airplane, which was already passing over the roof.

"Patrice! Patrice? You're hurt?"

Auguérand, raising himself up on his elbow, held out a bunch of keys, and murmured, feebly: "Everything…quickly."

"Everything? Destroy it?"

"Yes."

Thismonard tried to search for the wound.

"No…go!"

"My poor old…"

"Quickly, go."

The dying man collapsed, and his forehead struck the step of the building in with the work had been born with a dull thud. The stone was already stained red.

Thismonard said: "The end of a dream!"

He had to step over the corpse to enter the laboratory. The sanctuary as still entirely impregnated with the master and his night's toil. There, four hours earlier, he had been laboring to complete the work of half a century, full of joy at being able to extend his benefit of the races of humankind...

Thismonard knelt down momentarily—but it was not the time for meditation; he chased away his own.

"Quickly, and everything! We have but to obey. I'm the executor of his will."

Then, methodically—for he had a very methodical mind—he started destroying. First, he emptied the carboys of elixir into the sink, in order that no one could use them, and while the years of human existence glugged viscously toward the sewer, he smashed the flasks, bottles and alembics, in order that no analysis could reveal the chemical composition of the liquids therein.

"His formulae! His treatise!"

He opened the writing-desk and took out armfuls of paper, catalogues, labeled files, stacks of notes; he stuffed the stove, in which the flames sizzled. The task did not take long; five minutes sufficed to annihilate a life.

"Have I forgotten anything? Oh! An idea! Of course, yes—that's the safest way."

With a liter of gasoline, he made a pool on the floor and set fire to it; he scarcely had time to throw himself backwards; his clothes and hands caught fire.

"A pyre for you, my great man! I'll offer you the funeral rites of Hercules."

He ran outside in order to lift up the cadaver and drag it into the conflagration, but, to his great amazement, Auguérand had disappeared. Only the bloody stone step attested to the scene of the drama.

"Someone's picked him up, carried him away, perhaps saved him. Who?"

A hired aircar was flying straight ahead, over the trees. The caltrops on the lawn had been retracted into the grass. How? In the distance, in front of the sanitarium, silhouettes were running away; others, closer, emerging from the trees, ran forward howling. The unemployed had climbed over the gate.

"There he is!"

"It's not him!"

"Yes!"

"No!"

"Elixir! Elixir!"

"Death to the Alboche!"

"Death to the traitors!"

"Elixir! Elixir!"

In an instant, Thismonard was surrounded by faces, fists and cries, and driven back against the wall. Behind him, the fire was crackling; further away, to the left, the animals in the menagerie was roaring and bellowing in terror.

"Fire!"

"It's been set on fire!"

"It's the Action!"

"It's the Alboche!"

"Elixir! Elixir!"

In the deafening racket it was scarcely possible to make out the voices, and he rubbed his burned hands with a mechanical gesture.

"Where's the elixir, you?"

"Thrown away."

"Auguérand?"

"Gone"

"His formula?"

"Burned."

"The elixir, you were asked!"

"Down the drain, I told you."

"Take that, you bastard!"

Thismonard fell, his left eye and brain traversed by a bullet.

They searched the house and the outbuildings for the inventor, without finding him anywhere. The already dense crowd in the garden mounted an assault on the balconies, came in through the windows, crowded into the rooms and smashed everything, only looting with difficulty for want of sufficient freedom of movement. Those who had succeeded in stealing some work of art were soon forced to let go of it, because it was digging into their sides, but they did so in such a way as to leave nothing but shards. Almost everything was destroyed within a hundred minutes.

The massacre of the animals offered the amusement of a sport; the tiger, rendered furious by blows of canes and human baying, lashed out with its claws and was riddled with bullets.

At eleven ten, fire broke out on the first floor of the house, lit by a prankster. The youth of the Schools arrived; it generously set out to put out the fire that it had demanded the previous day. That disaster might yet be circumscribed.

At one o'clock, nothing more was rising above the clinic but swirls of inoffensive smoke. In the absence of any kind of brigade, the students had spontaneously taken on the role of the police, and carried it out with the conviction that young people bring to the exercise of any temporary authority. They evacuated the area, only permitting their own people to go into the buildings. They could be seen prowling around inside, in quest of things they would not specify to anyone; it may be supposed that they were searching for a forgotten flask, some vestige of the great secret, the fortune.

These efforts had no compensation at all; the Auguérand formula remained as undiscoverable as his person.

The fact spread into the streets and throughout the world. Already, Paris was experiencing a vague sadness; no one admitted it out loud, very few people having dared, and the newspapers made no mention of it, but it was not necessary to express it to feel it. All thinking people estimated that they had undoubtedly been too hasty; they blamed it on the panic.

They went to bed with that thought that evening, and the on the morning of the twenty-seventh, Paris had a very clear notion of having experienced a fit of madness the previous day.

The public services resumed their normal functioning as if nothing had happened. In spite of that affected reserve, however, the sentiments that the world had professed against us the day before spread among us against the perpetrators of the vandalism.

The curiosity-seekers who had headed on foot toward Neuilly that day were almost as numerous as the protesters of the day before. Their ranks filed slowly along the avenue, with long gazes at the twisted gates, the devastated gardens, the brown-tinted fragments of walls, which they pointed out to one another in low voices. Until nightfall, the march-past continued, reverently, at the pace of a funeral.

During the week that followed, the ruins of the villa were the goal of an incessant pilgrimage; people came from far and wide; a few cities sent wreaths; the mourning as affirmed, opinion settled. Auguérand's discovery became inestimable from the moment that it was lost.

For a long time, the doctor's disappearance invited speculation; no one had seen him except for Thismonard, who was no longer there to say anything, and his testimony would not have cleared up the mystery anyway. The Direct Action claimed the honor of having "set fire to the glory-hole" but not of having shot the inventor. He was generally believed to be dead, but some claimed that he was still alive; some even claimed that an ambassador had taken him away in a hired aircar.

Might he not be in hiding, in Germany or elsewhere? Might he not reappear one day? Some conserved the hope, but they grew old waiting.

One certainty, at least, remained granted: human life could be prolonged.

What had been found once could be found again.

Everywhere, people started searching.

251

THE SUPREME CONFLICT

I. The Supreme Conflict

War was imminent, and even seemed inevitable, At least, this time, it really would be the last, and for good reason—necessarily, since after that supreme clash, there would be no one left on Earth to engage in other battles.

Who, then, would be able to nip the evil in the bud, prevent the conflict from breaking out, and to obtain arrangements that would satisfy everyone, or temporarily appease appetites and angers? Who would even dare to try to solve the insoluble problem, even though it was a matter of life and death for the last two peoples that still existed, and who were standing face to face, one of the two being too many if the other were to continue living on the diminished globe? The human populations, like all animal and vegetable species, only knew, and only could know, natural law, and natural law knows only one sole objective: to survive, to the detriment of others, to escape death by inflicting it on one's neighbor.

In such an urgent situation, the Society of Nations remained ineffective, for the most serious and most powerful reason of all: it no longer existed. It had disappeared a long time ago—so long that no historian or archeologists would have been capable of saying that it had ever existed.

For centuries had passed—so very many centuries, that nothing remained of us and our works. Furthermore, the new world was so different from ours that it would have had great difficulty in imagining what we were; physically and mentally, the generations of that time were so far from us that they no longer retained, of our appearance and mores, the vague notion that remains to us of our prehistoric ancestors.

To be sure, it must not be concluded that the last humans were ignorant of everything. On the contrary; our modern science, compared with theirs, would seem infantile. But they arrived so late, behind us, that our obsolete silhouette was lost in the perspective of the ages, and we had become, in their eyes, the contemporaries of the people who lived in caves and shaped the first flints.

Shocking as such an opinion might appear to us, it was not scientifically erroneous, since the planetary era that we call the Quaternary Epoch has not yet finished; the world in which we reside so proudly at the present moment is exactly the same as the one in which the humans of the Stone Age were installed, and whose difficult conquest they undertook. We inherited it from them, and are still in possession of it; it is the one in which and on which we live. Our effort is merely the continuation of theirs; our progress is merely the evolution of their initial gesture; our shelter is merely theirs, ameliorated and enlarged. But when the day comes when the present cycle will have completed its normal revolution, and the planet, re-made anew, will have ceased once again to be what it was for a few hundred centuries, no logic can oppose our history being confounded, at that distance, with that of our elders.

That epoch had arrived. Without being totally unaware of us, the prolongators of our species only recognized in us a kind of anthropoid. They did not deny us, but they only cared about our individuality, our history, our mores, our religions or our ideas in the same way that we occupy ourselves with the hordes that trampled the muddy soil of the primal forest and prowled in the moist air of new continents before the glacial period.

The globe was no longer the same. By virtue of the cooling of the sun and the consequent anemia of the Earth, everything had changed. The world map presented a new configuration. Europe was icebound, along with Asia, three-quarters of Africa and Oceania too. Of the two Americas, nothing more remained than a transversal strip elongated between the tropics. The cold having drawn gradually nearer, the two polar regions had grown progressively, advancing toward one another. Two enormous ice-caps, threatening to join up, had petrified everything and restricted life to the ribbon of the Equator. Even there, it was in distress.

An audacious explorer who risked a crossing of the hyperborean ice of Spain or Algeria would not have been able to recognize, beneath the immobilized ice-sheet, what had been continent and what had been ocean. The gentle Mediterranean, with its frost-covered waves, was imprisoned beneath a chill of which the present-day winters of Greenland or Spitzbergen can only give us an approximate idea.

One thing, however, still testified to our vanished existence: two Egyptian Sphinxes and a Pyramid, recently discovered under the mass of ice and snow, had revealed the existence of a gigantic humankind; the scientists had analyzed with amazement the vestiges of the race that had erected those colossal dwellings, which provided a scale for its formidable proportions.

For everything was small in that finishing world; everything was slender and reduced; shelters as well as individuals, occupiable space and its inhabitants. The remains of terrestrial life, strangled between the two tropics, had taken refuge on the soil of Guianas and Guineas; another continent, of recent creation had been formed by the alluvia that had succeeded in fusing the Antilles five thousand years earlier. That part of the globe, the youngest, was also the most fertile, fattened by the detritus of northern death.

That disparate condition was sufficient, and had sufficed, to engender envy in the race that found itself fatally less favored than the other. By a simple comparison of its lot with that of the opposed people, it found itself driven to irritation against a state of affairs that it considered to be iniquitous. No less logically, it eventually came to find intolerable that which it had found unjust; and, aided by poverty, was bound to pass, without any great effort, from theoretical and verbal recrimination to the effect of protest of action—the kind of action that kills.

Diplomats, who still existed, found themselves, as in our day, reduced to impotence, for words can do nothing against the harsh realities of hunger or thirst. There was, however, one difference between the fashion in which the vital problem was posed to the peoples of that time and the fashion in which it is posed to the peoples of today. One might even say that the difference was essential, although the final result would remain identical: modern men had fight in order to eat; the last men were about to fight in order to drink.

For water was in short supply. Let us try to understand why.

II. Between the Tropics

The time in which these things are happening is a long way—an exceedingly long way—ahead of us. Myriads of stars are still scintillating in the depths of space, but they are no longer those which we see today. Stars have gone out; others, which appears to us as nebulae, have condensed, ignited and shine with a bright glare. The sun, already habitable, is watching the family of planets to which it gave birth become etiolated; they persist in rotating around the original Center, but they are dying or dead. The Earth is struggling: a supreme scintillation, like that of a lamp whose oil is about to run out, emanates therefrom and still radiates, so feeble and so pale, dying out and flaring up again in fits and starts. The death of the globe has only one more obstacle to overcome: human genius.

For nine hundred years, in fact, the progression of the cold seems to have been halted; humankind has been able to find a means of drawing up to the surface of the terrestrial crust the last flickers of heat that still persist in the central nucleus. The work of decrepitude is continuing regardless in the depths of the planet, but as long as a single calorie remains in the entrails of the globe, it will belong to that sickly tyrant who will reclaim it for personal use. In order to prolong the agony of the race, humankind is delaying the death of a heavenly body.

To tell the truth, however, humankind is only delaying its superficial and visible death; as for its profound death, that is being hastened, since the consumption of the final reserves is being hastened for the species' own benefit. About that, however, it does not care; the ferocious egotism that has characterized the human species in its relationships with everything surrounding it, is still operating in its customary fashion in this instance. The human motto remains: "Us first!"—or, more precisely: "Everything for us alone!" And unanimous effort, in perfect serenity, is directed toward the realization of the common desire.

In spite of that effort, and the result obtained, the victory of humankind has been precarious, and its benefits temporary. Animal and vegetable life, maintained with such difficulty on the surface, cannot go on much longer. Poorly protected by the excessively thin layer of the atmosphere, terrestrial heat is radiating into space, lost. The exhausted soil no longer produces anything, save for the miserable plans that consent to live without warmth and almost without water. A minuscule world! Pines and maples scarcely hoist themselves above the grasses, stunted in the lifeless air, and forests of birch and oak only attain the height of our wheat.

The sun, impotent to melt the marine ice-sheets in order to cause subsequent evaporation, moves across a uniform, metallic sky devoid of nuances; no vapor rises from the oceans any longer, no refraction breaks up the light, with the result the pinks of dawn and the purples of dusk will never illuminate a horizon again. When it happens that an imperceptible cloud has traversed the sky, the news is hawked around the entire world, and rain only falls at centuries-long intervals. All the springs have run dry; rivers no longer exist. The soil, no longer furnished, has become dry and friable. In places where there were once virgin forests, glaucous lichens carpet the tropical plains; in the shelter of greenhouses, the most truculent of flowers is the timid edelweiss.

There is little wind, because of the uniform envelope of cold, condensed around an atmosphere without contrasts, but there is sometimes a slow invasion of frost, so slow that no breath of wind is perceptible, so glacial that it vitrifies stems. Nothing moves. A harsh brightness outlines forms and casts sharp shadows.

The races of wild animals, without refuge and without nourishment, have gradually become extinct, with the exception of reindeer and wolves, which humans were able to save, a few bears, and the last condors, which have survived miraculously and were perishing for lack of prey. As for domesticated species, a few still exist, thanks to the protection of the masters who have secured a subterranean refuge for them, beside them, and chemical nourishment. Even the sturdiest have become etiolated, however; by now, no more than a few pairs of bison remain, reduced to the stature of mastiffs, and a few mountain dogs scarcely as big as cats.

Humans had suffered less, in relative terms. Buried in their densely-packed cities, which were in reality nothing more than enormous, geometrically-figured ant-hills, mechanically served and artificially lit, they only went outside in exceptional circumstances and for very short periods. It is also necessary to note that the task of going up to the surface and risking death by exposure to open air was exclusively incumbent on certain social classes, charged with determined missions: the acquisition of the water that now constituted the vital problem par excellence, figured in the first rank of the necessities whose urgency was capable of driving a few humans outside their native territory.

All other needs, science supplied with the aid of metallic elements found in the depths of the Earth. Since time immemorial, humans no longer ate; they merely nourished themselves. Chemistry had procured them the means of combating the non-existence of organic resources. Official laboratories sent bottles of pills and various essences designed for communal alimentation to domiciles. As a rule, that distribution was free. By contrast, water was only distributed with extreme parsimony. On many occasions, endemic maladies resulted from the penury of the precious liquid, or even its insufficiency. Many a time, too, social crises were occasioned by restrictions from which the mass of the people suffered intensely, and several of them took on a character of menacing acuity.

In spite of the watchfulness of the public authorities, in certain malefactors—who were, for the most part, of privileged origin—a possibly-hereditary tendency to waste water had been observed; they bought it at fantastic prices, or even fabricated it clandestinely at home, for employment in ablutions or other superfluities. The discovery of this sect of lunatics had provoked riots. The factories making artificial water were carefully guarded, and its rationing carried out with strict severity.

That very severity, however, provoked revolts—but the disturbances did not last long and order as son restored, thanks to the mathematical organization of the populations, whose lives were detached from any abstract ideology.

In these conditions of existence, which confined each people to its original lodging, and forbade in an almost absolute fashion any long displacement on the surface of the ground, it seemed that the excessive promiscuity of beings of the same race could easily engender civil wars, but it also seemed that humankind scarcely had anything to dread, henceforth, from collision between nations—but the eventuality nevertheless came about, and that supreme act of folly had frightful results.

III. Future Silhouettes

It would be wrong to imagine that these last representatives of the human species were still similar to us. Physically, intellectually and morally, they were more different from us than we are from prehistoric humans, for two reasons. Firstly, they were more distant from us, by virtue of a duration much longer than the period that has now elapsed since the Stone Age. Secondly, the conditions of material life had changed infinitely more than they have done between the beginning and our day. The weather, the climate and all kinds of urgency had modified the thoughts of these beings along with their needs; simultaneously, the gradual transformation of organic functions had had the fatal result of transforming the organs themselves.

The stature of the last humans, much inferior to ours, had participated in the reduction of the habitable world and the consequent diminution of beings and things. The strongest of them scarcely attained the dimensions of a seven-year-old child, but their cranium was twice the size of ours. Their heavy head, mounted on a thin and fragile neck, oscillated incessantly. The bone-structure of their bodies, which had, over many generations, become unaccustomed to all physical effort, had been extremely impoverished by heredity, and their musculature was no less atrophied. Their limbs were incredibly small, thin and short, the arms being incapable of labor, the limbs useless for walking, and the feet tiny.

On the other hand, the hands were highly-developed—not the palms, which, no longer having anything massive to hold or anything heavy to carry, were scarcely more ample than a rose-petal, but the fingers had become immeasurably long, and spatulate at the end by virtue of habitually operating keyboards. Those fingers were manifestly much more skillful than ours in the manipulation of delicate instruments.

Machines of every sort, invented by human genius to reduce to a minimum the expense of his animal strength, had long been able to free them from all labor. Motion and locomotion being the work of the machines by which they were surrounded, the masters, liberated from all personal effort, had suffered the punishment of their idleness and become etiolated. No longer acting, no longer eating, drinking too little, hardly breathing, always sitting or lying in front of machines, they had skimpy torsos, and shortened intestines, but bulging abdomens. If their bones were frail, their joints seemed enormous, knotted by a congenital arthritis; they did not live for many years.

The entire body was pale and glabrous, as if dusty. The bald head and face no longer presented the slightest vestige of any down. Even in youth, the epidermis resembled silky paper that had been rubbed for a long time. The useless teeth had disappeared; the inferior jaw, no longer functional, had been reduced to the pint of only offering an imperceptible thickness, but that degeneration, on the one hand, and the habit of swallowing without chewing, on the other, had occasioned a frightful prognathism of a chin that was both exceedingly short and exceedingly jutting. The mouth was a short, narrow slit between thin blue-tinted lips, designed for sucking tubes or swallowing pills. The nose was similarly reduced, while the nostrils, adapted to the function of detecting the possible presence of noxious gases, and the permanent effort of breathing the dryness of the rarefying air, could raise their wings toward the eyes and open their black and horny fossas as wide as possible.

The lower part of the face being diminished by atrophy, while the forehead, by contrast, had developed excessively, the eyes had now descended into the bottom half of the face. Alongside the yawning nostrils, scarcely above them, those eyes were deep-set beneath the protuberance of the frontal bone. The very large iris, shining with keen thought, was uniformly steel-gray; the pupil, accustomed to passing from total darkness into overly brought light, was like a cat's, alternately round and slit-like. Between the violet eyelids, deprived of lashes, those human eyes were incessantly blinking or squinting, in a perpetual desire to see or to understand, and their expression was cruel.

Although they rarely did anything, these little monsters were perpetually in motion, agitated by trepidations, shaken by furtive spasms—but they no longer paid any heed to it, for their hereditary neuropathy, the consequence of long overloading of the nervous system, had become the condition of the race, and they trembled as one breathes.

The slept little, a slumber haunted by dreams. Their thoughts gave them no repose; but their hearts were dry, emotionless, pitiless and inexorably egotistical.

What were their mores? They had none, in the modern sense of the word. They had no mores, but only customs and habits—or, more exactly still, a way of life. They had laws, to be sure, and very strict ones, but the moral rules that are, for us, the very basis and principle of laws, no longer existed for them. They admitted social necessities, which they reinforced with sanctions, but without recognizing any other origin or any other value than necessity. They lived mathematically.

During too many successive eras, human beings had seen the passing of all dogmas, all conceptions of poetry and reason, all myths and all symbols, all idealistic or realistic possibilities, and their long lassitude had led them to total indifference. Abstractions, in any form, no longer interested them. The experience accumulated by so many generations and so much history had ended in a refusal to any longer to get excited for any reason whatsoever; those calculators no longer knew how to establish any distinction between good and evil.

They did not love anything. They had suppressed all passion, as a futile expenditure of strength—which is to say, a loss, and, in consequence, a danger. They lived chastely and impassively, not fearing death and not enjoying life. But the day was at hand when their egotism was about to find itself confronted by a similar egotism, and when their existence, scarcely pleasant as it was, would come under threat from the mere presence of a rival race—and when it was deemed that each one could only survive by virtue of the disappearance of the other, then, pitilessly, the abolition of each one was decided by the other.

IV. The Attack and the Riposte

Thus, the last descendants of the human species, divided into two groups, had divided up the last habitable zone of the terrestrial globe. On the equatorial slice of that icy ball, the people of Min occupied the subsoil of the continent formed in the place where the Caribbean Sea had once been; in the same segment, but almost at the antipodes, the people of Dû lived in the depths of a vast territory created by the fusion of the Malay archipelago and Melanesia.

These beings, who resembled us so little, physically and mentally, differed very little, on the other hand, from one another. Although the former appeared to be the descendants of ancient emigrants of the European race, and the latter the representatives of an autochthonous race, the same evolution over thousands of centuries had brought them to the same point of degeneration. For those little monsters, immobilized in their subterranean cells, the unique labor was the haunting of figures; their days and nights were spent seeking the solutions of problems. Their considerable brains had attained a capacity for labor and production in comparison with which we are embryonic creatures. The conquests of their minds would be unimaginable by ours.

The science they had acquired, which furnished them with everything, no longer left them anything to do except think, to discover more or to invent more, and endlessly to augment the patrimony of auxiliary forces that they annexed to their increasing debility. That they were now, in spite of that science, condemned to a disappearance that could not be long delayed, was something known, but which did not trouble them.

That in each of the two States, the calories still disposable were equitably distributed to all, was also a matter of regulation; but when the Dû learned that the Min had invented a means of drawing the residue of nuclear activity in their direction, and capturing the last molecules of hydrogen—which is to say, monopolizing heat and water—that news was equivalent, for them, to a condemnation to perish of thirst and cold.

They felt neither anger nor indignation, since such states of mind were forbidden to them, but at that very moment, a cold and formal decision was unanimously made to inflict on the adversary the death that the enemy was threatening to in-

262

flict on them. Only the immediate and total abolition of the Min could permit the Dû to continue to live; that abolition was imperative; and every mind was applied to its realization.

There was then, without any patriotism or enthusiasm, a general mobilization of sound combatants; it was effected immediately, that very minute, and it was very simple. The conscripts to the war went calmly to their rooms and sat down, their forehead in their left hand, their right hand on the table. From time to time a finger twitched, and that was all; the most terrible battles were unleashed.

For, in truth, we have no idea of what war might become, nor of the intensity of destructive power that it might have in the future. We have only known, until now, its relatively benign manifestations, by comparison with what it will produce in time, and future historians will not fail to be struck by a psychological singularity that is a feature of our present epoch. Without any doubt, our 20th century will appear to them as a period of transition, the critical moment when humankind literally dreamed of suppressing war and, at the same time, prepared for the practical inauguration of an era of truly devastating conflicts.

Indeed, in 1920, our philosophers were in agreement with our politicians in declaring that the collisions of human masses, launched against one another, represented barbaric behavior, unworthy of the new times, and that it was appropriate to avoid it. In saying that, they were right, since the raising of armies and attacks were, in sum, merely the repetition of prehistoric methods, amplified but not modified.

War thus practiced was still what it had been at the dawn of the ages; its brutal and impulsive method, with the contribution of individual heroism, still shared in the initial and simple character that it presented when one beast launched itself at another; the tactics and strategy were no more than a theorization, a technical regulation of the movements of one pack against another, one horde against another.

Artillery, whose progress amazes us, was merely an ingenious extension of the ballistics invented by apes throwing coconuts. Stones projected by slings merely represented an intermediate phase between that primate invention and ours. The most monstrous of shells is merely an improvement of that same coconut. All the forms of modern war therefore proceed, as our philosophers assert, from the primitive epoch, and it can rightly be sustained that they are obsolete. They cannot last much longer. We have a right to better ones.

Science will take responsibility for procuring us the ameliorations for which it is permissible for us to aspire. Human science is only at its beginning; it has scarcely existed for a hundred years; what it has furnished in those hundred years, permits us to imagine the support that it will furnish twenty thousand years from now. It is to science, and not to military men, that civilized people will address themselves, from now on, to obtain the means of killing those who annoy them, and of liberating the space that they covet when that space is encumbered by other occupants.

Neither the Min nor the Dû had an army. Why would they have had one, and what use would it have been to them? Humankind had had none for a hundred or two hundred centuries, and had only done battle with greater efficacy in consequence. The reason is quite evident. War had never been anything but the competition of life; it could only disappear when life itself disappeared. The day when people had decided to abolish their armies, with the innocent illusion that they were thus abolishing war, they had merely given it its most homicidal form; in the desire to suppress it, they generalized it.

What were combating armies, in effect, but emissaries of a country, representatives of a race posted as an advance guard, in order to cover and protect their fellows? The bloodiest battles, therefore, only constitute skirmishes between these advance guards; once that curtain of troops has been removed, collision is contrived between the peoples themselves, and battles, instead of striving to crush an opposing army, henceforth strive, with much greater force, for the very annihilation of the enemy race.

To that task, the scientists applied themselves methodically, and, alone in the depths of their laboratories, a few individuals sufficed for the task. There was no longer any question, as at the end of the 20th century, of operating with the feeble resources procured for the Europeans of 1980 by physics and mechanics, chemistry and physiology, or electric waves scarcely capable of destroying a million lives in a few minutes...

The Min could do better than that; the Dû could do more.

The method of the Dû consisted of a progressive disorganization of matter. Animal, vegetable, or mineral, every substance was disaggregated, without, however, losing its form. It was reduced to a molecular dust, which maintained its apparent cohesion, but which died and collapsed at the slightest breath. Their means of combat thus presented the benefit of being sure and universally effective; on the other hand, it was relatively slow, since its total action took place over twenty-six hours.

The method of the Min, by contrast, offered the advantages of instantaneity, but it only affected organic substances; it struck the with immediate death by commotion.

The Dû, having decided to attack at twenty-seven minutes past midnight, emitted their waves at thirty-four minutes past. At sixteen minutes past one, the first harmful effects were identified by the Min. A rapid investigation revealed the origins of the damage, and the riposte was immediately decided. At two forty-three, the commotion was launched against the Dû, who vanished from the world.

The last war had lasted exactly a hundred and thirty-two minutes.

In spite of the victory of the Min, their disaggregation was to continue, logically. It was consummated the following day, and the prescribed hour.

When the pale sun rose for the second time, humankind no longer existed—for the human race, by whose hand all other species had perished, was only to perish, like the rest, at human hands.

SF & FANTASY

Henri Allorge. *The Great Cataclysm*
Guy d'Armen. *Doc Ardan: The City of Gold and Lepers*
G.-J. Arnaud. *The Ice Company*
Cyprien Bérard. *The Vampire Lord Ruthwen*
Aloysius Bertrand. *Gaspard de la Nuit*
Richard Bessière. *The Gardens of the Apocalypse*
Albert Bleunard. *Ever Smaller*
Félix Bodin. *The Novel of the Future*
Alphonse Brown. *City of Glass*
André Caroff. *The Terror of Madame Atomos; Miss Atomos; The Return of Madame Atomos; The Mistake of Madame Atomos*
Félicien Champsaur. *The Human Arrow*
Didier de Chousy. *Ignis*
Captain Danrit. *Undersea Odyssey*
C. I. Defontenay. *Star (Psi Cassiopeia)*
Charles Derennes. *The People of the Pole*
Georges Dodds (anthologist). *The Missing Link*
Harry Dickson. *The Heir of Dracula*
Jules Dornay. *Lord Ruthven Begins*
Alfred Driou. *The Adventures of a Parisian Aeronaut*
Sâr Dubnotal *vs. Jack the Ripper*
Alexandre Dumas. *The Return of Lord Ruthven*
Renée Dunan. *Baal*
J.-C. Dunyach. *The Night Orchid; The Thieves of Silence*
Henri Duvernois. *The Man Who Found Himself*
Achille Eyraud. *Voyage to Venus*
Henri Falk. *The Age of Lead*
Paul Féval. *Anne of the Isles; Knightshade; Revenants; Vampire City; The Vampire Countess; The Wandering Jew's Daughter*
Paul Féval, *fils. Felifax, the Tiger-Man*
Charles de Fieux. *Lamékis*
Arnould Galopin. *Doctor Omega; Doctor Omega & The Shadowmen*
G.L. Gick. *Harry Dickson and the Werewolf of Rutherford Grange*
Edmond Haraucourt. *Illusions of Immortality*
Nathalie Henneberg. *The Green Gods*
V. Hugo, P. Foucher & P. Meurice. *The Hunchback of Notre-Dame*
Michel Jeury. *Chronolysis*
Octave Joncquel & Théo Varlet. *The Martian Epic*

Kurt Steiner. *Ortog*
Eugène Thébault. *Radio-Terror*
C.-F. Tiphaigne de La Roche. *Amilec*
Théo Varlet. *The Xenobiotic Invasion*
Paul Vibert. *The Mysterious Fluid*
Villiers de l'Isle-Adam. *The Scaffold; The Vampire Soul*
Philippe Ward. *Artahe*
Philippe Ward & Sylvie Miller. *The Song of Montségur*

MYSTERIES & THRILLERS

M. Allain & P. Souvestre. *The Daughter of Fantômas*
A. Anicet-Bourgeois, Lucien Dabril. *Rocambole*
A. Bisson & G. Livet. *Nick Carter vs. Fantômas*
V. Darlay & H. de Gorsse. *Lupin vs. Holmes: The Stage Play*
Paul Féval. *Gentlemen of the Night; John Devil; The Black Coats*
('Salem Street; The Invisible Weapon; The Parisian Jungle; The
Companions of the Treasure; Heart of Steel; The Cadet Gang; The
Sword-Swallower)
Emile Gaboriau. *Monsieur Lecoq*
Steve Leadley. *Sherlock Holmes: The Circle of Blood*
Maurice Leblanc. *Arsène Lupin vs. Countess Cagliostro; Lupin vs.*
Holmes (The Blonde Phantom; The Hollow Needle)
Gaston Leroux. *Chéri-Bibi; The Phantom of the Opera; Rouletabille*
& the Mystery of the Yellow Room
Richard Marsh. *The Complete Adventures of Judith Lee*
William Patrick Maynard. *The Terror of Fu Manchu*
Frank J. Morlock. *Sherlock Holmes: The Grand Horizontals; Sher-*
lock Holmes vs Jack the Ripper
P. de Wattyne & Y. Walter. *Sherlock Holmes vs. Fantômas*
David White. *Fantômas in America*

SCREENPLAYS

Mike Baron. *The Iron Triangle*
Emma Bull & Will Shetterly. *Nightspeeder; War for the Oaks*
Gerry Conway & Roy Thomas. *Doc Dynamo*
Steve Englehart. *Majorca*
James Hudnall. *The Devastator*
Jean-Marc & Randy Lofficier. *Royal Flush*
J.-M. & R. Lofficier & Marc Agapit. *Despair*

J.-M. & R. Lofficier & Joël Houssin. *City*
Andrew Paquette. *Peripheral Vision*
R. Thomas, J. Hendler & L. Sprague de Camp. *Rivers of Time*

NON-FICTION
Stephen R. Bissette. *Blur 1-5. Green Mountain Cinema 1*
Win Scott Eckert. *Crossovers* (2 vols.)
Jean-Marc & Randy Lofficier. *Shadowmen* (2 vols.)
Randy Lofficier. *Over Here*

HEXAGON COMICS
Franco Frescura & Luciano Bernasconi. *Wampus*
Franco Frescura & Giorgio Trevisan. *CLASH*
L. Bernasconi, J.-M. Lofficier & Juan Roncagliolo Berger. *Phenix*
Claude Legrand, J.-M. Lofficier & L. Bernasconi. *Kabur*
Franco Oneta. *Zembla*
L. Buffolente, Lofficier & J.-J. Dzialowski. *Strangers: Homicron*
Danilo Grossi. *Strangers: Jaydee*
Claude Legrand & Luciano Bernasconi. *Strangers: Starlock*

ART BOOKS
Jean-Pierre Normand. *Science Fiction Illustrations*
Raven Okeefe. *Raven's L'il Critters*
Randy Lofficier & Raven OKeefe. *If Your Possum Go Daylight...*
Daniele Serra. *Illusions*